A Royal Pain

RETAIL TO RICHES, BOOK 2

LAURA HEFFERNAN

EMPRESS BOOKS

$\mathcal{B}$eing a $\mathcal{P}$rincess is for the birds...

Lila's mother-in-law hates her. That would be bad enough in a regular family, but Lila married the Prince of Corchenne, and his mom's the queen. She's determined to make amends, but then her scammer brother shows up. The opposite of what she needed. Lila's trying to make friends while Caleb's trying to make a quick buck. Now Lila's stuck trying to get everyone to see Caleb's true colors before he does something completely unfixable.

Pierre claims to love Lila despite her relatives, but if she can't fix her brother's mess, it will destroy the royal family—and also the economy of Corchenne. Can their marriage survive the monarchy's disapproval and the weight of royal expectations?

Copyright © 2022 by Laura Heffernan

Cover by La Voisin Art

All rights reserved. No part of this book may be reproduced in any form or by any means without the prior written consent of the Publisher, excepting brief quotes used in reviews.

This book is a work of fiction. Any resemblance to real people, places, or situations is merely a coincidence.

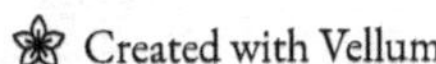 Created with Vellum

Chapter One

Although I'd seen pictures online, nothing prepared me for my first sight of *Chateau de Serpentine* up close. It absolutely took my breath away. The little girl inside me who'd watched *The Princess Bride* dozens of times with her best friend's mom growing up couldn't quite believe I'd come from working retail at SidMart to living with my prince husband in an actual castle.

Well, temporarily living, anyway. We didn't plan to stay forever. Pierre and I were on the tail end of our honeymoon traveling around the world, and it was only appropriate to meet his family before we headed home to Boston. My nerves made me nauseous, but I needed to know my husband's birthplace.

Since Pierre and I had wanted a quiet ceremony, his mother Queen Claudette I of Corchenne hadn't attended our wedding. Well, that and because we worried she might try to stop it, like his brother. But that's another story. Hopefully, Queen Claudette would be willing to forgive our faux pas and start the type of mother-daughter relationship I'd always dreamed of having. To that end, we were staying here for the entire month of September before leaving Corchenne's mild climate and returning to the Northeast in time for winter.

In my lap, my little Yorkshire terrier whined and wiggled. Lost in thought, I'd stopped petting him. Preacher was keeping me from hyperventilating. The entire country was going to meet me at once, thanks to the joy of television. Why hadn't we gotten married in the nineteen thirties?

"Almost there," I said, stroking his silky fur. "Isn't it beautiful?"

Set at the top of a hill, the castle towered over the surrounding countryside. With literal towers on each of the four corners. A long, winding path served as the driveway that would lead us home, although Pierre told me the royal family also had a gondola to carry them up and down when the roads got icy.

I glanced down at the book in my lap, a gift Pierre presented me with after we got into the car at the airport. It was large and heavy, clearly ancient. Gold edged the pages, and the words OFFICIAL GUIDE TO BEING A PRINCESS were embossed on the front. I'd laughed, but after paging through it, the book contained some good advice. Not a lot, but some. Good manners were apparently timeless. Reading helped me avoid thinking about all the ways I could embarrass myself in front of the entire country.

Even if the book contained some antiquated ideas, I appreciated the gesture. Pierre knew I was terrified of meeting his mother. I would do almost anything to get her approval, including studying this book.

The castle must take up two or three blocks. Last year, when I first found out Pierre was royalty, I'd read that it housed something like forty *unused* bedrooms. Not including the suites for residents. I'd thought the article exaggerated, but after counting windows on the second floor, the writer might have underestimated.

Each corner boasted a turret, a gorgeous tower with carved snakes winding up the outside. That explained the name. The Corche flag flew above each turret, a blue iris on a white background with a matching blue border. A larger version of the flag flew near the massive double doors, along with two others that weren't taught in my college world geography class.

I nudged my husband. "What are those smaller flags?"

"The top one is a serpent protecting a bunch of grapes. It's the sign of the sovereign, showing that Queen Claudette is currently in residence at the Chateau. That one comes down when she's not here."

"Interesting." So many intricacies of royal life never occurred to me. Imagine having people raise and lower a flag each time you left the house. On a slow day, I'd be tempted to come and go just to watch. Then again, the queen probably didn't have many "slow" days. She had a country to run. "You have people lower a flag every time your mom runs out to the grocery store?"

"Her Royal Majesty the Queen does not 'run out for groceries,' as you so adorably put it." He kissed the tip of my nose. "But no. It's only lowered when *Mére* travels abroad. Also both times she went to the hospital to give birth."

"That makes a little more sense." Heavy stress on the little.

"The lower flag is for Henri. It's similar to *Mére's* to indicate the Crown Prince, but it uses a darker royal blue instead of the iris color," Pierre continued. "It also matched my father's, except for the size."

"Do you have a flag?"

"Of course," he said. "Someone should run it up the pole once the car arrives. It has a light gray background with the serpent, the crest of the younger son. Now that you're my wife, they'll have made one for you as well. *Mére* should present it to you at your first official function as Princess Lila."

Yikes. Although of course I'd known what marrying Pierre

entailed, hearing myself referred to as "Princess Lila", someone who attended official functions, terrified me to my core. I was no one. Born to hard-working parents in rural New Hampshire, a girl who moved to Boston to go to college, then dropped out of law school. Shortly thereafter, I wound up staying in the area to work at SidMart, a large big box store, mostly because Boston was such a great city, and I couldn't afford to move anywhere else. Also, my brother had essentially swindled me out of my student loans and stuck me with a fixer-upper that needed to be restored before I could get my money back. At least that led to Pierre making me an irresistible offer that led to our marriage.

What would even be on my flag? Fenway Park was a Boston icon, yet an unlikely choice. A blue vest to represent the common worker? While I'd appreciate that symbolism, I didn't need to see that reminder greet me each time I arrived at the castle. Grapes? This was a wine-producing country. Plus, it was relatable. Everyone liked wine, and I needed people to relate to me.

Maybe the people of Corchenne would like having a regular person princess. I knew more about daily life struggles than Queen Claudette or the Crown Prince. Pierre got a taste of how us plebes lived while he was working in Boston, but Prince Henri never took the silver spoon out of his bu—er, mouth.

I couldn't do anything but wait. It wasn't worth worrying about hypothetical royal events at the moment, so I turned my attention back to the window. We'd climbed about halfway up the hill, which gave me a dazzling view not only of the Chateau but of the surrounding area.

To the south, glistening blue waves crashed against large boulders, a gorgeous private beach that probably protected the castle from attack back when it was built. Palace guards would have had little trouble stopping invaders who climbed over the rocks. The last Corche war was two hundred years ago, so now the coastline perfected the images for postcards. To the north, west, and east, thousands of vines dotted the landscape in all directions. With the weather just starting to turn, the red and golden leaves were truly spectacular.

Pierre had told me Corchenne's primary exports were wine and grapes. When the fields unfolded as far as the eye could see, I realized how much farmland the castle oversaw. I'd always pictured something like Napa Valley, a separate part of the country dedicated to growing crops. Then again, Corchenne was significantly smaller than the United States. It might even be smaller than Napa.

"Does your family own all of that?" I asked him.

He leaned past me to peer out the window. "Not anymore. Decades ago, the royal family owned most of the land and allowed sharecroppers to plant on it. But my great-grandfather split up the farms and gave them to the workers. He felt they'd have more pride working on their own property."

"Your great-grandfather sounds like my kind of guy," I said.

"Oh, yes. The advisors hated him," he said. "Grand-père had many radical ideas, such as allowing women to vote and providing healthcare to all residents of Corchenne."

"A socialist, then." I shook my head in mock disapproval.

"The horror!" Pierre pretended to shudder.

When the limousine pulled to a stop, it was impossible to miss the giant television cameras pointed at us. Not all the networks were familiar, but I spotted at least one American channel. My hand shook as I clipped a leash to Preacher's collar so he wouldn't dart away. The last thing I wanted was to spend my first day in the country chasing a dog down a mountain while someone posted a live stream.

"You know, on second thought, what if I stayed in the car?"

Pierre followed my gaze out the window, then put an arm around me. "It's going to be fine. Everyone will love you."

"That's so much more believable if 'everyone' meant like three relatives rather than thousands of your subjects. What if I fall flat on my face? What if I puke?" Oh, no. I was going to puke.

He took both my hands in his. "Look at me. Take a deep breath."

Together, we counted to twenty.

"Are you going to be okay? We talked about this, but if it's too soon, tell me."

"Oh, no. Waiting will just make the anticipation stronger."

"Most people are interested in seeing me. That's where the focus will be. All you have to do is walk beside me and smile."

At the moment, I'd have preferred to walk ten steps behind him, out of the frame entirely. But that wasn't the deal. We'd spent a lot of time preparing for my official arrival at the *Chateau de Serpentine*. Delaying the inevitable wouldn't help.

Closing my eyes, I counted silently until I could breathe more easily. "Here goes nothing," I breathed. A tremor in my voice contradicted my brave words.

Preacher turned his head and licked my hand, just once. Then he met my eyes like he could feel my buried concerns rising to the surface. Would the Queen come out to greet the younger son who'd been away for years? Would she welcome me or treat me like a commoner, the way her older son did? Or would a line of servants show us into the house?

My last question was the first answered. The royal chauffeur, Bernadette, brought the car to a halt on a gravel path between an enormous stone fountain and the equally imposing front doors. The entrance had to be three stories high, and I wondered at the strength and skill required to maneuver them open and shut on windy days.

"That's your front door?"

"Somewhat," Pierre said. "To the side, there's a person-sized opening. That's what we normally use. The massive doors are from when the entire village slept in the castle on frosty nights. Now, we only open them for official events. The family has a separate, private entrance around the back. The servants also have several doors around the exterior."

"Then why are we opening the main doors?"

"I've been gone for five years," he said. "The public wants to see me return home."

"Right. The public." I swallowed hard. "I keep trying to forget about them."

"When we're in public, it's best never to 'forget' about them," he said . "But you'll get used to it. I barely notice them now."

Behind us, the trunk of the car opened, and Bernadette unloaded our baggage. Each suitcase barely touched the gravel before a blue-and-gold uniformed servant swept it up and into the house.

"Let's get out," I said. "I can carry my own bags."

"You absolutely cannot."

I glared at my husband. "Excuse me?"

"First, we're royalty. The citizens of Corchenne are home right now, waiting to get the first official glimpse of their beautiful new princess. No one knew about our engagement. Everyone missed our wedding, and we flew in discretely. They don't want to watch you struggle to carry a fifty-pound suitcase up a steep stone staircase." He paused. "Also, the servants are paid well. Working here is an honor. Let them do their jobs. They might lose their jobs if they don't have work. That doesn't help them."

"Fine." He certainly knew which arguments would make me relent. I wouldn't be responsible for getting royal servants fired ten minutes after I arrived. Although I wasn't sure I bought his reasoning, I also didn't want the people's first impression of me to be watching me argue with their Prodigal Prince.

Instead, I pulled out a mirror to double-check my hair and make-up. A stylist had flown in with us to pull my honey-blonde strands into an updo. Just another thing I would probably never get used to: having a personal stylist. Oh, and flying on a private plane. Makeup that wasn't bought on clearance.

Pierre squeezed my hand. "Ready?"

Leaning over, I kissed him tenderly. His hands came up to cup my face, and when we pulled apart, I remembered all the reasons

I'd signed up for this royalty nonsense. Despite who his family was, I loved Pierre with all my heart. "I am now."

He knocked twice on the roof of the car. The side door immediately opened. Preacher leaped out, to my horror. He almost knocked our poor driver over. Bernadette wore a dark blue uniform with a matching headband in her long, dark hair. She was a medium-sized woman with big, innocent-looking brown eyes. She almost appeared fragile, but Pierre assured me earlier that she was an expert in three different martial arts and carried a gun. We were safe with her.

To her credit, Bernadette took my dog's enthusiasm in stride. She didn't even flinch, instead pulling out a dog treat. "Hello, Little Fellow. May I?"

My dog gobbled the proffered snack in one bite, then started begging for more. Bernadette scooped him up before reaching into the car to take his leash from me.

"Sorry!" I said, my cheeks flaming. "It's been a long drive. I can take him."

"Don't be silly. You've been traveling all day. You must be exhausted. I'd be more than happy to take him for a bit. Our cooks always have some treats on hand for all our guests. Both two and four-legged."

I adored her immensely.

"If you're ready, Your Highness?" With the hand not clutching my thrilled dog and his leash, Bernadette helped Pierre out of the car before setting Preacher on the ground several feet away.

Pierre turned to offer me his hand. Taking it, I stepped to the ground. "Thank you. This may be the nicest reception I've ever had. I can almost pretend I'm not terrified."

"It is my pleasure, *ma chérie*. You deserve all this and more." He kissed me lightly, this time for the benefit of the onlookers.

I drew myself up to my full height and threw back my shoulders, trying to look both taller and thinner. My chin pointed toward the sky, instilling false bravado in me. I pointedly avoided making eye contact with any of the reporters. If I looked into a camera, I'd probably have a panic attack.

A line of people in identical dark blue and gold uniforms extended from the car to the door. For a moment, I stared, wondering how they would help us get inside.

"You have twelve servants?" I finally asked.

"Of course not," he said. Well, that made me feel better. It didn't explain why a dozen people wore matching outfits to greet us, but at least–"At last count, I believe there were three hundred and seven members of the palace staff. These people are assigned to our wing."

Duh. Right. Twelve people were a lot to clean one house, but obviously a castle needed a lot more. But then his words sunk in. "These people are working just for us? We don't need a dozen servants! I don't even need one."

He leaned closer. "We'll discuss it later. Smile for the cameras."

The cameras. Right. I'd been trying to ignore them for my sanity. But at the reminder, I said a silent thank you for the glass of wine I'd chugged before getting into the car.

We started at the end of the line, and Pierre introduced me to each member of our staff. I tried to focus on each person in front of me. There were the maids, the steward, Pierre's Chief of Staff. So many people. *Our staff.* Holy moly.

Everyone bowed or curtsied to me, which made me feel like a character in a storybook. Drawing on months of preparation, I greeted each of them with a nod and slight curtsey, exactly the degree appropriate for a princess to greet someone of a lower station. Thank you, *Princess Diaries*.

Committing each person's name and position to memory would take some time, but I vowed to do it. The staffers had to know I wasn't any better than they were. Just luckier.

"You ready to go in?" Pierre asked, one hand on my back.

"Ready!" I took a deep breath. "Here goes nothing."

Chapter Two

OFFICIAL GUIDE TO BEING A PRINCESS: *A princess shall keep her home prepared to receive guests at a moment's notice.*

The gorgeous and imposing exterior of the Chateau should have prepared me for the grandeur inside, but it didn't. The royal family didn't allow photographs to be taken of most of the castle's interior, so I'd found very few images online to sate my interest. At one point, Pierre and his former roommate Blaise dug up some old family photographs, which I enjoyed looking at, but even those didn't prepare me for marble floors, stone ceilings so high my footsteps echoed, or massive portraits that couldn't even be accurately described as "life-sized." Dinosaur-sized, maybe. The cost of just one of those enormous, ornate picture frames was probably more than what the average American family paid for a month's rent. And there were dozens.

"Don't you worry about people breaking in and looting the castle? There's so much expensive stuff just lying around."

"We typically do not, for three reasons," Pierre said. "One, Corchenne is a small country. Our crops do well. Second, in recent decades, the royal family has been very generous with our citizens. We have free health care for everyone, unemployment compensation, paid maternity leave…"

"Ooh. You know I love it when you talk dirty to me," I said. "This place sounds like a dream."

"Unhappy subjects tend to revolt, you know. My mother has no wish to become a modern-day Marie Antoinette."

I snorted. "What's the third reason?"

"While the castle appears inviting and rather open, we have excellent security. Cameras throughout, full-time guards on staff, both inside and out. Alarms on the priceless artifacts. Anyone who tried to steal a picture frame would be caught before they got it off the wall."

That made sense. Even so, it felt weird to be surrounded by so much luxury. I'd already spotted at least four chandeliers, and we hadn't even reached the wing where we'd be sleeping. I couldn't believe we had *our own wing*. Most people I knew didn't even have guest rooms.

"I can't believe you grew up here," I said for at least the millionth time. The hall contained life-sized marble statues of former monarchs.

Pierre shrugged. "We didn't, not really. Henri and I mostly stayed at a smaller estate with our nannies and tutors."

"You didn't live with your parents?" I couldn't fathom that. Sure, my parents drove me up the wall sometimes, but they'd always been there when I needed them. Also when I didn't want them. I reached over and squeezed his hand. "You never told me."

"I didn't think about it," he said. "It's all in the past. It's not as sad as it sounds. My parents traveled a great deal, and it wasn't considered a good idea to bring the Crown Prince and his heir along on most official visits. We didn't want to risk the entire royal line being wiped out at once."

"Yeah, that makes sense," I said. "Still, I'm sorry."

He paused and looked at me. "Our lives were very different growing up. But that doesn't mean I was unloved or unhappy. Henri and I had each other. Our nannies were kind, and they gave us plenty of affection. Just like growing up without ridiculous amounts of money doesn't mean you suffered."

I thought for a minute, letting the words sink in. "I get it. You don't want people to feel sorry for you."

"The poor little rich prince? Absolutely not." He took my hands in his, kissing the backs of each softly. The touch of his lips sent an electric shock up my arms. "Besides, look how amazingly it all worked out."

"Amazingly? I wouldn't go that far. What if there's a pea under my mattress? I shall toss and turn all night."

"Ah, that would be a tragedy. I suggest we go to our rooms immediately to investigate."

He didn't have to ask me twice. We bypassed the rest of the public areas of the castle and headed straight for our room. I'd get a full royal tour later.

When Pierre opened the door to our suite, my mouth dropped open. "Suite" wasn't even appropriate. This must be bigger than the three-bedroom apartment I'd shared with Madison in Boston. There was a set of double locks on the door. We had our own front entryway, again with the marble floors. Cold, impersonal, but lovely. A table sat against the left wall under a mirror. Vases at either end overflowed with fresh blue and white flowers.

The room was the size of an Olympic swimming pool. Here, a thick blue-patterned area rug brought the warmth lacking in the hall. The far end was dominated by the largest bed I'd ever seen— a four-poster majesty, with a canopy on top and heavy dark blue curtains hanging down on either side. Carved nightstands matched the wood of the bedposts, and at the end sat a gorgeous wooden bench with a plush blue velvet cushion. It was the most comfortable bed I had ever seen.

But the room didn't stop there. The near side of the room contained two armchairs that flanked a gorgeous blue-and-white-striped couch. The entire setup faced a fireplace, which sat under a twin-bed-sized television. Beyond the living area, we also had a small kitchenette that was hopefully stocked with microwaveable meals and chips, plus a small marble dining table and chairs. We could comfortably live here for weeks without getting cabin fever.

We could probably go three days without seeing each other.

Pointing at one corner, I asked, "Why do we have a tiny replica of our bed? They can't expect one of us to sleep on that."

"Don't be silly. That's for Preacher. I insisted they use the finest fabrics, despite knowing he'll sleep with us most of the time."

A cry of joy escaped me. "This is unbelievable! You didn't have to get me something so fancy. But I appreciate it."

Pierre's face turned red. "This is one of the less ornate suites, I'm sorry to say. Some of the visiting royals insist on being treated like it."

If I was going to stay here, I needed to adjust my thinking. Constantly pointing out the opulence surrounding us would both make me look hopelessly uncultured and irritate everyone around me.

"I'm sorry," I said. "It's a shock."

"You haven't even seen the best part." He moved across the room to a set of double doors I assumed concealed a closet and threw them open with a flourish. "Madame, your dressing suite."

"I have a *dressing suite*?" Part of me was terrified to think about what that meant. The rest of me was delighted. I raced around the bed to see what awaited. In here, plush royal blue carpet covered the floor. It felt like walking on a cloud.

Pierre's description of the room as a dressing suite was accurate. This room was no more a closet than I was a cantaloupe. Rows of drawers lined the lower half of the room on three sides. Above them were rods for hanging clothes, except for the wall directly opposite me, which had row after row of shoe racks. The fourth side contained a floor-to-ceiling mirror that must be about four feet wide, next to a clothing rack.

An island in the middle of the room housed more, smaller drawers, plus a makeup mirror. The most amazing thing about this entire room was that it wasn't empty. Clothes hung everywhere: ball gowns, gorgeous skirts, the kind of slacks that cost more than I used to make in a week. And the shoes. Oh, the shoes. I'm ashamed to admit a little drool formed in the corner of my mouth when I noticed the red soles on several pairs.

Tears welled in my eyes. "Oh, Pierre. This is too much! You didn't have to do this! It must have cost—you didn't have to. I love it all, but it's too much."

"While I would love to take credit, I actually didn't. My aunt provided most of this, directly from her closet. When we leave, several items will go back to Bridget or be donated. The rest will stay here for future visits."

"Won't your mother need this suite for other visitors?"

He shook his head. "We have many rooms, and I am her favorite son. This room is ours, at least until Henri takes the throne."

I threw my arms around his neck and kissed him. He put his hands on my hips and pulled me close. Our kiss deepened. When we parted, we were both out of breath.

"How much time do we have?" I asked.

A seductive smile spread across Pierre's face. "Oh, we have plenty of time to explore the room. I, personally, can't wait to test out that bed. After all, it might be defective. We should make sure it's safe."

"Absolutely," I said. "What a terrific idea."

~

Trying out the luxuriously soft bed eased the tension inside me. After we got up, Pierre and I took our time getting ready to leave, familiarizing ourselves with the benefits of living in a castle.

By the time I exited the massive shower, wrapping myself in a massive, fluffy cornflower blue bathrobe, I'd nearly forgotten that the Queen of Corchenne waited for me so she could determine whether I was worthy of being married to her favorite son.

Bernadette must have returned Preacher from their walk while I was showering because he now lay curled into a tiny ball on the royal blue bed in the corner. The corner of his tongue poked out, and he appeared completely content.

When we first started traveling, I'd been worried about how he'd adjust, but it turned out that dog was at home anywhere. Good thing—although my best friend Madison would have happily watched him during our extended honeymoon, I would have missed the little guy.

Humming to myself, I sat down in front of the vanity to touch up my hair and makeup. Someone helped me on the plane because of all the waiting cameras. When Pierre offered, a professional seemed excessive for a private meeting. Now I wished she were still here. I'd have to try to "borrow" some of her techniques.

There seemed to be a lot more toiletries than I'd brought. All unopened, mostly brands I'd only vaguely seen mentioned in some of the fashion magazines sold at my old job.

One look at Pierre's frowning face, and my newfound serenity evaporated. "What's wrong?"

He stopped pacing to look at me. "It's nothing. I just received a message from my steward that Henri has been informed of our arrival."

Henri. Ugh. To say he didn't support our relationship was an understatement. The last time I saw him, he'd offered to pay me to leave Pierre. When that didn't work, he tried to make it look like I'd betrayed my then-fiancé. Pierre had been less than pleased.

My hand paused with an eyeliner halfway to my face. As silly as it sounded, part of me had hoped to avoid my brother-in-law for our entire visit. Or for as long as humanly possible. More than a couple of hours.

"From your expression, I deduce that he's excited to see me as

I am to see him?" Since Henri hated me whether I looked good or not, I continued applying my makeup. The queen was waiting.

For me.

The *Queen of Corchenne* was waiting for me. Lila Sinclair, of the SidMart Sinclairs. I'd come a long way from that blue vest. I still pinched myself at least once a day. This fairy-tale relationship might never feel real.

"He's not hoping to see you at all," Pierre said, bringing me back to reality. "He's asked to have dinner with me and *Mére* alone. Claims he has pressing royal business for the three of us only."

"How charming." I ran a brush through my hair before twisting it up and turning my head, examining my handiwork from different angles. A stylist I was not, but it looked pretty good. Then again, if I were eating by myself, my hair didn't matter. "Well, I can order something. What's your national takeout?"

Even if I were allowed to use the royal kitchens to make myself a meal, I preferred not to burn the castle down on my first day. I was very aware of my talents, and cooking was not among them.

"Don't be ridiculous," he said. "I'm not going without you."

"You're not? Why?"

"Because we're a team, Lila. Husband and wife, prince and future princess. The rest of my family needs to include you in our business. If I let Henri set the tone tonight by excluding you, you'll never be invited to anything. He'll take me away more and more, doing everything in his power to drive a wedge between us."

A sound of disgust escaped me. "Why would he do that? I know he doesn't think I'm good enough for you, but we're married now. When does he let it go?"

Pierre walked over and wrapped me in a hug. "I wish I could say. With my last girlfriend, it ended when she took his payoff and walked away. As we know, that was never about suitability. You refused to be bought. I thought he would start working to accept you, but it appears I was wrong."

"What do we do?" I nuzzled into him, wishing I could stay wrapped up in his arms forever. Here, I felt safe. Everything else was a big question mark.

"I'll talk to him, *ma chérie*. I promise, my brother won't come between us a second time." After kissing me gently, he released me and opened the apartment door. Jules waited outside. I'd had no idea he was there. Did servants linger by the door all day, in case we needed something?

I hoped royals could do things for themselves sometimes. I hated having to ask Jules every time I wanted a cup of coffee or a late-night snack. Not that I knew where the kitchens were yet, but eventually, I'd find them. Having more than one still left me a little shell-shocked.

Pierre said, "Jules, please find my brother's chief of staff and let him know Lila and I would *both* be delighted to join him and our mother for dinner. Talk to the kitchen to make sure they're aware to plate four entrees instead of three. Then, arrange for an interpreter to sit beside Lila."

"An interpreter? I thought everyone in Corchenne spoke French and English."

"They do, but French is the official language, and Henri cannot be trusted to speak so you understand him."

"Can't you translate for me?"

"I can," he said. "But it will be less awkward to have a professional doing it. Otherwise, you'll be competing with my family for my attention the whole time."

"Gee, sounds like it'll be a great meal!" I didn't try to hide my exasperation.

"Is there anything else I can do for you, sire?" Jules asked.

For a moment, I'd forgotten he was there.

"No, thank you." Pierre paused. "Actually, yes. Ask the chef if he can prepare the chocolate mousse, please? It's Lila's favorite."

"Certainly." He vanished before I could tell Pierre it wasn't necessary to have specific desserts made for me.

Then again, if things went badly, like Pierre and I suspected, it would be nice to drown my sorrows in chocolate. Being a royal family wasn't all it was cracked up to be.

Chapter Three

Once Jules disappeared, I remembered I was supposed to be preparing for my meeting with Queen Claudette before dinner. We were expected to appear in the throne room at four o'clock sharp, and it was already three-thirty. I didn't have the first clue how long it would take to get there in this massive building, and I didn't particularly want to introduce myself to my mother-in-law while wearing a bathrobe.

"Isn't the throne room a bit formal for this? I don't feel like we're throne room people. We could meet in the kitchen?" I moved to the closet and started leafing through the items hanging on the rack. That shower must've taken longer than I thought, because someone had unpacked my suitcase, ironed my clothes, and hung them up. My comfortable, functional items looked out of place next to my new princess clothes. Pulling a floor-length, light blue silk dress with a sweetheart neck from the stuff Bridget had sent, I held it up to myself and turned to find a mirror. "How's this?"

"A little formal. That's a ball gown," Pierre said. He wore a gray suit with a dark blue shirt that made him look positively edible. "You're married to the second in line for the throne. At some point, I expect you to be officially named a princess. If Henri dies childless, you could wind up being the mother of a future king or queen. The throne room is appropriate for *Mére* to meet you."

The word "mother" rang in my ears, so loudly I barely heard the dress I was holding clatter to the floor. To hide how flustered I was, I hung it up and grabbed another one. Turning toward my husband, I held the new dress up to get a better look. Knee-length, full skirt, also blue. Good thing I looked great in the royal colors, because Bridgette had sent me a ton of them. Pierre nodded his approval.

Finally, I found my voice. "Mother? Kids? Us?"

"Yes, of course. Don't you want kids?"

"Um, sure? I mean, yeah, maybe? Honestly, I never thought about it," I said, stepping into the dress and turning so he could zip me up. "When you asked me to marry you, it was a sham, so fake kids weren't part of the negotiation."

He nodded. "True. I couldn't tell you we needed to have kids to preserve the line of succession while hiding my heritage. But I always expected at least two. You don't?"

For a moment, I closed my eyes and pictured Pierre and I holding two bouncing, smiling children. A girl with my long blonde hair and blue eyes, a boy with Pierre's dark good looks. Then I imagined the girl throwing up on me as the boy yanked on her hair, then ran away screaming. I thought about mountains of dirty diapers and sleepless nights and...

"You look terrified," Pierre said.

"I'm okay. I think," I said as I stepped into a pair of low silver heels. "But one thing at a time, please? Right now, I'm trying to deal with meeting your mother and eating dinner while Henri glares at me. I'm not ready to throw a talk about our future offspring into the mix. We just got married."

He nodded. "I understand. I'm sorry I didn't think to bring it up earlier. I guess I assumed you would know that marrying me meant having baby princes and princesses."

"If I'd thought about it, I'm sure I would have been." My hands shook as I swept eye shadow across my lids. I needed to be careful not to turn myself into a raccoon. "It's definitely a conversation we should have. Just not today, okay?"

Pierre cupped my face in his hands and kissed the tip of my nose. "Certainly not today. One thing at a time. If it comes up, I'll tell *Mére* that we plan to wait a few years."

"Thank you. That helps."

"Of course." He looked at his watch. "Are you ready? It takes a few minutes to get to the throne room. We don't want to appear looking rushed."

I swallowed. It was now or never. For most people, meeting their spouse's parents was nerve-racking. Most people weren't meeting royalty. The thought of offending Pierre's mother had me so worried I barely slept for a week before we arrived at her home. Or as she called it, *Chateau de Serpentine*. My mother-in-law lived in a freaking castle. That thought just kept hitting me.

It only took a second to apply a last layer of lipstick. "I don't know. Am I ready?"

"You look beautiful," Pierre said. "Relax. She'll love you because I do."

"Are you sure? Henri doesn't." Far from loving me, when I'd met Pierre's brother, he'd threatened to have me arrested. I mean, sure, he thought we were planning to commit marriage fraud, but still. Even after hearing we were truly in love, he doubled down on his threats. It was a big mess.

I didn't want to think about what Henri said to Queen Claudette about me. Under the circumstances, I couldn't imagine

Henri's mother welcoming me with open arms, even if Pierre was her favorite son.

"You convinced me to return home, so she should be grateful. It's what she wanted."

"Except we're not planning to stay here for long."

"She doesn't know that," he said.

"She might suspect if she's been following either of us on Instagram." When we first met, my husband had intended to walk away from his title and influence forever and become a private American citizen, living the quiet life. I'd convinced him we could do a lot more good using his connections. "Or if any of her advisors have."

After the wedding, we'd been traveling, researching how we could help. I'd spent time in places I had never dared to dream of visiting back when I worked retail for minimum wage. We'd donated close to ten million dollars already to help combat climate change, and I was scheduled to speak to Congress on the topic next month.

A thought that filled me with slightly less dread than the prospect of meeting my husband's mother.

"What if I forget the protocol? What if I go to curtsy and fall on my face? What if—"

"—She adores you? She welcomes you to the family, names you a princess, then announces she wants you to be her heir instead of my brother or me?"

"That's not funny. That's possibly scarier than falling on my face."

"Okay, I apologize. But it's going to be fine. You've been studying Corche customs so much, I suspect you know more than I do at this point." Putting his arms around me, he kissed me again. "Let's go. You'll see there's nothing to worry about."

"Fine." Throwing my shoulders back, I took one last look in the mirror. I cleaned up pretty nicely, if I said so myself. A year ago, yoga gear from the local big box store where I'd worked comprised almost all my wardrobe. The type of stuff that fell apart after you washed it a few times. Now, as surreal as it seemed, I wore clothes fit for a princess.

Clothes literally belonging to royalty. I wasn't sure what Bridget's official title was, but she must have one. Thankfully, we were close to the same size. I hated the idea of buying an expensive wardrobe for our trip when that money could be used for important things. Once we returned home, I didn't expect a tremendous need for fancy, floor-length gowns. Nor did I want to buy a bunch of suitcases to fly them back.

After I finally finished getting ready, Pierre stepped out to make a call. On his way, he admitted a familiar-looking Black girl about my age. She had a friendly smile, dozens of dark brown braids dyed magenta at the ends, and gorgeous brown eyes. She also looked a lot taller than I expected after our Zoom meeting.

Upon seeing me, my new social media director bowed. We'd had a brief virtual conversation shortly after the wedding where she reminded me I had become a face of the royal family, that they were working to get my new accounts verified on social media, and not to post anything that might embarrass anyone or create a scandal.

She needn't have worried. After a video of someone renaming my former place of employment "STDMart" had gone viral, I didn't feel any need for internet fame. Mostly, I hoped no one connected me to that store. I wasn't ashamed of having worked for a living, but there were things you didn't need to be famous for.

"Good morning, Madame Delilah."

"Candace?" We'd only spoken a couple of times, and the formal way she addressed me made me wonder if I'd misremembered what she looked like. But the similarity to Blaise was uncanny. That made sense, considering she was his little sister.

"Yes, madame."

This would never do. I wasn't the kind of person you greeted with a curtsey or called "madame." When Pierre said it, the word felt like a pet name. Not when it came from a stranger.

"Seriously, none of that nonsense. I'm Lila. No bowing and scraping."

Her lips twitched. "I thought you might say that, but it's important to err on the side of formality. Remember that."

I waved one hand. "Consider yourself erred. Or whatever. Did I post something I wasn't supposed to?"

Candace shook her head. "Not at all. I'm here to give you your new phone."

She withdrew a rectangular device from her pocket. I tried to stop her with a shake of my head. "Thanks, but I have a phone that works just fine. I don't need a new one."

"Your existing phone is ancient, and it looks it," Bridget said. "But that's actually not the point. This one is loaded with top-of-the-line security features. It's virtually unhackable."

"Can I still play Animal Crossing?"

She shifted her gaze from side to side, then leaned forward and said in an exaggerated whisper, "Yes, but don't tell anyone who you are. I'll get in trouble."

I grinned at her. "Your secret dies with me."

"Anyway, I've got your new social media accounts installed on there," she said. "I picked it up from Pierre's head of security on my way here."

"I have social media already."

"Yes, but now you have official Corchenne royalty accounts, verified and everything."

"Oh, wow." When Pierre and I got married, I'd ended his social media hiatus by announcing the news to the world, and I'd gotten plenty of new followers. But being officially recognized by the apps would give me access to a whole new platform.

Taking the sleek new device from her, I turned it over in my hand. It was bigger than my old phone, heavier. A thick covering protected it from damage, much nicer than the plastic case I'd picked up on clearance at SidMart for three dollars back when I worked there.

I tapped the screen to turn it on. "No face ID?"

She snorted. "Of course not. What if someone kidnapped you and held it up to access your phone?"

The thought made me shudder. "Couldn't they also kidnap me and force me to input a password?"

"You'll meet with the head of security later to discuss that possibility. I'm making sure you've got the phone because meeting the Queen is a photo opp." She pulled a piece of paper from her bag. "Here is a full list of all your official new accounts and passwords. You'll need to change the passwords to your own as soon as you can. Then shred the list. Even if the passwords won't work, you don't want anyone else to find it."

"Thanks." Taking the list, I scanned it. "Hold on. This email address is wrong."

"Pardon?" She said something quickly in French, which I interpreted to mean that she thought she hadn't understood me.

Shaking my head, I pointed. "It says 'delilahleon' here. That's not my name. I'm Lila. Lila Sinclair."

"You are married to his royal highness, Pierre Leon."

"Yes, but I didn't change my name. I don't know the custom here, but in America, each spouse gets to choose. I like my name, and I kept it."

She tsked and shook her head. "Well, that will never do."

"It's not a big deal to get me a new email address, is it? I never go by Delilah, either. I would honestly prefer if no one knew Lila was a nickname, although you somehow found out."

"Her Royal Majesty's staff did a thorough background check. There's not a lot we don't know." She tapped her lips thoughtfully. "Perhaps I can change 'Delilah' to 'Lila'. That means getting a whole new address, but it only takes a few minutes. I don't know how the queen will feel about your refusing to use her last name for official business."

I sighed and set the list on a nearby end table. "Then don't tell her. I'll keep using my old email. But I'm not sending anything that calls me Delilah Leon. It wouldn't be authentic."

"I will speak to Alexandre," she said, sighing as heavily as if I'd asked her to rename the castle after me. "Back to the phone. Which, by the way, has your email installed. This device is one hundred percent secure, and it's only got official accounts on it. No need to worry about posting from the wrong account."

"What if I post from the wrong phone?"

"That won't happen, because I'm under orders to take your regular phone and secure it in the vaults until you leave." She held out one hand.

Putting my hands on my hips, I shook my head. "No way. I need to be able to reach my family and friends."

She started to speak, and I held up one hand to stop her. "Look at my phone. Is there any chance I would confuse this with a Queen-issued royal device?"

Candace took in the Ruth Bader Ginsburg cover on my five-year-old iPhone and pressed her lips firmly together. It took me a minute to realize she was trying not to laugh. "Uh, no, Madame. Not likely."

This time, I didn't correct her. We had enough to navigate as we learned to work together without me snapping at her for using the manners she was expected to use with everyone else. Hopefully, as she got to know me, we'd become more informal. Well, she would. Personally, it was tough for me to get more informal than I already was, unless I started wandering around the castle in my jammies.

No wonder they didn't think I was good enough for Pierre.

Biting my lip, I forced myself to focus on the matter at hand. "You said the accounts were set up. Do I have any followers yet?"

"The monarchy has verified royal accounts on social media platforms," she said. "This morning, I officially introduced you on all of those accounts and asked our followers to welcome you to the family."

That made me smile. I'd never expected her to help me find my footing. "Thank you."

"I also followed all the official accounts for you: Queen Claudette, Prince Henri, Prince Pierre, a few others."

I wrinkled my nose. "You followed Henri? Honestly, I prefer not to hear what he has to say."

"His Royal Highness is a representative of the throne and a member of your new family. Many official statements come from his account." Darn it. That meant blocking him was also probably out of the question. "I can't tell you not to unfollow anyone, but it looks better if you have those connections. Helps give you credibility."

"Does that mean you told them to follow me back?"

"Of course," she said.

"Great! It's nice to have a handful of followers from day one."

"A handful?" Candace blinked several times. "As of nine o'clock this morning, you had three million, two hundred forty-seven thousand, three hundred sixty-two followers on Instagram. Twitter was nearing five million."

I choked. "That's not funny."

"I never joke about a royal's influence." She met my eyes, dead serious, and I felt light-headed.

"Let's sit down."

Wait. We were already sitting down. To her credit, Candace didn't point that out. I put my head between my knees and tried to remember how to breathe.

Preacher came over and jumped up beside me, putting his chin on my knee. As usual, stroking his fur made me feel much better. Slowly, my heart rate returned to normal.

Millions of people were interested in my thoughts. Me? Little Lila Sinclair?

"But I'm nobody," I finally choked out.

"You're not nobody," Candace said firmly. "First, you're a smart, educated, and interesting woman. It will help to remember that. You bring a new point of view to discussions. You're also married to Pierre de Leon, the son who vanished years ago and has been living out of the public eye. After he fell in love with and married a commoner, you convinced him to return to Court. The people are delighted he's back. Most of the replies to our posts say 'thank you'."

For the next several minutes, she suggested things to post and topics to avoid (anything controversial, anything sexual, and anything negative about other countries or their leaders). By the time we finished, I felt better.

Well enough to try out my first post from me: a picture of Preacher, the new royal Yorkie, lounging on that ridiculous-yet-amazing dog bed. Candace had told me when we met that a staffer could handle my posts, but to inspire people, I needed to be authentic.

I also needed to figure out what I wanted to inspire them to do. A general "don't be jerks" message sounded nice, but wasn't exactly life-changing advice. That was Future Lila's problem, though. At the moment, I just needed to keep my head above water.

"One more thing," Candace said after explaining the extra log-in procedures, super security, and what to do if I forgot my passwords and locked myself out or lost my phone.

"Uh-oh. I don't need to consult with you before I post, do I?" Because I wouldn't. Although I looked forward to seeing how Pierre and I could use our influence as a royal couple to make the world a better place, I had no intention of being a mouthpiece for the monarchy.

"We won't have post approval, but palace staff will read everything from your accounts," she said. "Queen Claudette wants to get to know you. In time, it will be more sporadic."

"She doesn't trust me."

"You're a stranger to her."

"I'm her daughter-in-law. I bet if Pierre had married Adrienne, she wouldn't have her accounts monitored," I said bitterly.

That wasn't entirely fair, since Queen Claudette had known Pierre's ex-girlfriend practically since birth. But also, history had shown I was a more trustworthy person than Adrienne. Especially where Pierre was involved.

"Social media barely existed when the two of them dated. It wouldn't have been an issue."

I huffed, but didn't respond.

"That's not the condition," she said.

"No? Then what?"

"Queen Claudette doesn't want you to post anything personal. Nothing about Lila Sinclair, the woman. This account is for Delilah, wife to the second son of Queen Claudette I."

I stared at her in stunned silence. "How am I supposed to influence people, get them to like me, if they can't know me?"

This was the entire reason we'd come back to Corchenne. Use my influence, make the world better. After less than a day, the Queen was putting a kink in my plans.

Chapter Four

OFFICIAL GUIDE TO BEING A PRINCESS: A princess must never appear flustered. Whatever happens, she must look as if it is precisely what she wanted to happen.

Pierre took my hand as we left our apartment. It calmed me. These days, I needed calming surprisingly often. I loved Pierre with all my heart. I wouldn't trade him for anything. But being the wife of a prince was both exhilarating and exhausting. I constantly worried that I wouldn't measure up. If this trip turned into a disaster, what happened to our future? Would Pierre allow his family to sway his opinion of me?

It was impossible to forget the way Pierre's brother Henri, the crown prince, spoke to me when we met. The way he looked down on me for having a low-paying retail job. He even tried to pay me to walk away from our relationship.

Beside me, my husband squeezed my hand. "Whatever you're thinking about, stop. Your scowl would terrify the Huns into retreat. *Mére* will think you hate her."

I shook my thoughts away before pasting a smile on my face. "Sorry, I'm just nervous. Will your brother be joining us?"

"I don't believe so. His flag was lowered shortly after we arrived. I believe he sailed to France for the afternoon. We'll see him at dinner. *Mére* dines later in the day."

Hearing it would be just the three of us made my shoulders relax. Henri was far from my favorite person. If there were a way to avoid him during our entire trip, I'd seize it gratefully. But for now, I'd accept a reprieve for a few hours.

As the doors to the throne room opened, I reminded myself not to gape at everything like some country bumpkin once we entered. Every thirty seconds, I found something else amazingly opulent in this building. The throne room must be the most impressive space of them all.

Pierre paused and turned to me as his mother's steward, Raul, announced our arrival. He kissed the tip of my nose, then my lips. "You're going to knock her dead."

"Is that the plan? I was hoping we'd have more time before Henri became King."

"If you're making bad jokes, you're ready. Come."

Like the other rooms we'd been in, the throne room had exquisite white marble floors threaded with gold. I wanted to assume it was fake gold but, well: castle. What must that have cost?

A plush dark blue runner created a path from the door to the raised dais, so thick I almost tripped on the edge. Rich-looking tapestries covered the walls in the Corche colors of blue and white.

Finally, my eyes went to the dais dominating the room where Queen Claudette held court. A massive throne sat in the middle, with smaller, equally ornate chairs on each side. Someone sat in the seat on the left, but when the Queen stood and moved to the front of the platform to greet me, she obscured my view. Not that there was any reason to look elsewhere with this woman in front of me.

She stood tall like her sons, with the same dark hair. Hers had been pulled back into a sleek chignon. She shared Pierre's powerful jaw and straight nose, to the point where examining her features felt like holding a mirror to our future.

To my surprise, her head was bare. I'd expected her to wear a tiara or crown like monarchs in storybooks. But then I realized Queen Elizabeth didn't wear her crown all the time, either. There were plenty of photographs showing that. This was an informal family meeting, not an official state event.

The steward stepped to the side of the walkway and gestured with one arm. Queen Claudette's eyes—my mother-in-law's eyes—fell on her son, and her face broke into a smile. For the first time, I relaxed. Maybe Pierre was right. She might be the ruler of a small country, but she'd been born a regular person. Queen Claudette loved her son and wanted him to be happy.

Then she turned to me, and the expression faded. Her eyes went cold, piercing right through me. A chill went down my spine, but I reminded myself to stay strong. Like Pierre told me all the time, she was as human as I. A very rich, powerful human who could squash me like a bug. Okay, he never said that. Still, we both knew it.

In a weird way, though, she brought me and Pierre together. I owed her that, at least. Although, on second thought, she probably wouldn't appreciate learning that her decision to have him move back to Corchenne led to our agreement to enter a fraudulent green card marriage, causing us to fall in love. At least not during our very first meeting.

"Pierre, darling! It's so good to see you." She stepped forward, taking his hands in hers and kissing each cheek before wrapping him in a hug. "I'm so relieved to see that you've finally decided to spend time here with the family. We've all missed you."

"It's good to be home. I've missed you, too. And Corchenne, of course," he said. "How are you feeling?"

"Oh, I'm fine, dear. Come, come. Don't keep me waiting. It's well beyond time for you to introduce me to your wife! I still can't believe you didn't invite me to the wedding."

"My apologies. There were extenuating circumstances." He turned to me and stretched out one arm. "*Mére*, I'd like to present my beloved wife, Lila Sinclair. *Chérie*, this is my mother, Her Royal Majesty Queen Claudette I of Corchenne."

"Delilah, I'm so pleased to finally meet your acquaintance." When she said "finally," she glared at Pierre in a way that made my lips twitch. I struggled to maintain a straight face. Now wasn't the time. "Surely my son meant Delilah Leon, though?"

"It's an honor to meet you, Your Majesty." I curtsied deeply, the way I'd practiced a thousand times. Pierre had warned me that his mother might not understand my decision to keep my maiden name following our marriage. I opened my mouth to give the explanation we'd practiced.

But as I brought myself upright, my gaze fell on the man standing beside Pierre's mother for the first time. The words shriveled in my throat, and I wobbled on my toes before toppling to the ground.

"Lila?" Pierre's voice cut through my stupefaction as Claudette let out a delicate laugh. "Are you okay?"

"She's fine, dear. I see your wife has spotted my newest advisor. It might be a shock to see a familiar face this far from home, but I hope a good one."

Until Queen Claudette uttered the phrase "familiar face," I'd hoped to be wrong. Lots of blonde men in the world stood approximately five feet, ten inches tall. Who wore the air of superiority and made my skin crawl.

Or not.

Struggling to my feet, I found my voice. "Caleb? What on earth are you doing here?"

Chapter Five

Despite my parents' inexplicable adoration, Caleb was the black sheep of my family. At least, as far as Hannah and I were concerned. A few years ago, he "borrowed" my sister's hard-earned money and never repaid a single cent. He talked me into investing in a "fixer-upper" by promising to do all the work. Then he fled to Brazil with the renovation fund. When he heard about my wedding, he had the nerve to ask me to send him cash for a plane ticket. We intentionally hadn't invited him.

Despite his promises, he never paid anyone back. An overly optimistic part of me had hoped Caleb would never find out who Pierre was. The longer my opportunistic brother didn't know about my rich relations, the better. He didn't have any social media, which I'd hoped would stop him from learning about me.

Instead, his lack of internet presence apparently made the queen think he was someone she wanted in the palace.

I didn't know what he was doing here, but somehow I suspected my mother was involved. She adored Caleb, talked to him all the time. Now, for whatever reason, here he was. Standing beside my mother-in-law, the Queen of Corchenne. Who just called him her new advisor.

He couldn't be up to anything good.

What could Caleb advise a queen on, anyway? Being shady? Lies and deception? Either she hadn't vetted him, or he was even more of a smooth-talker than I thought. Knowing the full reach of Queen Claudette's power and influence, I suspected it must be the latter. But how?

This couldn't be happening.

Bile rose in my throat. It took all my effort to tamp it down.

"Sister!" Extending both hands, Caleb approached.

I forced myself not to step backward. He grabbed my hands and kissed both cheeks in the French way. Also, apparently, the Corche way. With extreme effort, I avoided rolling my eyes. No matter how surreal this experience got, today was my first meeting with Queen Claudette. I needed to be on my best behavior.

"What are you doing here? Aren't you supposed to be in Brazil?"

"I needed a change of scenery," he said. "Besides, after I missed your wedding, I wanted to congratulate you and Pierre in person."

"That is very kind," Pierre said, extending one hand. "It's a pleasure to see you again."

Although Caleb had met Pierre a few times when we first bought the house next door to him, they'd only ever been neighbors. Cordial, nothing more. The look on my husband's face told me he remembered everything I'd ever said about my brother. He was very worried to find Caleb in the throne room, cozy with the queen. We had to warn Pierre's mother. I could only hope Caleb hadn't already gotten into the royal vaults.

Yes, the family had plenty of money. That wasn't the point. I wasn't about to let my brother take advantage of my new mother-in-law. Especially when I had only known the woman for about fourteen seconds.

"Caleb has been telling me about a wonderful new opportunity," Queen Claudette said. "I never considered investing in a Brazilian company, but maybe now is the time to extend our family's holdings."

"Have you spoken to Henri about this?" Pierre asked. "Or consulted with your financial advisors?"

"Careful, my son," she said. "You come dangerously close to insulting me. You may have been a big-shot investment banker in America, but I'm your mother and your queen. I'm nearly twice your age, and I've been around the block a few times."

"Of course, *Mére*." He bowed deeply. "I didn't mean to imply that you don't know what you're doing. I've simply never seen you show an interest in Brazilian investments."

"You've been away," she said. "I'm always looking for new opportunities."

New opportunities were great, but new scams were not. Not even if scamming the Corchenne royal family finally convinced my parents that their son wasn't perfect.

I cleared my throat gently. "If I may, Your Majesty...?"

"Yes, dear?"

"It's been a long time since I've seen my brother. Could we perhaps have a few moments to reconnect in private?"

"Certainly," she said. "There's a sitting room to the left. Pierre and I will join you shortly. But first, let's record this moment for posterity, shall we? Candace assured me that your social media accounts have been set up."

"Um, yes. They have. But she said not to get personal. I'm not sure that family photos—"

"Nonsense! What could be more appropriate and momentous than introducing your brother to your mother-in-law, the queen?" The way Claudette looked at me suggested the answer was "nothing". If she'd really wanted my opinion, I would have gone with, "getting boils on my lady bits."

With no other choices, I took a group selfie and posted it, "accidentally" forgetting to tag anyone. Let Candace complain about my poor hashtag use later. If Caleb hadn't been peeking over my shoulder, I would have put my thumb over the camera. The internet didn't need to meet him.

My husband kissed my cheek before I left the room to have a private talk with my big brother. "Thank you," he murmured. "Don't worry, I'll talk to her."

"I have total faith in you."

Like the throne room, Queen Claudette's attached sitting room had marble floors, floor-to-ceiling windows bordered by silken drapes, and furniture I was afraid to sit on because I might wrinkle it. Caleb and I had barely entered the room when a server appeared to ask if we needed anything.

Yeah, a new brother?

"No, thank you," I said. "By the way, I'm Lila."

"Michel."

"I'd love a drink," Caleb said. "A glass of your finest red wine, if you don't mind."

"That's not necessary," I said.

"It's not a problem, Madame," Michel said with a deep bow. Before I could stop him, he left the room.

Immediately, I whirled on my brother. "What are you doing here?"

"Her Royal Majesty told you. I'm here to offer a great business opportunity to the queen."

"Since when do you rub elbows with royalty?"

"Oh, I don't know, since my baby sister married into the family?"

I glared at him. "So, after you stole from Hannah and screwed me over with that awful house we *finally* sold, now you're going to con my relatives, too? No way, no how. I'm going to have Pierre arrange a flight home for you immediately."

Whirling around, I headed for the door. Caleb's voice stopped me in my tracks. "I wouldn't do that if I were you."

"Why ever not? You don't think the queen would be interested in hearing how your grand investment opportunities make no one but you any richer?"

The door opened as Michel re-entered, carrying a tray with a snifter of wine and two glasses. We stopped talking until he placed it on the coffee table. I thanked him, and he left. Caleb continued to watch me with a bemused expression on his face.

"You don't take enough advantage of your situation," he said.

"I want to use my situation to make the world a better place," I replied. "That's the best way to take advantage of it."

He snorted. "Right. You could build a spaceship. Space L for Lila. Why not go further? With your husband's money and resources, you could buy a planet and name it after yourself."

Why on earth would I do that? And who would I pay?

"I don't think planets are for sale, Caleb. Anyway, you're changing the subject. I will not let you con my mother-in-law."

With an overly exaggerated sigh, Caleb fell onto the couch. He picked up a glass of wine from the end table and sipped it before replying. "You never had any faith in me."

"I had all kinds of faith in you three years ago," I said. "Remember when I purchased a property with you, intending for you to fix it up and sell it so we could split the profits? I used my student loans to pay for it. You ditched me. If Pierre hadn't saved me, I'd be working on that place until I turned fifty."

"I didn't do that to hurt you," he said. "I met Fernanda, and we fell in love. When her visa expired, I didn't know what to do. But then she got pregnant, so I followed her to Brazil. You'd have done the same thing."

He had me there. That we currently stood in Corchenne was strong evidence that I would have done the same thing, despite my intent to return to Boston in a few weeks. The difference was, Fernanda wasn't allowed to go back.

"You had options, Caleb. You could have finished the work

before you left or hired contractors. Taking our money and disappearing was not the only choice."

He stared at his wine again for a long moment. "You're right. I'm sorry."

Surprised, I sat in the chair across from him. I'd never expected to hear an apology from my brother. "Wh-What did you say?"

"I messed up. I made a huge mistake. We left so fast, got married right away. Later I realized Fernanda pushed for a quick wedding because she didn't want me to do the math."

"What are you talking about?" My mind flitted back to a distant memory of Mom bemoaning the fact that Aberto was born less than nine months after Caleb fled the country. "Are you saying–?"

"Aberto's not mine." He swallowed, and tears prickled at the corners of his eyes. "That's the real reason I'm here. I've left Brazil for good."

My heart went out to him. There were many, many things I could–and did–say about my brother, but he loved that little boy. "Fernanda cheated on you?"

"She lied to me," he said. "When we met, she was in love with someone else. He dumped her after she got pregnant, so she pretended the child was mine."

My whole life, this might be the most vulnerable I'd ever seen Caleb. "That's awful. I'm so sorry. How did you find out?"

"The other man changed his mind. Realized he was in love with Fernanda and came to Brazil."

"Oh, Caleb." As much as I resented my brother for the things he'd done, no one deserved to be treated that way.

He refilled his wine. "Yeah. When I confronted her, she told me everything. At that point, you'd already left Boston for your whirlwind honeymoon tour. Hannah, point-blank, refused to let me stay with her, and I couldn't stand the humiliation of telling Mom and Dad. Instead, I used the last of my money to come here."

"Okay, I understand why you're embarrassed, but don't you think Mom and Dad will eventually notice they no longer have a grandchild?"

"I'll tell them at some point," he said. "After I get back on my feet."

"Which you're doing in Corchenne." We'd come full circle. Although I felt bad for his situation, I still didn't want my brother here to screw over my new family. And I absolutely didn't miss the irony of the con man getting conned by his wife.

I filed that thought away for later. Hannah would appreciate the schadenfreude. Caleb would not.

He nodded. "After Fernanda left me, there was no point in staying in Brazil. I'm still a U.S. citizen, and there's more opportunity elsewhere."

"Opportunities like..." I couldn't say "screwing me over," but didn't know how to end that sentence. Better to let my voice trail off.

The door flew open. Raul entered, bowing deeply before he faced us. "Presenting Her Royal Majesty Queen Claudette and His Royal Highness, Prince Pierre de Leon."

Caleb rose instantly to his feet. After an awkward moment, he cleared his throat, and I did the same. Was this how we entered rooms now? Would my husband always require a royal pronouncement? I envisioned Raul standing in the doorway of my bedroom, informing me that Pierre was about to enter the royal bedchamber, and I had to swallow back a giggle.

Queen Claudette swept into the room with Pierre a few steps behind her. She took her place on the sofa and patted the seat beside her. "Caleb, dear, please sit."

Dear? Caleb dear? Oh, no. Things were worse than I'd thought. Here I'd allowed myself to hope that Pierre and I interrupted the beginning of his pitch, but between that and the "advisor" comment, it sounded like my brother had made himself very comfortable with the royal family.

As if his mind followed the same train of thought, Pierre spoke. "Caleb, when did you arrive in Corchenne?"

"He's been here about three weeks," Queen Claudette said. "Caleb has been invaluable in helping me understand what makes my new daughter-in-law tick. He's also suggested several upgrades to the palace. Last month, he even spotted a rotting floor in one of the gazebos. Imagine if he hadn't been here, and it had collapsed."

I desperately wanted to ask if Caleb had caused the floor rot. I wouldn't put it past him. Instead, I considered the rest of her words. If he had been in Corchenne for three weeks, Caleb arrived a few short days after my wedding. Barely enough time to come to Boston and realize I'd gone. That was less than a week after I'd refused to buy him a plane ticket. If I'd paid him then, would I have avoided this embarrassment now?

Probably not. My brother was a leech, fueled by cash. He absorbed whatever he got and instantly wanted more. More likely, he would've ruined my wedding and still flown here after Mom and Dad "loaned" him cash for a new venture.

Now he'd attached his little suction cup to my mother-in-law. From the way she looked at him, it was going to be difficult to pry him loose.

"Caleb, why don't you tell everyone about this project?" Another tray appeared in front of Queen Claudette as if by magic, and she suddenly held a teacup. The china appeared to be so delicate, I couldn't imagine picking it up for fear of breaking it. "I find the idea fascinating."

Caleb leaned forward, perching excitedly on the edge of his seat. "Picture this. You've got all that fertile farmland out there. Most of the year, it's growing grapes. Which is great. I love grapes, I love wine. But what about after the harvest? Soon, the fields will be bare. Nothing but dirt. All winter, that land sits fallow until someone is ready to plant again."

"I believe that's called a 'renewal period', in farming terms," I said.

"Right. And fine. We let the land renew. We don't plant. But what if we use the land to grow animals? Livestock that we don't have room to raise anywhere else?"

Livestock? My brother wanted to bring in cows? Pierre and I exchanged a look.

"Are you suggesting we turn the vineyards into a place for sheep or cows to graze during the offseason?" he asked.

"Don't be ridiculous. Although the manure would probably be great for your grapes, they'd trample the land too much. I'm looking for something lighter."

"Chickens?" I asked hesitantly.

"Now you're getting the idea!" Caleb said. "The bird market is enormous right now. All we'd have to do is make sure they're fed. The rest is smooth sailing."

"That sounds very innovative," Pierre said diplomatically. "However, the royal family doesn't own most of the vineyards on the island. They were gifted to the people who worked on them decades ago. Before we could use them, we need permission from the current owners."

"Doesn't that make it perfect?" Queen Claudette beamed. "Imagine Caleb finding a way for us to give income to our people year-round by renting the land from them when they don't need it. They'll be delighted."

When you put it that way, using the farm betweens season sounded great. But I knew nothing about farming or renewing farmland or—any of this.

"Did you commission experts to analyze the fields?" I asked my brother.

Queen Claudette stiffened her back and looked down her nose at me. "Surely, my dear, you aren't suggesting that I would consider an investment proposal without first performing due diligence?"

"Of course not, Your Majesty," I said hastily. "I just didn't know how far you two had gotten since Caleb arrived. My apologies."

"My guy did a full farmland analysis, and he thinks we can

swing this," Caleb said. "We've got a shipment coming soon. This is going to be huge."

"How does it work?" I desperately sought any way to help the queen see reason. "The Corchenne government buys the animals, they pay to rent the land from the farmers and… Then we sell the animals when it's time to plant? So they're only owned for a few months? Where do they go after that?"

That truly sounded like the worst idea I'd ever heard, but I knew as much about farmland as about colonizing the moon.

Caleb beamed. "Now you've got it! I'm so happy you're on board."

"On board" was a stretch, but Pierre spoke before I could contradict Caleb. "This sounds like an interesting proposition. What does Henri think, *Mére*?"

She waved one hand. "Oh, you know your brother. So stodgy and unflappable. He gets so set in his ways. Once he makes up his mind, changing him takes moving a mountain."

That description fit the man I'd met perfectly. However, if he could stop their mother from making a huge mistake, I would swear my undying fealty to him on the spot.

"True," Pierre said, "but he has a good head for business."

"Your brother isn't interested in expanding his holdings at the moment," she said. "He's taking more of an interest in international relations."

Pierre said, "that's something Lila and Henri have in common. Lila loves meeting people and learning from them."

"What about you?" Caleb asked. "Do you see yourself investing in bird farming?"

Pierre pulled a business card from his pocket. "I never make these types of decisions on the fly. Send a proposal to my business manager, and we'll be in touch."

My eyes shot daggers at him until I spotted the name on the business card. Blaise. Pierre's former roommate, a chef, and someone who would absolutely never, ever return Caleb's calls.

Smart. I should have fake business cards made up with Madison's info. She would love rejecting Caleb on my behalf.

"Sounds great!" Caleb said. "I look forward to working with all of you."

Over my dead body. This "opportunity" would never pan out. He'd take whatever he could get his hands on and skip the country, never to set foot in Corchenne again. Any money she gave him would be lost forever.

We had to get Queen Claudette to listen before my brother ruined everything.

~

The moment Pierre and I finally extricated ourselves from the sitting room, I dragged him outside. "This is awful. The absolute worst!"

"The worst thing possible?" Pierre quirked an eyebrow at me. "Worse than the planet getting hit by an asteroid?"

"Of course not," I amended. "Okay, one of the worst things that could happen to me. Not as bad as losing you, obvs, but since you might leave me after my brother steals your family fortune—it's bad. He's got his hooks into your mother already. We need to save her."

He cupped my face and gave me a slow, lingering kiss on the lips. Mmm. An excellent way to calm me. "Everything will be okay. Number one, he will not steal my entire family fortune. As my mother so bluntly pointed out in there, she's an intelligent woman who knows what she's doing. She's probably just humoring him. Number Two, I love you and would never hold you responsible for your brother's actions."

"You say that now. To think I was starting to feel sorry for the creep!"

"Oh?"

Quickly, I filled him in on the things Caleb said to me. "Of course, for all I know, it's another lie."

"That's easy enough to find out."

"It is?"

"Certainly. I'll ask my chief of staff to look at the records, find a birth certificate. Alberto, right?"

"Right. But if Fernanda lied about the father, Caleb's name might be on it."

"True. One thing at a time. I'll also have him look for proof that they married in Brazil and evidence that either of them filed for divorce." He paused. "You know, if he's telling the truth, your brother is probably feeling very vulnerable right now."

Although I hated acknowledging that Caleb was a person with emotions and not a supervillain, it wasn't in my nature to ignore someone in pain. "I know."

"He could be trying to change."

I'd given Caleb the benefit of the doubt repeatedly over the past twenty-five years. I could have empathy without wanting to give him anything. But I didn't want to argue with Pierre. We needed to present a united front. "For now, I'll assume that he's telling the truth about Fernanda. He seemed to be in genuine pain. But I still don't trust him. Did you warn your mother?"

"When you were speaking with Caleb, I told her a little about your history, especially the financial stuff. She admonished me not to treat her like a child. We may need to tread carefully."

"Do you think it would help at all if I spoke to her?"

"Not yet. I'll keep trying. Meanwhile, you do everything you can to dazzle her. The more she trusts you, the better."

"On it," I said, trying to sound more confident than I felt.

"Maybe we should invite him to dinner this evening. I can talk to him, get a feel for this project. It might help matters between you and Henri to have a buffer. Someone else to occupy attention."

"You'd subject yourself to hours in a room with my brother, just for me?"

"Of course." He smiled gleefully. "I can't wait to hear all about Lila growing up."

Chapter Six

OFFICIAL GUIDE TO BEING A PRINCESS: Start at the outside of your silverware and move inward with each course. Any mistakes are the fault of the table-setter.

Before entering the royal dining hall, I ducked into one of the many bathrooms to check my hair and makeup. Everything needed to be perfect for this first meal. No chinks in my armor, as it was.

Well, as perfect as sharing my first meal with a brother-in-law who hated me, a mother-in-law who knew I wasn't good enough for her son, and my own brother, the spawn of Satan, could be.

Smoothing a loose strand of honey-blond hair behind my left ear, I forced myself to swallow that last thought. Queen Claudette hadn't brought Caleb here to spite me. He'd shown up, and she was doing the gracious thing by hosting him.

She didn't know our history. She wasn't there when he saddled me with a rundown house and six figures of debt. No one told her he'd stolen money from our sister. And while Caleb was busy ingratiating himself to my mother-in-law, he certainly hadn't brought up how our parents idolized him and reminded Hannah and me every day that we'd never live up to his amazingness. If I were rude to my brother in front of everyone, it would only make me look petty and small.

To calm myself, I hummed a song from *Encanto* while I finished freshening up. When I worked at SidMart, that was one of about four approved movies to air throughout the day in the electronics section. It played over and over and over.... At least it was catchy.

Pierre knocked at the door. When I called for him to open it, he poked his head in. "Were you just talking to me?"

"No, sorry. I was, er, ranting about Caleb. You know, the usual."

Coming in, he approached and met my eyes in the mirror. "Finding him seated beside my mother was quite a shock. I know you're dreading this dinner more than a root canal, but it's important to keep him close until we know more about his plans."

"That's not a fair comparison," I said. "With a root canal, they give you drugs to knock you out."

He smiled thinly. "You've got this. We've got this."

I took a deep breath before applying my lip gloss, then released it. "Thanks. I think I'm ready."

Pierre took my hand and helped me up, then walked me to the door. "Besides, if he hurts my mother, I'll let you sic Preacher on him."

"My hero," I said.

We walked hand-in-hand through the halls connecting our turret to the main castle, down the stairs, and into the royal dining room. When we arrived, I felt better, stronger. Pierre and I were here to get to know my new relatives. Have a nice dinner. That was it. One thing at a time. Rome wasn't built in a day, and Caleb wouldn't single-handedly bring down the Corchenne monarchy before dessert arrived.

Unlike so many other rooms we'd passed through so far, the royal dining room had dark blue tiles on the floor, carved with the de Leon family crest. A massive fireplace dominated one wall, with a gorgeous portrait of the royal family. It must have been painted decades ago: King Henri I dominated the frame, with Queen Claudette by his side and the princes flanking them. Pierre and Henri looked like teenagers. Everyone wore formal clothes, serious expressions, and their crowns. I was no art critic, but the work looked exceptional to me.

On either side of the fireplace sat buffet tables. Enormous mirrors hung on the walls beside the fireplace. The far wall contained floor-to-ceiling windows similar to the ones in the throne room. Queen Claudette hadn't arrived yet, so I moved to take in the spectacular view of the vineyards.

"I never tire of looking at this," Pierre said, coming with me.

"I can see why." The coppery leaves stood out against the dark blue water. Sometimes I forgot we were on an island. "This may be my favorite spot in the whole castle. Other than our room, of course."

"It's definitely the best view. Father insisted we move the royal dining room here when I was young. He wanted to enjoy the vineyards while we ate." Sadness filled his words, and I glanced again at the portrait on the wall.

"I'm sorry, Pierre. You must really miss him."

"He's been gone a long time. I am at peace. But sometimes, it's important to remember what we've lost so we appreciate what we have."

Behind us, the double doors flew open. Raul strode in, then stopped and stood at attention. "Presenting Her Royal Majesty Queen Claudette and His Royal Highness, Prince Henri, accompanied by Mr. Caleb Sinclair."

We stood at attention while the three of them moved to the table. Out of the side of my mouth, I whispered, "Promise if we ever become queen and king, you won't do that."

His lips twitched. "You have my solemn oath."

The dining room table held eight chairs on each side, plus one at each end. Given how much longer the room stretched on, I suspected additional leaves could be added. The chairs were made of a gold-colored wood with blue cushions that matched the iris blue of the country's flag. A few shades lighter than the floor tiles. Good thing we were checking out the room when everyone else arrived. I never would've been able to figure out where to sit without Raul leading me to my chair.

As expected, the monarch took the head of the table. She put the windows to her back, facing the door. Henri likely would have sat at the other end for state meals, but since there were only five place settings, he stood behind the chair to Queen Claudette's right. Pierre trailed behind me and Raul, pausing at the chair on his mother's left. Raul pulled out the next seat down, and I sat. A moment later, Caleb settled into place across from me.

Goblets full of water stood at each place setting, but now uniformed servers came around to offer wine. I started to say no because wine loosened my tongue, but then I remembered Pierre's comment about the two of us trying for a family right away. Better not to cause speculation on why Pierre's new wife wasn't drinking. It was embarrassing enough when my parents thought were getting married because I was pregnant.

Queen Claudette asked Henri about his trip to France, which gave me time to get used to sitting there. The attention would turn to me soon enough. Meanwhile, I listened with half an ear while servers carried silver trays of food into the room.

By the time a steaming bowl was placed in front of me for the soup course, my mouth was watering. We hadn't eaten since getting off the plane several hours ago. I would've happily poured the entire bowl into my mouth if I'd been alone. Instead, I sat patiently while one of the servers—whose nametag identified her as Deidre—unfolded a napkin and placed it gently in my lap. So weird. It took a lot of willpower not to tell her I was perfectly capable of handling my own napkin.

I waited hesitantly, unsure of my next step. At home, one of my parents would say grace before we ate. It was the height of rudeness to start first. Queen Claudette was not overly religious, according to Pierre, but that didn't mean I could start eating before she did.

Oh, man. I hoped we didn't have to wait for a royal taste tester to approve the meal. I might pass out.

Thankfully, as soon as everyone was served, she simply reached out to her sons with each hand and squeezed gently. "Thank you for this food. I am grateful all of you came tonight."

"We're thrilled to be here, *Mére*," Pierre said.

"Then what are you waiting for? Eat before it gets cold!"

She didn't have to tell me twice. Careful not to slurp or spill, I picked up the spoon furthest on my left and dug in.

"Your Majesty, did I ever tell you I am the one who brought Pierre and Lila together?"

Not five minutes into the first course, Caleb's words made me choke on my minestrone soup. I coughed and sputtered. Pierre rubbed small circles on my back. When I could finally breathe again, it took half a glass of wine before I stopped seeing red enough to follow the rest of the conversation.

"Oh yes," Caleb was saying, "I found Lila's house when it was first listed for sale, and I was the one who convinced her that real estate would be a brilliant investment."

Yeah, great. It only took every second of my time and every spare penny for more than a year. If Pierre hadn't come along when he did, I'd still be eating dried beans three times a week to pay for paint.

As if he could read my thoughts, Pierre squeezed my hand where it lay on the table. "Yes, *Meré*, I am forever grateful that Lila moved next door to me so we could meet and fall in love. Just think, if Caleb hadn't chosen that property, I might still be a bachelor."

I choked back a snort of laughter. Queen Claudette's perfect mask slipped, just for a second, and her brown eyes shot daggers at the three of us.

"What a tragedy that would be," Henri said dryly. "Would anyone else like more wine?"

Four crystal goblets shot into the air. Well, at least Caleb joined me on Queen Claudette's "Least Favorite People" list for a few seconds. We all drank and finished our soup in silence. It tasted fantastic. I could've eaten a vat of the stuff and still wanted more.

The quiet didn't last, though.

"Tell us, Caleb," Henri said once the soup bowls had been cleared, "what was Lila like as a young girl?"

My brother looked delighted at the question. "Oh, Delilah was a fascinating child."

I bit my tongue to keep from correcting him. Now wasn't the time. He knew well that I never, ever used my full name if there were any way around it.

"You know, Caleb and I didn't play together much," I blurted. "He wasn't interested in his little sister. He doesn't have many stories."

"That's right!" Caleb laughed, a touch too loudly. "I almost forgot about the time you set up a free hospital to educate your dolls about the benefits of public health care."

Pierre's lips twitched. "I see my wife has always had a strong sense of social justice."

"One of many things you love about me, right, darling?" To the Queen, I said, "I'd love to get involved with the Corche people. Do some charity work, if I can. Do you think you could recommend some organizations?"

She waved one hand. "I'll have my assistant set up some photo opps for you. I hope you weren't planning to provide free health care yourself?"

"Ah, no, Your Royal Majesty. I'm not a doctor." My face flamed. "During college, I learned that I grow faint at the sight of, er, medical things. All of them."

"Lila's talents are better used in other areas," Pierre said smoothly.

"I'll bet," Henri muttered under his breath.

I dearly wished he sat close enough for me to kick him. Barely had I finished the thought when Henri yelped and jumped in his seat.

"Wanting to help the less fortunate is lovely, dear," Queen Claudette said, ignoring her sons completely. "But now that you're in the public eye, you must pick the right cause. Nothing too sordid or scandalous."

Why would helping people be sordid or scandalous? I wanted to enhance the lives of Corche citizens, in whatever way I could. Currently, I had no idea what that was.

"What do you recommend, your Majesty?"

If I'd hoped she would give me permission to use anything other than her title, I was destined to be disappointed. "I'll be hosting a fundraiser next month to buy new equipment for the children's hospital. I'd be delighted if you would help me with the planning."

"As monarch, aren't you in charge of the hospital?" I asked, wrinkling my brow. "Couldn't you buy the equipment yourself?"

Caleb barked out a laugh. "Don't be naïve. That's not how these things work."

"Why not?" I insisted. "The monarchy has more money than God. The royal family could give money to the hospital and even get a tax write-off. Not that you probably need it—do you pay even taxes to yourself?"

"We do indeed pay taxes," Queen Claudette said, lifting her nose in the air. "I can see that your education in the Corche government has been sadly lacking. Pierre, you'll see to fixing that."

Her condescending attitude had me biting my tongue so hard I tasted blood. But it wouldn't do to toss my wine at the Queen and call her an ogre. Instead, I gritted my teeth and tried to think of any other topic of conversation. Obviously, I'd have to add "educating the Queen" to my list of ways to improve the world.

"*Mére*, Lila can inform herself on any subject she chooses," Pierre said. "She studies daily to learn about the language, the people, and the resources of the land. And she has a point—we could put more money into the hospitals without asking anyone else to donate."

"How would you know?" Henri asked. "You haven't even opened the folder of budget documents I gave you."

"I read many things when you're not peeking over my shoulder," Pierre said as Henri glared at him across the table. Then, as if realizing how much animosity flowed toward us, he took a bite of his dinner and chewed enthusiastically. To his mother, he said, "This beef is divine."

"And I love the wine," I said, eager to get the conversation onto safer ground than my political goals. "Was it made here in Corchenne?"

"Of course it was," Queen Claudette said. "Do you think I would bring in foreign wine to welcome my son home?"

"What mother means," Pierre said quickly, "is that we have such amazing vineyards here on the grounds, we wanted you to sample our offerings. We've been blessed with abundantly fertile crops for the past few years. We love to share that bounty with family and friends."

Henri snorted. "Did you hear that on CNN? What do you know about our crops, Mr. Boston?"

"I still have advisors here to keep me apprised of things," Pierre said.

"Would you have returned to solve problems?"

"Certainly. But I trusted you to handle matters while I was away. You are more than capable. Luckily, there was no need for me to interfere."

Queen Claudette cleared her throat as if this was the four millionth brotherly squabble she'd interrupted. Probably was. "We're celebrating the harvest later in the week with a festival. It's a grand affair—music, grape picking, wine making, cheese. It's one of my favorite events!"

"Also a great way to meet people," Pierre added. "Get to know the locals."

"Caleb, I hope you'll be able to come see it," Queen Claudette said. "And Lila, too, if you're not too busy."

Nothing like being an afterthought. I smiled tightly. "I'd be delighted."

"*Meré*, I've been giving some thought to the matter of Lila's title," Pierre said.

"Oh you have, have you?" Queen Claudette replied. "Silly me, but I thought it was the queen's job to assign titles, not the absentee prince's."

"Of course. I didn't mean to imply otherwise. However, I know you're busy. I thought you might have more pressing matters at hand."

Across the table, Henri mouthed something that I strongly suspected was the French equivalent of "suck up," based on his expression. He didn't comment, though.

"Go on," my mother-in-law said. "I imagine you think she should be named a Princess of Corchenne?"

"That is the tradition, of course," Pierre said without hesitation. "And I believe Lila would be a credit to that title."

"Traditionally, Corche princesses own land in Corchenne. Or at least their fathers do," Henri said.

"What about their husbands?" Pierre shot back.

"You don't own any land here," Henri said. "Not yet."

I watched the two of them like a ping-pong match. Henri's last comment seemed to have hit home, but then Pierre leaned forward. "That's not entirely true. There is *Grand-meré's* land."

"That's not yours!" Henri shouted.

"It is *our* family vineyard—"

"Enough!" Queen Claudette clapped her hands loudly. We all turned to look at her. "We have a guest, and you two are being abominably rude. Pierre, I will consider your request. What land did you have in mind?"

"*Maison du Vin Mousseux*, on the west shore," he said immediately. Clearly, my husband had thought about this. "It's been empty since the old baron died. We could hire someone to bring back the glorious sparkling wine we sold decades ago."

"It's all horribly overgrown. No one has tended that land for years," Henri said. "You'd know that if you ever took an interest in your country."

"Lila's not afraid of hard work," Pierre said, ignoring the barb. It was an old argument between the brothers. "She remodeled an entire house practically by herself."

Yeah. No thanks to my useless brother, I didn't say. Instead, I turned to my husband. "When a landowner dies, the crown takes his property?"

"No, not at all. The Baron took the land over from my grandmother before she passed. He was my mother's cousin. We are his closest living relatives."

"*I* am his closest living relative," Queen Claudette corrected him. "As such, I will decide how to handle the land and attached titles. It is high time someone put those vineyards back in order. Thank you for the suggestion."

She lifted her glass, showing the matter closed for now. But I didn't miss the way she looked at me while she drank. Not as a loving mother-in-law meeting her son's new wife. The narrow-eyed suspicion of a Mama Bear who feared that someone was coming to steal her cubs. To seduce him into giving her lands she didn't deserve and a title she didn't earn.

Pierre's request hadn't done me any favors, although I appreciated the intent. If I wanted Queen Claudette to accept me into the family, I had my work cut out for me.

Chapter Seven

After an endless day of travel, stress, and meeting hostile relatives (mine and Pierre's), I wanted to crawl into bed and sleep for about seventeen hours. Unfortunately, Pierre and I had already made plans for the next day that didn't involve spending the whole time unconscious. I barely kept my eyes open long enough to take off my makeup and hang my borrowed dress in the closet before collapsing onto the amazingly soft sheets. The only way I could have been asleep sooner was if I'd worn my pajamas to meet the queen.

What felt like three minutes later, daylight flooded the room. My cruel traitor of a husband stood at the window, holding the pull cord for the curtains.

"Why would you do this?" I moaned. "I thought you loved me."

"If it were my decision, we would stay in bed all day." His

weight settled onto the edge of the mattress beside me, and his firm hand stroked my cheek. "Time to get up, *ma chérie*. We have much to do today."

"Like meeting more of your relatives who hate me?" I grumbled, rolling over and attempting to pull one of the massive pillows over my head. Pierre swiped it easily and tossed it onto the bench at the end of the bed. "Or trying to stop my brother from stealing the kingdom? Darn. We really should do that one first."

"Like meeting my favorite relative, who I'm sure will adore you every bit as much as I do."

I snorted as I struggled into a sitting position. "Right. Just like your brother and mother do."

Pierre pulled me into a hug and stroked my hair. I nestled into him, savoring the closeness. We had a busy agenda for the next few weeks; I knew better than to let these moments slip by. "*Mére* will come around, eventually. She doesn't dislike you, per se. She just takes time to warm up to people."

"She didn't need time to warm up to Caleb. She's ready to adopt him, maybe try to marry him to Henri to make it official." I was being childish, and I knew it. Seeing my brother appear at Court annoyed me, but seeing him accepted like the long-lost prodigal son really chafed. Especially since I actually returned with the long-lost prodigal son, and we hadn't received nearly the same warm welcome.

"Your brother is a special exception, as you know," Pierre said. "He's spent years learning how to charm people. If you'd shown up spouting nothing but compliments and lies, they'd love you, too. Also, he arrived before us. We have no idea what his initial reception was. He'll show his true colors soon enough."

"I hope so." Rearranging the pillows, I leaned back against them and accepted a cup of coffee from the tray Pierre had set on the nightstand. "Thanks. You made me breakfast in bed?"

"Well, I brought you breakfast in bed. Do I still get points if I didn't cook it?"

I recalled the last time Pierre had prepared me a meal, on our third date. Although he'd reheated a pre-made dinner, it had been inedible. After one bite, we'd ordered takeout. "You get more points for not making it yourself."

After handing me a napkin, Pierre lifted the lids off several plates on the tray and moved the whole thing over to the middle of the massive bed. Almond-filled croissants and toast and grape jelly—"Fresh from the vineyards," Pierre assured me—and scrambled eggs and Eggs Benedict and French toast. I couldn't believe the mountain of options in front of me.

"How hungry do you think I am?"

He laughed and held up two sets of silverware. "This isn't all for you. We're sharing. And I, personally, am famished. All that bowing gave me quite the workout yesterday."

I snatched up a croissant and bit into it. It melted in my mouth. Pure heaven. Bliss! So amazing. I swooned. "What's going on today?"

"Aunt Bridget is on her way to meet us, as I said."

Mentally, I pulled up a picture of the family tree. "She's a Duchess, right?"

"Yes. Fourth in line for the throne, after me. But she finds court to be dreadfully boring, so don't be surprised if she begs us to have kids as soon as possible, just in case."

I rolled my eyes. "Not this again."

"Sorry, not now," he said. "She's the one who donated those clothes for you to wear while we're here. I knew you wouldn't want to buy a lot of things to wear once."

I glanced over at the dozens of dresses, shirts, skirts, and tailored pants hanging in the closet. Most of it in silks, linen, and other expensive fabrics, all gorgeous. "She has excellent taste. Thank you very much."

"Don't thank me. It was her idea. Bridget is also going to..." He stopped and studied me. "How do I put this delicately? She's going to serve as your royal tutor."

I raised my eyebrows. "My royal tutor?"

"Yes. I know you've been studying Corche custom, and

you've done a great job, but there's no substitute for having a guide. Bridget is also royalty, although not a queen. She can attend functions with you when I'm busy. She'll be by your side when I'm not."

"So she's my babysitter. Someone to make sure I don't stick my foot in my mouth." My tone gave away exactly what I thought of this plan.

"Not exactly. Yes, she'll be helpful, and you can learn a lot about courtly graces from watching her. But it's more about having a friendly face in every crowd. It's not uncommon for me to get called away to talk about all kinds of political affairs, even during social events. I thought you would appreciate her company."

When he put it that way, the gesture brought a smile to my face. He was being thoughtful, not insulting. I hadn't memorized all of Corche custom yet. I didn't know how to address a baron or how deeply to bow to a duke, despite having watched *Bridgerton* fifteen times. In the twenty-first century, how much ceremony was expected? Not a clue, but Bridget probably knew.

"Thank you. That was very sweet of you."

"That reminds me. She's got a few ball gowns for you to try on for tomorrow's event." Pierre glanced at his watch. "And she'll be here in about fifteen minutes."

Soon. Well, she could show up whenever, as long as I got to finish my breakfast. There was no point in wasting a lot of energy choosing an outfit if she was bringing me clothes to try on. Instead, I drained my coffee cup, speared a piece of French toast with my fork, and went to grab one of the royal blue robes I'd spotted in the closet the night before. Full length, velvety, with the family crest on a front pocket, these robes were literally made for royalty. The one I pulled out might have been cut specifically for me. It felt amazing.

Exactly fifteen minutes later, someone knocked sharply on the outer door of our apartment. I glanced at Pierre. "Well, at least she's punctual."

He laughed and went ahead of me to greet our guest. "Oh, I doubt that. She probably had someone come ahead with the clothes so you could start looking. Bridget's never on time for anything."

The door opened, and a short brunette with dancing brown eyes swept past my husband. "I heard that, Pierre! I'll have you know, I've been standing outside that door tapping my foot for at least ten minutes now. I've been dying to meet my new niece. I can't believe you kept her from me this long. You know I would've hopped a plane to meet you on your travels if anyone had told me where you were."

Pierre laughed. "One of many reasons I didn't. It's good to see you, Bridget."

Bridget approached me and curtsied deeply before squeezing my hands with hers. "Lila! It is an absolute pleasure to meet someone who brings such joy to one of my beloved nephews."

"Thank you, Your Grace." I didn't know what I'd expected, but from Pierre's description, his aunt had sounded like a stuffy old schoolmarm. Nothing like the vibrant woman standing in front of me. "Not to sound rude, but I was expecting someone older. You and Pierre appear to be almost the same age."

"My youngest nephew is a year older than me," she said. "*Pére* remarried after his first wife died in childbirth. *Mére* was quite a bit younger than he."

"It's really none of my business."

"Of course it's your business! We're family!" She waved one hand. "It's all good. Anyway, call me Bridget. None of that 'Your Grace' nonsense. I'm only a duchess because my sister married a prince before I was born. Anyway, Pierre tells me you need new clothes and hate shopping."

"I wouldn't say I *need* new clothes."

Pierre had been standing back and letting Bridget take the lead, but now he cleared his throat. "How many evening gowns did you pack?"

"I have one!" Purchased from a clearance sale at the local Nordstrom Rack several years ago. But the style was classic.

"It's cool, Lila. I've got way more clothes than anyone needs. And I've brought quite a lot. You wouldn't want people to think the Prince was being stingy with his bride, would you?" Bridget winked at me.

"Couldn't they think that his new bride is frugal and environmentally conscious enough to want to reduce unnecessary consumption?"

She laughed. "Right. That's a good one."

Stepping aside, she motioned toward the door. Two men entered, wheeling a rack stuffed with so many clothes, I could barely tell where one garment started and the next began. Blues and greens and reds and swirling floral patterns all melded together. It looked like when I used to pull dressing room duty back at SidMart.

"Oh, wow. I can't possibly accept all this! You've already given me an entire wardrobe!"

"Of course you can't take *all* of it," Bridget said. "No one looks good in every color. I brought options so we could figure out what would work best for your complexion and body type. I've seen pictures, but there's no substitute for trying things on in person."

That made sense. As overwhelmed as I felt, the only way to get thro was one piece of clothing at a time. Stepping forward, I pulled a long, dark blue dress with a silver swirly pattern off of the rack. Holding it up to myself, I turned around, looking for a mirror. The fabric swished when I moved. It felt amazing against my skin.

"This is gorgeous!"

"Thanks," Bridget said. "It's a nightgown, though, so not ideal for your introduction to the public."

My face grew warm as I stuttered out an apology. "But, seriously, I have my own nightgowns. I can't take yours."

She laughed. "Oh, that's not mine. The front of the rack is all things I made for you, based on what Pierre told me."

"Made? You sewed these?"

"Sure I did. What, you think the royal family doesn't have any skills?" She rolled her eyes. "Pierre, you didn't tell me that you married my mother."

"I think you'll find that my wife has many, many talents, Bridget. But I made it sound like you were bringing her clothes from your personal wardrobe."

She shrugged. "A lot of it is. *Mére* freaks out when I wear too much stuff I made myself, so I brought it to you to pacify her."

I noted the present tense. It hadn't occurred to me that Pierre's grandmother could still be alive. Or step-grandmother. That was worth exploring later. "She'll be okay with me wearing stuff you made?"

"I doubt it, but we won't tell her. Since we're not exactly the same size, it wouldn't occur to her that I could've altered anything to fit you. And on that note..." She pulled several beautiful gowns off the rack and shoved them at me. "Go change. We've got a lot to do today."

Before I could take the gowns Bridget offered me into the dressing suite, Pierre stepped forward. "I'd love to be part of this, but I'm sorry to say I have an appointment that cannot be missed. Bridget, would you be so kind as to show Lila to my office when you're finished?"

"Of course. We want you to get that fabulous first look when Lila walks into the ball all dolled up." When she spoke like that, I felt like a princess.

"I quite look forward to it. Only I'll be escorting her. We'll walk into the ball together." With a bow, he turned to go.

A moment later, he popped back into the room and cleared his throat. "Lila? Uh, look who I found outside our door."

The look on his face had my heart sinking before my brother's familiar voice entered the room. "Good morning, sister dear!"

It took all of my effort to avoid spitting out, "What do you want?" Instead, I gritted my teeth together. "Caleb! What a surprise. I'm sorry, I'm a little busy at the moment."

"No problem. I came to ask if I could take Preacher out. I haven't seen him in a long time, you know."

That's because you abandoned your pet and moved out of the country, I wanted to say. There was no point.

At the sound of his name, my Yorkie sat bolt upright on his bed. Then he spotted Caleb, and the little traitor raced into his arms, yapping excitedly.

"I guess that's settled," Pierre said. "I believe his leash is on the table by the front door."

"Hold on," I said. "How long will you be gone? We're only going to be twenty minutes or so."

"No problem. I'll come find you."

Bridget cleared her throat. "Our agenda is packed. Lila, can you give him a key to put Preacher and his leash back inside when he's done?"

I sighed heavily. That was a terrible idea. "I don't have a key yet. Pierre couldn't find a second copy, so it'll arrive later today."

"Ah, well. It was just an idea." Caleb stood, setting Preacher on the ground. "Sorry, buddy."

My dog whined. His sad face broke my heart. It would help if someone took him out while I tried on these gowns. We lived in a palace, after all. Surely, no one was going to break in during the few minutes between when I left and Caleb returned Preacher.

"Fine, no problem. I'll leave the door open. Just lock the knob when you bring him back." I couldn't spend any more time on this, not when I had a million things to do. Swiveling around, I turned to Bridget. "Are you ready to get started?"

The first dress on the rack was a stunning, form-fitting blue-green silk gown with a V-neck. Just looking at it made me feel like a mermaid. Since Caleb was still lurking like a big weirdo, I went into the dressing suite to try it on. The fabric slid over my hips like a hot knife slicing through butter, and I swear, I grew three inches taller in it.

When I showed it to Bridget, she let out a wolf whistle. My brother had finally taken the dog and left. "Not to toot my own horn, but I am good!"

I chuckled. "You really hit it out of the park with this one. And it's only Dress #1."

The second dress was an empire-waisted yellow gown with capped sleeves and a sweetheart neckline. Beautiful, not my color at all.

"You can't win 'em all," Bridget said as she took it back. "Next!"

She handed me a lilac cotton dress that was pretty, but not a ball gown. After that, the dresses sort of blurred together. Shimmery satins, silks softer than a kitten, in a variety of colors. Finally, we got to the last two.

Bridget held up a one-shouldered white gown similar to something I'd seen Kate Middleton wear. On her taller frame it was sleek and stunning. On me? I'd look like I was going to a toga party. We bypassed that one entirely. The final option had ruched gray fabric, fitted at the top, but flaring out at the end. I expected it to be confining, but it fit me like a glove.

When I walked out to show this last one to Bridget, she gasped. "Oh, that's amazing. I love the blue, but this is the one. Wear it tonight."

I spun around, admiring the skirt as it flared around me. Then my eyes landed on my feet. The boots I'd worn on the plane were comfortable, but not exactly appropriate for a formal ball. "What do you think about shoes?"

There were many pairs in the dressing suite, but I hadn't examined them. Part of me still worried that if I breathed wrong, I would break the spell and wake up as the old, SidMart-working Lila who had a mortgage the size of Rhode Island and a hopeless crush on her oblivious next-door neighbor.

"I know just the pair. C'mon, Cinderella."

Bridget led me to the shoe wall—seriously? I had a shoe wall now—and reached for a pair of silver glittery heels. They must be three inches high, which would keep the dress from dragging without making me feel like a stork. I slipped them on and moved in front of the floor-length mirror.

She was right. Absolutely perfect. There wasn't even any point in trying anything else.

Next, she moved to the island and started opening drawers. It hadn't even occurred to me that they might be full of accessories. My mouth dropped at the sheer volume of it all. This was so much extravagance. So many things that would get worn once, or not at all. I shook my hesitation aside. This wasn't the time. Tonight, I needed to make a good first impression on the public at a royal affair. That meant not wearing jewelry I'd bought on clearance at work.

After seriously considering a strand of pearls with matching earrings, we decided on a circle pendant rimmed with sapphires and diamonds, a show of the Corche colors for my debut. Then we found a pair of dangling sapphire and diamond earrings. My hands would remain mostly bare, though. I refused all rings other than my engagement and wedding bands. Pierre had gifted me the most amazing family heirloom: a metal serpent twisted into a ring with an enormous emerald on top. It was stunning, and worth— well, let's not talk about that.

Part of me desperately wanted a tiara, but I wasn't a princess yet. There was no guarantee I would ever be. Queen Claudette seemed hesitant to even make me a Baroness.

It would be super embarrassing to remain forever title-free, but we'd only known each other for a few hours. Maybe she knew I wasn't princess material, just like Henri said.

"Do I need a purse?" To distract myself, I started opening drawers. It had to be here somewhere.

"You do not!" Bridget crowed. "Run your hand down the sides of that baby."

When I found the opening on my left hip, I gasped. "You didn't."

"I did!"

"I can't believe you gave me pockets! I love you even more now." I barely resisted throwing my arms around the woman who was, for all intents and purposes, a total stranger. Then then she wrapped me in a hug, dispelling my fears.

"Oh, I'm so glad you love everything," she said. "Now, take it all off. It's time for your grand tour, and I don't want you to mess up that dress before the ball."

"Are you kidding? I will wear this forever and never ever take it off. I want a dozen of them. It's the most flattering thing I've ever seen. It looks better than my wedding dress, which was amazing."

"If you spill coffee on it, you can't wear it to the ball."

"Darn it. Fine." With a sigh, I took everything off and put it away carefully. All my gorgeous things would be here later.

~

Since this trip had been full of glitz and glamour, I should be more immune to the castle's opulence. Nope. Every room was absolutely stunning in each exquisite detail, from the main halls and sitting rooms to the bathrooms with chandeliers. Seriously.

We ended the tour at Pierre's office, where my husband was already inside with his chief of staff. Jules had run Pierre's affairs for years, including when he was in Boston. Now it was time for my husband to catch up on the non-urgent business that came up while we'd been traveling.

When we peeked through the door, Pierre sat behind an enormous pile of documents, pen in hand. Looking up, he waved me in. "Thank goodness you're here! I'm getting a cramp in my signing hand."

"With all due respect, Your Highness, the stack would be much smaller if you came home more often."

Bridget snorted. Pierre turned a withering look on Jules, who met his gaze steadily, without a trace of contrition.

Finally, Pierre said, "You may have a point. But if you tell my mother I said that, you're fired."

"Of course, sir." Jules turned toward me and Bridget. He bowed in greeting. "If you don't mind, I will take my leave while you speak with your family."

"Not at all," Pierre said. "Take a longer break. I can certainly write my name a hundred times without you peeking over my shoulder. Lord knows, I did it enough in school. Meet me back here at three?"

Jules nodded on his way out the door, and I examined the room where my husband worked. After poking my head in some of the other offices, I'd expected heavy dark wood, a high-backed chair, maybe some deer heads over the mantle or similar. Wooden paneling, yet another chandelier.

The reality was quite different. Large windows let in significant light. Under the windows, a black leather couch and armchair faced a sleek glass and metal coffee table. A matching wet bar stood in the corner. The sleek metal and glass desk sat beside a sturdy metal filing cabinet. That must hold all the important stuff. Few things cluttered the surface of the desk other than a computer. But the best part was on the walls behind the desk: bookcases. Plural. Like *Beauty and the Beast* bookcases from floor to ceiling. No wonder he knew exactly what to install in our Boston apartment.

Bridget nudged me. "Gorgeous, isn't it? Wait until you see yours."

"Mine?"

"Yes, of course." She headed for a door that I'd thought a closet. "It's attached, but you've also got an exit onto the hall, so you're not constantly walking through."

My office was smaller than Pierre's, but by no means small. Instead of a couch, I had a love seat and chair in one corner. My desk was made of beautiful, carved white wood, creating an L-shape with extra chairs at one end. My bookcases were covered with glass. A stunning chandelier hung from the ceiling.

"You're serious? All of this, just for me?"

Bridget shook her head. "Of course not."

"Yeah, I didn't think so. It's too much."

She pointed. "That side of the desk is for your chief of staff."

"I'm sorry, my staff? You mentioned earlier that your assistant could work with me while we're here. Is that right?"

"Yes, certainly." She picked up her phone and shot off a text. "She'll be here soon."

The words still lingered in the air when someone knocked on the hallway door. I looked from Bridget to the door and back. Twice. "How did you do that?"

"Zoe has been in the office I use all day. She knew I'd want you to meet her when we finished your tour. Bring her in, and we'll get everyone settled."

Trying to exude confidence, I strode to the door and opened it. A woman with short, dark hair and brown eyes waited. She wore a navy suit, and a held a clipboard. It made her look so efficient, I thought about buying one of my own.

I held out my hand. "Hi, Zoe, I'm Lila."

Ignoring my hand, she curtsied. "It's a pleasure, Your Highness."

"Oh, please, don't do that. I'm not—" Bridget cleared her throat. My face grew warm. "I mean, I haven't been crowned. The Queen hasn't given me a title. Please, come in. We have a lot to talk about."

"We certainly do," Zoe said, walking briskly by me. "I requested a copy of your official schedule for the week. Pierre's staff was handling it, but I'll take things from here. With your permission, of course."

This was so overwhelming, I was more likely to beg her to help than say no. And while Pierre's staff was competent to manage it, they also had plenty of work to do without taking me on. "Oh, yes, please. I need any help I can get."

"The most important thing, for now, is your sessions with Duchess Bridget here. There is much to learn, and not a lot of time. That reminds me—how is your dancing?"

"My dancing?" I wanted to smack myself on the forehead. With everything else going on, it hadn't even occurred to me to think about the thing that people typically did at a ball.

"Yes, Madame. You have a ball starting in—" she checked her watch "—five hours, twenty-three minutes. If you require dance instruction, we should start immediately."

Right. The ball. Formal dancing. Lessons. So much happening today.

"I should be fine. I'm sure Pierre and I will be too busy to dance much."

"Since the ball is being held in your honor, you'll be expected to lead the first dance, at a minimum," Zoe said.

I glanced to Bridget—excuse me, Duchess Bridget—for confirmation. She nodded.

To Zoe, I said, "In her quest to have the perfect daughter, my mother signed me up for Girl Scouts. I got the horseback riding badge, the sewing badge, and the ballroom dancing badge. It's almost like she was preparing me to become a princess."

Zoe's lips twitched. "Excellent. Let's have a quick demonstration, then. Your Grace, would you do the honors?"

"Certainly." Bridget bowed deeply, extending one hand to me. "May I have this dance?"

"With no music?"

Zoe pulled out her phone and began tapping. The opening strings of a waltz soon filled the room. I took Bridget's hand. She pulled me toward her. Her right hand went to the small of my back, and she took her left hand in my right. My other hand rested on her shoulder.

We paused while Bridget closed her eyes and listened to the beat of the music. I cocked my head to do the same, but kept my eyes open. The moment she moved, I wanted to follow her lead. It had been fifteen years since Girl Scouts ended.

I'd spent a lot of my teen years dancing in clubs. None of that was remotely useful in remembering how to waltz. Formal ballroom dancing was more about counting steps and following my partner's lead than about feeling the music and letting it consume you.

Eventually, it came back to me. A simple box step. Back, back, together. Front, front, together. One, two, three. One, two, three. Always in a circle. Once I mastered that, I even managed to smile. Bridget whisked me around the room to the tempo of the music. It was a lot more fun than I expected a formal ball with thousands of strangers to be. As we twirled in circles, I felt free.

One song turned into another, then a third. By the time Bridget declared herself too tired to continue dancing, my feet ached. Unfortunately, while she could sit on the couch and rest, my work had barely started.

Zoe brought in a pile of books and spread them on the coffee table in front of us. The titles on the spines made me groan. *The Corche Code: An English Translation. Corche Law. Corche Law for Dummies. The Corche Charter*, translated.

"It'll be okay," Bridget said, as if she could tell how badly I wanted to bolt.

Instead of answering her, I muttered, "I love Pierre, I love Pierre" under my breath until I felt strong enough to pull the first book into my lap and open it. It was heavy, with thick pages and thick black letters on the front. I was having law school flashbacks, and I hadn't read a single word yet.

At least law school taught me I could do this.

With a sigh of resignation, I dove in.

After our third time through the Corchenne Constitution, Bridget motioned for me to put it away. "Thank you for putting up with me. I know this isn't exactly how you wanted to spend your first full day in your husband's home."

"Don't be silly! I love reading three-hundred-year-old documents," I said with as straight a face as I could manage.

She snorted. "You don't have to lie to me. Pierre told me one thing you hated about law school was being forced to read documents written in 'stuffy old English.'"

"To be fair, this is stuffy old French," I pointed out. "Well, a translation of stuffy old French. Does that make it Frenglish?"

"That makes it something I very much appreciate you taking the time to read thoroughly," she said gently. "Accept the compliment."

"Thanks. You're right. This isn't exactly how I dreamed of meeting my husband's family, but it *is* important. I want Queen Claudette to see that I'm very serious about both Pierre and being a credit to Corchenne. Doing that requires me to learn as much as I can about Pierre's lands, the laws, and the people."

"Law school really missed out the day you left. You're an excellent student."

Those words brought a smile to my face. "No, you're an excellent teacher. If I absolutely needed a royal tutor, I'm glad it's you. You make this all so much less boring."

"I appreciate the sentiment," Bridget said. "You're slouching. Drop your shoulders. Put your head back."

"Yes, ma'am." I laughed.

"I'm serious."

"Right. Sorry." I adjusted my posture, using the big mirror on the wall for guidance. "How's that?"

"Better. You'll need to practice."

"Toto, we're not in Kansas anymore," I muttered. Back at Sid-Mart, no one cared when I slouched.

"Look, like it or not, you're royalty now. Your life is different. Pierre has been living life under the radar for long enough that you've had a pretty easy go of things. Even on your honeymoon, people weren't on the lookout for you the way they will be now that you're home in Corchenne. You're going to have to behave like the royalty you are. You'll meet your security detail in a couple of hours. Pierre's talking to the head, Alexandre, right now. Any time you leave the chateau, you'll go with at least one bodyguard and a chauffeur. No more driving yourself."

"That's cool. I'm from Boston; I hate driving. Also, I don't have a car."

"The royal vehicles are at your disposal. Provided you also take a driver and your security detail," she said. "Any time you'd like me to go with you, check with Zoe to see if I'm free. I've moved into the castle for the duration of your stay."

Until she'd said that, it hadn't occurred to me to wonder where Bridget lived. Pierre made it sound like she had a home somewhere else, but didn't specify. "Where's your home? Can't you drive back and forth?"

"My vineyard is on the north shore of the island," she said. "About forty miles away. An hour by car, depending on road conditions. Today I took the helicopter, but that's too much fuss for going back and forth every day."

Wow. Not in Kansas, indeed.

"I want you to know how much I appreciate everything you're doing for me. I can never hope to repay all this."

"You make Pierre happy. That's payment enough. Just be a credit to me, and to him, and everyone wins."

"I'll do my best," I vowed.

"I have faith in you. Now, who manages your diary?"

"This feels like a stupid answer, but...me? On my shiny new phone?"

In response, Bridget laughed. "Zoe's details are in the phone, so you can message her anytime. She also has access to update your calendar, but check with her before you schedule anything."

"This is too much," I said. "I hate to sound ungrateful. I absolutely appreciate everything you're doing for me, but how busy can I possibly be? I'm no one."

"Oh, sweetie. You're the woman who captured the heart of Corchenne's second most eligible bachelor, and the one who brought him back home after years away. The entire country is waiting to welcome you."

She probably meant that to be comforting. Instead, a wave of fear swept through me. The entire country was ready to meet me, but was I ready to meet them? I was no one, a girl from Boston. I used to work for minimum wage while eating dried beans for dinner. What happened if I introduced myself to the entire country at a fancy ball, and they figured out I was nothing but a fraud?

Chapter Nine

After I'd convinced Bridget (and myself) that I'd make a good impression at the ball, she left to rest before dinner. Since I had nothing scheduled for the next hour, this seemed like a good time to chill in my office and check my DMs. There were several official "Delilah Leon" emails waiting for me, but since I didn't know any of those people, they could wait. I needed to make sure my bestie knew how to reach me on my fancy new phone since I wasn't supposed to use the old one in public anymore. For years, Madison and I texted all day, every day. Being married to a royal meant certain compromises. Some I was willing to accept, but reducing contact with my best friend wasn't one of them.

I'd just finished regaling her with a description of the prior night's meal—and the bombshell of Caleb's arrival—when the inside door to Pierre's office creaked open behind me. A glance at the clock told me it was nearly time for lunch. Since his schedule was also clear, maybe he'd come to get me.

"Are you ready to get a bite to eat?" I called without turning around. "I just need to finish this email to Madison first."

"Madison?" A familiar voice responded, but it wasn't my husband. "Please send her my regards."

Ugh. I suppressed the urge to roll my eyes. Henri topped the list of people I had no need to see.

After minimizing my open windows and locking the screen, I spun around on my chair. "Not to be rude, but I doubt she wants to hear from you."

"Is it because I never called her after our night together?"

To my horror, my best friend and Henri had hooked up when he'd flown to Boston to try to ruin my wedding. She didn't know what he'd done, and the two of them shared a very expensive bottle of tequila with Pierre. When we'd talked the next morning, she'd been outraged on my behalf.

"No, I think it's because you tried to blackmail me into leaving your brother at the altar," I said. "She's got a bad habit of holding grudges against people who try to ruin her friends' lives."

"A pity," Henri said. "She was fun."

"She is utterly delightful," I said before deciding to dispense with the small talk. "What are you doing here?"

"I wanted to speak to you."

"Okay, well, it's been lovely catching up, but I have to find Pierre for lunch." Shoving my chair back, I started to stand, but the look in Henri's eyes stopped me.

"Please, wait," he said. "I need your help."

A bark of laughter escaped me. "Oh, that's awesome. You want me to help you? Why on earth would I do that?"

"Because *l'ennemi de mon ennemi est mon ami*."

He might as well have been speaking Elvish, for all I understood. "Well, that clears things right up. We done here?"

"I apologize, sometimes I forget you do not also speak

French," Henri said. "It means, 'the enemy of my enemy is my friend.'"

Enemies? Other than Henri and his mother, I didn't have... "You're talking about Caleb."

"Yes." He leaned against the edge of my desk, the most casual I'd ever seen him. Usually he was so stiff and formal.

Now that I was paying attention, I saw the hint of dark shadows under his eyes, a bit of stubble that suggested he hadn't shaved this morning, and wrinkles in the shirt beneath his suit coat. As Crown Prince, Henri took pride in looking impeccable. If he would ask me of all people for help looking like he'd been tossing and turning all night, he must be desperate.

"Well, I know why I'm not happy to see my brother," I said. "What about you?"

"He is getting too close to *Mére*. He's trying to convince her to invest an immense sum of money in a scheme that's guaranteed to fail. She won't even discuss the possibility that it's not a goldmine."

"Is that usual? Does she normally consult you on this type of thing?"

"Since Father died, yes. She wants me to know everything about running the country. I have my own duties, but she counsels me on the king's and queen's duties."

"Is that normal?" A thought struck me. "Oh, no. Is your mother sick?"

He smiled. "Nothing like that. She's hoping to retire while she's young enough to enjoy life. *Mére* took the crown at nineteen years old, and it's been a long time. She's looking to hand over the mantle to me. Not immediately. The intent was that I would be crowned when I turn forty, although if I'm not married by then, she may reconsider."

"You can't find a nice girl to settle down with? What a shame. It's not the blackmail habit, is it?" I didn't bother to hide my sarcasm. Even though Henri was here, asking me for help, part of me wondered how he was planning to twist this situation to his advantage. Nothing got by Henri.

"There's no need to hold a grudge, Lila. You got what you wanted."

"No thanks to you," I grumbled.

"If I apologize, can we call a truce? I need your help."

I thought for a moment. Pierre loved his brother very much. A lifetime of being at odds with Henri sounded exhausting. We'd want our future children to play together. Maybe it was time to put our differences behind us. I stuck out my right hand. "Deal."

He shook it. "I apologize for trying to break you and Pierre up. Now I see how much you care for each other."

"Thank you," I said. "Do you want me to talk to Caleb for you? To be honest, I don't think he'll listen to me."

"No offense, but I agree," he said. "Your brother doesn't strike me as the type of person who listens to anyone trying to tell him what to do. He has ignored all attempts my stewards have made at steering him away from seeking an investment from *Mére* or the kingdom."

"He's a con artist." No reason to beat around the bush. "Whatever he's offering your mother, it's something you don't want her wrapped up in, even if she weren't the queen. But if the people find out she got scammed by her new daughter-in-law's brother..."

"We'll have a national pitchfork shortage when people line up to run you off the island," he said.

Not the worst outcome, since Pierre and I intended to return to America before the first frost. But we had every intention of being allowed to visit Corchenne later. Becoming the national pariah wouldn't fit with that plan at all.

"So how can I help? You don't think your mother will listen to me, do you?"

He shrugged. "Telling her about Caleb's history can't hurt. But she also knows that you don't trust him. It may take more than that. I need to know what he's up to. He's been very close-lipped about the project, and he's somehow convinced the queen not to tell me anything."

"Talk to Blaise. Pierre gave Caleb a business card with his name on it, telling him to set up a meeting. Caleb couldn't know the meeting would never go anywhere."

"I did. They spoke this morning. Everything Caleb said was meaningless double-speak. He talked about 'revitalizing tourism' and similar buzzwords, without adding any value to the conversation."

"Yup. Sounds like Caleb."

How were we supposed to stop my brother if the queen refused to listen? What little he'd explained of his plan sounded terrible. Any plan that involved giving him money would absolutely not pan out for the investors. Caleb would make sure of it. But I couldn't hide the checkbook of the queen. I sighed, casting my eyes around the room for inspiration. Unfortunately, what they landed on was the clock.

"Listen, I want to help with this, Henri, but I have to go if I want lunch before I need to start getting ready for the ball. It's my first formal public appearance. There's no way to know how long it'll take."

"Certainly." He rose to his feet. "My apologies for keeping you from your duties."

"No problem. I'll let you know what I find out."

"*Merci.* I'm counting on you, Lila."

As I watched him go, the sinking feeling in my chest had nothing to do with the enormity of the task. For the thousandth time, I wondered what on earth I'd gotten myself into by coming here.

By the time Bridget's sea of hair and makeup people left me later, I felt better about my role in all of this. I might be a fraud, in over my head, but I looked like royalty. Compared to this, I'd been make-up free on my wedding day.

Expertly applied shadow, mascara, and liner made my blue eyes look huge. Blush brought color to my cheeks where otherwise fear had turned me into a ghostly white.

Taking a deep breath, I said to the mirror. "I belong here. I am a member of the royal family. I can do this."

I spent so long twirling before the mirror, looking for chinks in my princess armor, that Pierre knocked to see if I were okay.

Opening the door, I said, "I've never looked so much like a Barbie doll."

He just stared. Suddenly, I felt self-conscious all over again.

My hands went to my bodice. "Is it too much? It's too much, isn't it? I knew it! The gown, the shoes. Maybe I should wear my hair down. I—"

Pierre stepped forward, taking both my hands in his. "Stop. You are the most beautiful woman I have ever seen. You will outshine even the queen, which is appropriate. This is our night. Your night, *ma chérie*. The people will adore you, much as I do."

His words calmed me, as did the amazing kiss he gave me. My lipstick could be redone. I pulled him toward me, taking strength from the feel of his arms around me. He was right. Together, we could face this ball. No, better than that. We would nail it.

When we parted, I felt better. For the first time, I stopped to examine my husband's royal attire. He wore a tuxedo, as expected. His tie was made from the same fabric as my dress, a touch that I hadn't expected. A matching square poked out of his breast pocket.

He'd put more gel than usual in his tousled black hair. It was different, but I liked it. While Pierre would normally bear some scruff at this point in the day, his cheeks were as smooth as my brother's lies.

"You look pretty good yourself." I whispered, not wanting to shatter the magic of a royal couple getting dressed for a ball together.

"This old thing?" he winked at me. "Come on, Alexandre wants to speak with us before we leave."

Right. I'd forgotten that Bridget said we had a security meeting this evening. After hours spent getting ready, I wanted to go. I suppressed a groan when we left the dressing room and saw the man waiting in our suite. He wasn't particularly tall, but he was solid as a brick wall. He had serious dark eyes and spiky black hair. His tuxedo must have been tailored to those muscles. Anything off the rack would have burst at the seams. He didn't appear to be carrying a weapon, but based on prior conversations, I expected that coat to hide a variety of expensive high-tech devices.

Last week, when Pierre mentioned getting a briefing from his head of security, I'd chuckled nervously, waiting for the punchline.

There wasn't one.

"It's nice to meet you," I said, shaking his hand. Wow, he was strong. "But is any of this necessary? Corchenne is a peaceful country. The last major threat was in 1984." I'd looked it up online.

"Yes, it most certainly is necessary." Alexandre eyed me up and down. "Especially because you seem rather defenseless."

At that, my spine stiffened. "I'll have you know, I once bought a month of capoeira classes on Groupon."

"Are you bulletproof?"

"Well, no," I admitted. "But I'll work on it."

Pierre squeezed my hand. "I know it's overwhelming, *chérie*. But I promise it's all about keeping you safe. It's been years since I took any self-defense classes. If you'd like, we can resume them together."

I smiled up at him. "Yes, please."

"I'll schedule the first lesson tomorrow, if you're free, Your Highness," Alexandre said.

"Zoe has my schedule, but she can probably fit you in. Tell

Jules to find a time that works for Pierre, then check with her. Most of my lessons can be moved around."

"None of your lessons are more important than self-defense," Pierre said. "We will start tomorrow. I will handle my aunt."

"Wonderful! I'm glad that's settled," Alexandre said. "For now, I need you to stay in the castle unless you have a bodyguard with you. If you leave with Bridget, she can bring hers. Try not to wander the public areas alone during the hours that we're open, when possible."

Begrudgingly, I agreed.

"Glad that's settled," Alexandre said. "Now we'll need to discuss your secret code phrase."

I glanced at Pierre. "Is that like a safe word?"

He laughed. "Not exactly. It's what you will say if you are being held against your will. Certain words will alert security to find you, even if you say everything is fine."

"Right." I snorted. "I'm so sure people will want to kidnap me."

"You are hopefully soon to be a Princess of Corchenne. The only one. Until Henri marries and produces an heir, enemies of the throne might wish to harm you," Pierre said.

When he put it that way, maybe a security detail wasn't completely ridiculous. But what were the odds?

"I didn't realize the Corche crown had enemies," I said.

"Everyone has enemies. I wouldn't be doing my job if I didn't prepare for every eventuality," Alexandre said.

Right. I wasn't here to make things difficult for palace staff. First the email address, then the security detail. If I argued at every turn, they would hate me.

"Okay, then. If I ever say anything nice about my brother—Caleb—you'll know that I'm in grave danger. Immediate, mortal peril from which I cannot possibly extricate"

Pierre's lips twitched. "Your relationship might get repaired someday."

"Before or after he finishes conning your mother out of a fortune?"

"Touché." He nodded toward Alexandre, who made a note on his phone.

"What's your secret code phrase? How do I know if you're in danger?"

My husband's ears grew red. "Now that you mention it, we'll have to create a new one."

"Why? What was it?"

"I would ask someone to consult with Adrienne about the state of her pomegranates." His ex-girlfriend. No wonder he was embarrassed. "They used to be my favorite, and it's been many years since I left."

"It's okay," I said. "I'm not worried you like Adrienne's *pomegranates* anymore."

Leaning on my tiptoes, I kissed him. Then Pierre excused himself to read some reports while Alexandre reviewed the castle's security protocol with me. There was a lot. Enough that I resolved never to leave the castle alone, because I might not get back in.

Chapter Ten

OFFICIAL GUIDE TO BEING A PRINCESS: A princess shall always dance at least six inches from her partner. Any closer would be unseemly.

Nothing could have prepared me for my first sight of the Corchenne ballroom decked out in royal splendor. Not the dozen or so Netflix movies I watched where a regular girl marries a prince (seriously, there are a ton of them). Not the videos of Kate and William's wedding or the images online showing events at Buckingham Palace. Even the seven hundred times I'd watched *The Princess Diaries* didn't properly convey what I was about to face.

That happened on TV, far away. Even the events with real royals seemed like fairy tales. Except now it *was* my world. Prince William and Kate had been invited to this event, as had Harry and Meghan. We didn't expect any of them to show up, but still. I, Lila Sinclair of Boston, formerly employed at SidMart, was at an event being held in my honor where actual royalty had been sent an invitation. Without an expectation that it would be thrown in the trash unopened. Supposedly, a member of the Spanish royal family might show up. The King had a daughter close to my age.

It hadn't sunk in yet that I *was* royal now. Well, sort of. A royal-in-law, at least. Pierre seemed to think that, since tonight was my "official" introduction to Corche society, his mother might present me with my flag and title at the end of the event. After last night's dinner, I wasn't holding my breath.

All those thoughts ran through my head in the blink of an eye, so fast I was practically dizzy, while Pierre led me down the hallway leading to the ballroom. I couldn't wait for my first peek.

Okay, fine, second. I'd snuck in earlier while they were setting up, after I finished walking Preacher. But someone screamed *"Chien! Chien!"* in an increasingly panicked voice. I was about to consult Google Translate when they repeated the words and pointed at Preacher, which delivered the message. No dogs allowed, even those accompanied by the guest of honor.

Now that I'd left my Yorkie in our room, I was free to gape to my heart's content. As long as I remembered to keep my mouth closed.

In every movie I'd seen with nobility, royalty, or balls, I'd thought the idea of well-dressed people getting announced and then walking down a giant staircase was created by Hollywood. A way of adding drama. But then Pierre took me to the second floor of the castle.

"Hold on," I said, drawing to a halt. "Isn't the ball on the ground floor?"

"Yes, *chérie*. But the formal entrance for family and officials is this way. They'll announce us, then we'll walk down the stairs to the ballroom."

I didn't think I'd have to descend steps in the getup. In front of other people. I was doomed.

"Are you okay?" Pierre asked.

"Yup. Fine. Just trying to remember how to walk."

"You'll be smashing. The stairs aren't steep, and there's a banister. Take it with one hand and hold onto me with the other."

He stopped talking because we'd reached a massive set of double doors. Only the right door was open. Strains of orchestra music flowed through, as well as the gentle roar of people. A large man I'd noticed guarding the throne room when we arrived stood just this side of the door, arms clasped casually in front of him. Pierre greeted him fondly, introducing him as Duncan.

I forced the edges of my lips upward in what I hoped resembled a smile more than a grimace.

Duncan abruptly pivoted and opened the door before stepping to the side.

"Why is he doing that?"

"We are the first royals to arrive. The single door is for important guests and nobility. Royalty gets both doors."

Oh, wonderful. Just in case anyone hadn't been looking when unimportant fancy people entered, now we had their attention.

Pierre nodded down the hall behind me. "Look, there are Henri and *Mére*."

"Will he escort her in?"

"Only if he wants to be disowned. No one escorts Queen Claudette. Not since my father died."

That made sense.

"Should we wait for her?"

"No, she insists on being the last to arrive. That way, all eyes are where they should be."

Duncan cleared his throat. "Excuse me, Your Royal Highness. They're ready for you."

Inside the room, a loud clear voice shouted, "His Royal Highness, Prince Pierre of Corchenne! Accompanied by his wife, her ladyship, Delilah!"

Pierre stepped forward, leaving me no choice but to walk with him. We went through the doorway, looking down into the most splendid room I'd ever seen. Glittering chandeliers hung on either side of the door, as well as at the opposite end, about half a mile away. In the middle, a larger chandelier twinkled so brightly, the International Astronomical Union might have given it a name.

On the ground, a row of tables held enough food to feed the entire city. Chocolate fountains, a massive cake, canapes... So many dishes. And the people. A sea of people, all watching me.

I forced myself to smile and wave, hoping that if I focused on minor tasks, I wouldn't hyperventilate. One step at a time.

"Breathe, *chérie*," Pierre said beside me. "You're cutting off the blood to my arm."

My cheeks grew warm as my gaze went to where I clutched his formerly pristine, unwrinkled jacket in a death grip. "Sorry. It's just—I feel like Eliza Doolittle."

The big-box store employee might very well be the modern version of a poor flower girl. The contempt with which many customers once treated me resembled the way people talked to Eliza before she appeared as a lady.

In the end, people believed she was a princess. They would believe in me, too. As long as I didn't pass out.

"Your accent is far more charming than hers," Pierre said, drawing my focus back to him. As long as I gazed into his eyes, I didn't want to puke. Unfortunately, I couldn't do that while walking down the stairs. "Now, one step at a time."

"The rain in Spain stays mainly in the plain," I said with an exaggerated Cockney accent. "Thanks, Henry Higgins."

"In your case, *chérie*, it's more like 'I went to pahk the cah in Havahd yahd.'"

His deadpan Boston accent was so perfect, I struggled not to burst out laughing. "That might be the sexiest thing you've ever said."

"That is the sexiest thing? I need to up my game," he said. "How are you feeling about tonight?"

That made me smile, barely. "Terrified. But I'll be okay. Thanks."

"I haven't doubted that for a single second. You look smashing, by the way."

I did look smashing. Access to royal resources really elevated my style. I'd come a long way from the five-dollar sneakers and yoga pants of Boston. Well, okay, I still had yoga pants, but they were as soft as our mattress. It felt like wearing butter.

In a not-sticky way.

Turning back to my husband, I beamed. "Thank you. Bridget has amazing taste."

"The most beautiful dress in the world couldn't touch the sparkle in your eyes, the way you smile. Or the way you're looking at me right now."

My cheeks grew warm. "Keep talking like that, and I'm going to drag you off to a dark corner and wrinkle your suit even more."

Pierre threw his head back and laughed, a booming sound that made me feel even more at home. Were people looking? It didn't matter. We had each other. The rest was all details, and there was no reason to sweat the details.

Finally, we reached the bottom stair. The herald announced Henri behind us, and all of a sudden, the attention shifted to him. The tightness in my chest eased noticeably as we moved away from the dark blue carpeted staircase onto the white marble floor.

Hundreds of people waited for us at the bottom. I forced myself to smile and meet people's eyes while we walked. Fortunately, the crowd parted to let us through as the herald announced Henri's arrival. We turned and waited while the Crown Prince and then his mother joined the ball.

Since the dancing hadn't started yet, we walked toward the tables where we might find champagne. But instantly, a couple stopped us. Then another. Then a trio of older men. So many people, all wanting to talk to me. Not one of them stood out among the mass. Eventually, I gave up trying to remember all the names. I held my own, smiling and keeping up, but I prayed Queen Claudette would start the dancing so I could speak with people one at a time.

Unfortunately, before we got to that point, Henri pulled Pierre away to greet the British Prime Minister. My husband had prepared me for this possibility, so I let him go without a fuss. To be honest, I didn't feel comfortable consorting with high-ranking officials yet, so I was thrilled not to go with them. At the same time, it felt like someone stripped away my security blanket when I needed it the most.

As if my fear had summoned her, Bridget appeared at my elbow. "Everything will be fine."

Gratefully, I smiled at her. "You won't leave me?"

"I will be nearby as much as possible throughout the evening. But first, let me get some champagne. It will take the edge off."

Apparently, "as much as possible" didn't include this very second. But she vanished toward the tables before I could protest. Great. Now I was doubly lost and alone in a sea of unfamiliar faces. It was almost enough to make me seek out Caleb.

Just kidding.

Someone cleared their throat loudly behind me. Turning, I found a tall, lanky man with graying black hair and the blue and gold coat I recognized as the uniform of the castle's staff. I wished he wore a nametag. It would take me forever to get to know everyone.

"Hi. I'm Lila." I held out my hand to shake, but he ignored it. Should I curtsy? No. He wore a palace uniform. The prince's wife didn't curtesy to our employees. Although maybe I could start a new trend. Hmm.

"My name is Luc, Your Highness." The man bowed. "I am your Royal Interpreter for the evening."

"Please, call me Lila." He protested, but I cut him off with a wave of my hand. "I am not royalty. I have no title. You may call me Mrs. Sinclair if you're not comfortable using my given name. But, really, that's just going to have me looking for my mother."

"Yes, Madame."

Yup. I'd just signed up for an evening of "Madame" instead of "Your Highness." To be honest, I wasn't sure which made me more uncomfortable. I changed the subject. "So you speak French and English?"

"Yes, Madame. Also Spanish, German, Farsi, Japanese, and Welsh," Luc said, a touch of pride in his voice.

Wow. "That's amazing."

His cheeks turned pink. "I am a Royal Translator. It is literally my job to know many languages. Officials flew in from dozens of countries. If you need to speak to someone whom I cannot translate, we will find someone else to step in."

"Okay." My head was spinning, and I hadn't even managed a sip of champagne yet. "Will you follow me to the dance floor if necessary?"

"No. We prefer you only dance with other English speakers, but if you find yourself on the floor with someone with whom you cannot communicate, try to simply smile politely. We'll discuss when you finish."

Great. Now I'd have to be worried that, while smiling and nodding politely to someone speaking in a language I didn't understand, I'd just agreed to sell next year's wine crop for ninety-nine percent off.

"Can you do me a favor?" I asked.

"Certainly, Madame."

"Can you make sure anyone I dance with knows I have no authority to discuss diplomatic concepts or enter deals? The last thing I want is to start an international trade war."

Luc's lips twitched. "I am only allowed to translate your exact words. Please do not worry. You should be fine. The royal family would not allow you to make your debut if you weren't ready."

I sincerely doubted that, but I appreciated that this total stranger had faith in me. Henri would have kept me from the public eye forever if he could, and Queen Claudette probably wished Pierre had married my brother instead.

Scanning the crowd, I prayed to find Bridget returning. Instead, I spotted my husband speaking with Henri and the most beautiful woman I'd ever seen in my life. While I watched, she threw her head back and laughed at something Pierre said. He whispered in her ear before nodding toward me. He looked perfectly at ease. If he had married someone like her, this might be his life now. Luxury and balls, not an awkward wife and a terrible brother-in-law.

Pierre was giving all this up for me. In a few weeks, we'd return to Boston, where he once again worked a day job at a decidedly non-glorious bank. We never went to balls back home. And even though I'd like to use our influence and wealth to better the world, I didn't anticipate a slew of invitations in our future. Especially not after the world found out about Caleb's scheme to steal from the Crown.

My jaw set determinedly. I had to stop him.

"Would you like to join them, Madame?" Luc asked, following the direction of my gaze. "Protocol says that you would not be interrupting."

Pierre looked so happy over there, talking to his equals. I was so afraid of embarassing myself, I would make everything awkward. "No, thank you. I'd rather wait for Duchess Bridget to return."

"I believe Her Grace has been waylaid by the Prince of Denmark." A voice at my elbow made me jump. The owner spoke with a velvety Spanish accent that would have made me swoon, pre-Pierre. "Pleased to meet you. I'm Juan, Spain's ambassador to Corchenne."

"The pleasure is mine, sir," I said, drawing on my lessons with Bridget earlier. "I'm—"

"Her Royal Highness, Princess Lila Sinclair of Corchenne. Most recently from Boston, but originally from New Hampshire."

"You've done your research." I didn't bother to hide how impressed I was, especially that he got my last name right. Almost everyone I'd met assumed I had taken Pierre's last name. The lack of feminism was appalling. "But I'm not a princess."

"It's only a matter of time, I'm sure. I always make it a point to be informed." The orchestra started playing, one of the waltzes Bridget and I practiced earlier. Over Juan's shoulder, Pierre said something to his companions, then bowed slightly. Turning, he locked eyes with me.

The crowd parted. We met in the middle of the room like in a fairy tale. Beside me, Pierre cleared his throat. He bowed deeply before holding out his hand. "Shall we, *chérie*?"

"It would be an absolute honor, my prince." I slid into his arms.

"You know, I used to hate the weight of my title, but I don't think I'll ever grow tired of hearing it from your lips. Much as I can't wait to get used to calling you my princess."

He led me through the steps, so I didn't respond right away while I focused on the music. A waltz, naturally. Thank you, Bridget.

"You really think your mother is going to officially make me a princess?" Although I wanted to manage my expectations, my heart soared .

Take that, Mom and Dad! Caleb may be your perfect son, but he's not royalty. Nope, that's me. Little Lila, law school dropout, never going to amount to anyt—

"Whatever you're thinking, stop," Pierre said. "You're practically vibrating, and not in a good way. This isn't normally how the waltz is done."

"Sorry. It was just... It doesn't matter. Tonight is about you and me. I've come a long way, huh?"

"You most certainly have." He paused, looking around the room. "To answer your question, it is tradition when someone marries into the royal family for them to be given a title. When my parents married, my father was Prince Henri I and *Mere* was simply Claudette. My grandparents made her a princess first, and then she became the queen following my father's coronation. They made her sister a duchess. It's not required, but it is tradition. I know *Mere* wasn't thrilled that I married an American without a wealthy family, but I do expect she'll get over it, eventually. If she doesn't, I'll have a word with Henri after she retires."

That warmed my heart. When I felt surrounded by people

who didn't want me here, it helped to know he was on my side. Pierre's opinion was the only one I needed. He wouldn't let his family's power and influence change the way he felt about me.

I hoped.

"Hey, I didn't realize your grandparents were still alive," I said.

He tilted his head for a moment, then nodded. "They're not. You're talking about Bridget's mother."

"She would be your step-grandmother, wouldn't she?"

"Technically, yes," Pierre said. "But my parents were already married before she came into the family. *Mere* was never close with her stepmother. I've met her a few times, and she's lovely, but she's not my grandmother."

The music stopped before I could reply. Pierre and I walked hand in hand toward where Bridget waited with Juan. After asking me if I minded being left alone, Pierre asked his aunt for the second dance.

"Shall we?" Juan asked after they left. "It is your night. You should be out on the floor, enjoying it."

On the dance floor, no one could talk to me. I could focus more on my feet, less on saying the wrong thing. As long as I didn't trip and knock someone over, I should be able to avoid embarrassing myself.

I glanced around quickly. Since Pierre was dancing with another woman, it should be okay for me. Juan seemed nice enough, and he spoke English. We didn't need an interpreter, and he seemed nice.

Pasting a wide smile on my face, I accepted his outstretched hand. "I would be delighted."

Thankfully, I had Luc by my side. Even though he wasn't translating, he gave me the barest of nods. I interpreted that to mean, at a minimum, Juan was either actually an ambassador to Spain or someone not likely to kidnap me and ransom me back to the throne. After the ball, I'd talk to Alexandre and Pierre about arranging some hand signals.

We moved to the middle of the floor before Juan turned to me. Thanks to my brief lesson in my office earlier, I slid right into the appropriate steps. Just like riding a bike.

At first.

About halfway through the song, Juan spun me around, leaving me facing the opposite direction. Against the far wall, a woman glared at me with such seething hatred, I missed a step.

My foot connected with Juan's shin. To his credit, he didn't make a sound. But he couldn't mask the pain that flashed across his face.

"I'm so sorry!" I said. "That woman threw me off. If looks could kill, we'd be lying on the floor. Do you know her?"

She had long, dark hair piled on top of her head, a gorgeous, floor-length red gown that hugged her body like a glove, and an air of authority. She appeared to be about my age. I vaguely thought I might have seen her in a magazine at one point, but I couldn't remember where. Famous parents, maybe?

"That is Princess Serena of Spain," Juan said.

That explained why I recognized her. On the plane, Pierre and I spent a couple of hours going through photos of current rulers and their families. Unfortunately, with so many of them, I barely recalled anyone other than the British royals I'd already been familiar with, the President of Germany, and, well, Henri.

"I don't think she likes me dancing with you," I said.

"No, she does not," he replied. "I'm not surprised, considering I just ended our relationship out in the garden a few minutes ago. She's always been extremely jealous. Finally, I could not handle her baseless accusations."

Wonderful. The Princess of Spain thought I wanted to steal her man. Maybe I should talk to her. Surely she would understand that, as someone who had been in the country less than two days and, by the way, was newly married to a prince, I didn't have any interest in starting an affair with Juan.

Before I could decide, Princess Serena spun on her toe and strode out of the ballroom, nose in the air. I swallowed.

"Are you okay?" Juan said.

With a start, I realized I was being unforgivably rude. I summoned my inner *Downton Abbey* Dame to reply. "My apologies. I was thinking perhaps I should go talk to Princess Serena. We've never been introduced, and I'd hate to upset her."

"You have done nothing wrong. The fault here is mine. But if it would make you feel better, after this dance, I'll ask her for a word."

"Yes, thank you. I'll let the duchess or Pierre introduce us later."

"As you wish," he said. "When this dance is over, I'll return you to Duchess Bridget and find Princess Serena. Enjoy the rest of your ball."

Even though Juan seemed nice, in this crowd, I preferred the comfort of a familiar face. When the song ended, I was happy to say goodbye. Bridget handed me my long-overdue champagne, then we strolled around the edge of the ballroom.

She discretely pointed out people to remember, throwing out interesting tidbits. Later, I'd have to ask Alexandre if he had written dossiers for all the guests. It was the only way to remember everything.

About an hour after it started, the music halted. There were no clocks, but the ball couldn't be over already. I turned to Bridget. "What's going on?"

She nodded toward the doorway at the top of the stairs. The double doors closed after Queen Claudette entered, but now they stood open again. Duncan waited at the top. As I watched, he brought a horn to his lips and played several notes.

Silence fell as everyone turned their attention to the top of the staircase.

"Are you ready?" As Pierre's whisper caressed my shoulder, I jumped. He hadn't been there a minute ago.

"Ready? For what?" I whispered back.

At the top of the staircase, Duncan took a deep breath, then shouted, "Presenting Her Royal Majesty, Queen Claudette."

"I believe this is the big announcement," Pierre said. "You're about to get your title."

This whole time, I'd been afraid to believe. But now, it was really happening! My heart pounded as Queen Claudette appeared in the doorway at the top of the stairs. She stood tall for a moment, letting us all bask in her presence.

Her Royal Majesty—my mother-in-law? I still didn't get what I was supposed to call her—looked positively resplendent. When she'd mentioned her gown earlier, I hadn't stopped to wonder what type of dress a queen would wear to a ball. Before Pierre and I entered, I'd been too terrified to pay attention. She looked absolutely amazing.

The cerulean fabric set off her eyes perfectly. Her gauzy skirt flowed and moved, but had enough layers to be modest. The top appeared to be the same material, but with a lace overlay and a wide vee, just deep enough to highlight the massive diamond necklace she wore. There must be a name for so many rows of jewels, but I didn't know it. Other than enormous. Still, she wore it well. For this event, she'd brought out matching diamond earrings. Below her three-quarter-length sleeves, Queen Claudette wore white elbow gloves. A crown of platinum and diamonds completed the look.

The ballroom doors closed behind us with a thud, making me jump in my nervousness. Queen Claudette's gaze swept over the crowd, pausing only briefly as she spotted me and Pierre. She clapped her hands twice, and all conversation stopped immediately. Teachers worldwide would love to know how she did that.

"Wonderful! I'm glad to see everyone is here," she said loudly in French. Beside me, Luc translated softly into my ear. I'd barely noticed him following us. "Thank you for coming to this little soiree of mine, especially on such short notice. You know how it is when family drops in unexpectedly."

A chuckle rippled through the crowd. A few people looked at me, and my cheeks grew warm. I forced myself to focus on my mother-in-law. If being a public figure flustered me, I'd be too nervous to accept my title.

Did I get a crown? Oh, I wanted a crown. It didn't have to be as ornate as hers. Maybe just a tiara. That would be okay.

Queen Claudette continued, "In recent days, I have been fortunate enough to welcome a new member of my family. Some people are born into your family, and some are born into your heart. This person is the latter, someone I might never have met under other circumstances, but who I feel fortunate to consider family."

Really? She liked me! She really liked me! I'd been so worried, but Queen Claudette was happy for us. She spoke warmly, from the heart. It didn't sound overly practiced or rehearsed, and I truly believed she meant every word.

"Some of you met the newest member of our nobility tonight, and the rest of you are in for a big treat. People have to listen to me. It's a treat to find someone people want listen to."

Huh? People listened to me? I glanced at Pierre. "Did he translate that right?"

Luc shot me a withering look. "I'm standing right here. And shhh. I need to hear Her Royal Majesty."

"Sorry. She's just saying a lot of awfully nice—"

"Shh!"

Queen Claudette was still speaking, but now we'd missed a few sentences. Luc picked up seamlessly and began translating again. "Without further ado, it is my great pleasure to introduce you all to the newest member of Corchenne's royal family."

With great fanfare, she waited for a steward to bring her a folded bit of blue cloth. It was darker than the Corchenne emblem, but not quite navy. Then she held it up. The fabric fluttered out to a large rectangle. It was my flag!

Ever since Pierre told me that members of the royal family got their own flags to show when they were in attendance, I was curious. But this wasn't the same shade as my old blue vests. A large, fancy S took up most of the flag's center.

Cool. I thought they were still upset over me keeping my name. This felt like my mother-in-law extending a much-needed olive branch. Beaming, I took a tentative step forward. Pierre's hand on my arm stilled me. Confused, I shot him a look. Then I noticed no one was looking at me.

No one was looking at Queen Claudette, either, although she was still talking about the importance of family. No, oddly enough, everyone's eyes had landed on...

"The new Baron of Mousseux, Caleb Sinclair!"

Chapter Eleven

OFFICIAL GUIDE TO BEING A PRINCESS: A princess must remain in control of her emotions in public. Only in private may she express frustration or anger, and only with the most trusted of confidants.

"Please, please tell me that means 'Baron of Moose,'" Hannah said when I got her on the phone the next morning. I'd made a video call while still hiding my face under a pillow. Caleb wasn't the only talented member of the Sinclair family. "Actually, no need to tell me that, because I'm going to call him Moosey from now on either way."

"It's the house of sparkling wine," I said. "Apparently, that property makes some of the best sparkling wine on the island. Wine that our brother can now make and sell. Or, you know, he can use the land to breed chickens for export. With him, it might go either way."

"At least she thanked you for bringing him to the country," Hannah said. "She could have skipped mentioning you at all."

I groaned. "Great. Now I can forever be known as the new

99

baron's sister, who married a prince just so the queen could be lucky enough to make Caleb's acquaintance. How did this happen? The Queen doesn't strike me as a stupid woman."

This whole trip was a waste of time. What a disaster. My brother inexplicably stole my title, my mother-in-law hated me, and I'd barely seen my husband for more than about eight seconds, other than during our dance at the ball, where the entire world watched us. Living in a fishbowl was draining.

The worst part was Pierre's disappointment at the queen's announcement. He'd wanted his mother to accept me, to love me like he did. Instead, she not only embraced my sworn enemy, but she also gave him the land where he was hoping to make a home for our kids someday. His grandmother's land.

I sighed. "Pierre was heartbroken. I don't know how to fix this."

"She really gave him the house you two were planning to live in?"

"Well, nothing was set in stone," I grumbled. "But Pierre wanted it so I could have a title. Honestly, it's enormous. We don't need a house that big. But we need a home on this island more than Caleb. I don't want to stay in the castle whenever we're here. It's so grand. Not me at all. In the smaller estate, we could put up the whole family if everyone came to visit. Plus, everyone else you know. And she gave him a flag! I was supposed to get a flag as a member of the royal family. Instead, I got nothing. He doesn't even need a flag. He needs to return to Brazil."

"How does he do it?" Hannah shook her head with a look suspiciously like awe on her face. "What radioactive substance gave him this superpower?"

"I'm starting to think he's magic," I moaned. "He charms absolutely everyone he meets. People just give him things. Like castles! Like *my* castle."

I knew we were going in circles, but I was too frustrated to make sense.

Hannah stopped laughing and leaned toward the camera.

"Hey, what is that property worth? Do you think Caleb could sell it and finally pay me back?"

Okay, maybe she wasn't quite as outraged as I'd thought.

"That's what you're worried about? Money?"

"Not *worried*, exactly. Just trying to find the silver lining in your bizarre scenario."

"I didn't cause this!" I protested.

"Didn't you? After all, none of this would have happened if you hadn't married Pierre."

When she put it that way, things weren't so bad. Sure, my brother was scamming the queen of a foreign country and my mother-in-law preferred him to me, but I'd found my person. Together, we could weather anything.

Maybe I should go tell him that.

We needed more time together during the day, with the lights on. Pierre shaving while I was in the shower wasn't exactly the kind of quality time newlyweds needed together. Maybe that was Queen Claudette's plan. Keep Pierre so busy he forgot who I was. Keep me lonely and irritated, so I nagged him. Drive a wedge between us until her son realizes what a mistake he made marrying a liberal American commoner.

Nope. Not on my watch.

Deep down, I knew that was ridiculous. Pierre loved me, and I loved him. With all my lessons, my schedule was as packed as his. Not because the Queen was trying to destroy our marriage (probably), but because we'd just arrived. It would take time to orient ourselves to the realities of royal life. Personally, I figured it would all click about four hours after we boarded our flight back to Boston.

Talking sense did nothing to ease my ever-expanding feeling of impending doom, so it was time to go find Pierre. Throwing back the blankets, I rushed out of bed and into the shower. According to the official schedule, Pierre was in a breakfast meeting, but I could ask Jules to pencil me in after lunch.

Easier said than done.

During Pierre's first break of the morning, I had French lessons. He was free at eleven, but I had History of Corchenne. For lunch, my husband would be dining with the ambassadors from Japan and Belgium. My presence there would be neither desired nor beneficial to anyone in the room. Unless they served Beef Wellington. Preacher liked Beef Wellington.

There! I pointed to a blank spot. "What about this? It looks like we're both free at two o'clock."

He narrowed his eyes and leaned in. "Ah, yes. His Royal Highness was planning to take part in a flight demonstration, but the rain has grounded him."

"A flight demonstration? My husband can fly?" Bizarrely, the image of him flapping his arms like wings came into my head. Maybe he was like Ironman! Pierre certainly could afford to hire tech people to make him fancy gadgets.

"Certainly, Madame," Jules said, his tone holding the slightest bit of reproach. "All members of the royal family serve a tour of duty in the Air Force once they turn eighteen. You didn't know?"

"He mentioned once that he'd served when he was younger." I thought for a minute. "A long time ago. I guess he never said what he did. He didn't talk about it much. I thought he was too close to the fighting. That it was a painful memory."

Jules snorted, a sound quickly turned into a cough. "They'd never let someone so important near the combat. Prince Pierre flew medical supplies in and out of the field offices. Far from the fighting."

Yet another reminder of how my husband and I were worlds apart. Never had I even considered serving in the military. The thought of pointing a gun at someone filled me with dread. Pierre must have learned to shoot, though, if for no reason other than to protect himself. I hated to be reminded there were parts of himself that Pierre kept from me. What other things highlighted how different we were?

Sure, when we met, he was pretending to be an ordinary guy, an immigrant in the United States working as an investment banker. At first, Madison and I thought his accent was French. I'd barely heard of Corchenne—the first time Pierre brought it up, we thought he was kidding. Then he'd had to spell it before we could even find it on our phones. He certainly hadn't mentioned that he was royalty. We'd been friends for years, sharing weekly movie nights and hanging out all the time. It never came up before we got engaged.

After I'd found out, though, I'd thought we'd revealed our most important secrets. Maybe I'd been wrong.

Jules tilted his head at me. "Is everything okay, Madame?"

Quickly, I shook myself out of my funk and pasted a smile on my face. "Great! Can you pencil me in for a meeting at two?"

"Certainly. It's wise of you to snatch up the time slot before someone else does."

"Someone else might ask for a meeting with him in three hours?"

"It happens all the time."

Here I'd thought people needed to schedule time with the royal family weeks in advance. "Are the princes always this busy, even when Queen Claudette is holding court?"

"Not at all," he said. "The harvest is a busy time. Things are typically slower over the winter. But Pierre has been gone for years. Many of the Queen's advisors and important Corche families want to see him in person. They want to know if America changed him and if he has the same values as when he left."

"Maybe we should stay longer," I said, more to myself than Jules. Pierre could get additional face time with his people close, and I would be warmer. The weather in Boston over the winter was atrocious. If I moved away, that would be why.

"If Prince Pierre wants to make his home on Corchenne again, everyone would be delighted."

Imagine the entire citizenry of a nation caring at all where you lived. Corchenne had a population of maybe a hundred thousand people. There weren't even a hundred thousand people in America who knew my name.

Well, there hadn't been before I married Pierre. Now there were, but I bet half of them knew nothing else about me. Or cared.

"Thanks, Jules." I started to leave, then thought of something else. "Is there someplace where we can have a picnic? Something overlooking the vineyard, not too far from the castle? If we only have an hour, I don't want to spend most of it traveling."

"You're aware of the courtyard attached to the throne room?"

"Yeah, sure." His suggestion surprised me. "Would Her Royal Majesty be okay with me using it for something personal?"

"Absolutely not," Jules said with total certainty. "However, there is a similar patio on the west side. From the main hall, head through the portrait gallery. You'll find a set of large glass doors. There's a lovely garden just off the patio. You'll be able to see the vineyards. They are spectacular this time of year."

"Didn't you say it's going to rain?"

"Conditions aren't ideal for a flight display because of the cloud coverage. It should be warm enough to eat outside and not too windy. There is a gazebo overlooking the grounds where you can enjoy your meal. It's private, but not a long walk."

That sounded perfect. Privacy, fresh air, good views, and Pierre.

"Is afternoon tea a thing here?" I thought I'd heard my mother-in-law mention it, but didn't know if it was just her or everyone.

"Anything can be a thing if you wish it," he said. "You're married to the prince. Shall I ask Chef to prepare something special for you?"

"I can do it."

"Please, allow me. It's part of my job. It would be my pleasure to speak with him for you."

I'd actually meant that I could prepare a picnic, not that I could go ask someone else to do it for me. Even I could put together a charcuterie board. Or buy one pre-made. They must have a market around here.

I still hadn't gotten used to having other people do things for me. My first instinct was to protest. There was no reason I couldn't walk to the kitchen and request a cheese and wine picnic after lunch. I didn't need to know the best cheeses or the most delicious wines. But then my eyes fell on the clock, and I realized I was late for my meeting with Luc.

"Only if you're positive it's not an imposition. Thank you, Jules." I said. He bowed. "I'm sorry. I still don't get royal life. Am I supposed to tip you?"

"I would be greatly offended if you did," he replied smoothly. "To tip would imply that Her Royal Majesty doesn't pay me enough."

"I certainly wouldn't want to do that," I said hastily. Upsetting people left and right, that seemed to be my forte. "Please let me know if I can do anything for you."

"Of course, Madame. But you are already doing the most important thing."

"Oh, yeah? What's that?"

"Keeping his royal highness happy." That brought a smile to my face, but then Jules continued. "And, of course, raising royal babies soon."

I groaned.

~

When Pierre arrived at the gazebo that afternoon, he looked from me to the picnic basket to the blanket I'd spread across the wooden floor with a big smile.

"Surprise!" I held up two flutes of sparkling wine.

He took it and settled cross-legged beside me before sniffing the glass. "After last night, should I be worried about what's in this?"

I snorted. "Of all the Leóns I've met, you're the one with the least to worry about. I don't blame you for your mother's actions. It's Caleb I'm mad at."

"I know, I know. Please allow me to apologize on her behalf again."

"That's not necessary," I said. "I didn't marry you so your mom would give me fancy castles or a title. I married you because I love you. But we decided to rejoin the public eye so we could make a difference. The only thing I've done since I arrived is not strangle my brother, and that doesn't exactly make the world a better place."

"For what it's worth, I appreciate you not bringing a family murder scandal to the monarchy."

"Never say never," I said with a sigh. But Caleb had ruined enough of my stay, so I pulled two plates out of the picnic basket beside me and started piling them with cheese, bread, and these gorgeous juicy grapes Chef had picked just that morning. When I took my first bite, my eyes rolled back in my head. A girl could get used to this.

Leaning over, Pierre took my hand in his. "Other than your brother, how are you finding the castle? Is there anything I can do?"

For a long moment, I pondered his question. "I'm honestly not sure. Your mother's secretary sent me a list of 'approved' charities this morning, but she just wants me to hold a fundraiser. I'm not supposed to do anything hands-on—apparently, it would be 'inappropriate.'"

"That sounds like *Mére*," he said. "What did you have in mind?"

"I don't know. There are seemingly endless options until you realize I need approval to do any of them. Nothing political. No charity affiliated with any religion—or one that's anti-religion. Nothing where I'm working with my hands or surrounded by sick people." I sighed. "Not that I'm not happy to be here. Of course I am. It's just all overwhelming."

"I'm sorry," Pierre said. "We've only been here two days. It will get better, I promise. Let me talk to Jules. I'll find time next week for the two of us to go into town, take a tour, talk to the people about what's on their minds."

"Is that sanctioned?"

Leaning over, he kissed me lightly. "Not at all, *chérie*. I'm the black sheep of the family, remember?"

"Looks like there are benefits to marrying the bad boy," I said with a teasing smile. I pulled him closer and closed my eyes, enjoying the moment. This was why I put up with my encroaching brother and a mother-in-law who was trying to turn me into a well-groomed puppet for the throne. The fire that consumed me when Pierre and I were together made everything worth it.

If only I could remember that until we got back to Boston. I couldn't wait to resume our lives together, away from all this.

Pounding footsteps made the two of us spring apart. Pierre stood and helped me to my feet before running his hand through his hair, smoothing it into place. I did the same as we both turned to look at what was causing the disruption.

"Excuse me, sir?" Jules poked his head through the gazebo's opening, looking as if he'd run about ten marathons to get to us. His breath came out in short pants. "I have an urgent matter to discuss."

"Certainly, Jules. Please come in," Pierre said.

"Would you like some water?" I asked, digging in my basket. He looked on the verge of collapse.

"Yes, thank you." The chief of staff looked from my husband to me, then back. "We need to speak privately, if you please. This requires the utmost discretion."

"Anything you can say to me can be said in front of *my wife*," Pierre said sharply. "And if you apologize now, I will not fire you for implying she'll post our conversation on the internet."

My cheeks flamed.

Jules turned to me. "Please forgive me, Princess Lila. I did not mean to insult you. I'm a bit flustered at the moment."

Pierre asked, "What seems to be the trouble, Jules?"

At that, Jules snapped to attention. "My apologies, sir. Sorry again to intrude. And to insult. I'm afraid there's no delicate way to say this."

"Just tell us," I suggested. "I might not be up on all the Corche customs, but in America, we find that saying what you're thinking gives people information you want them to have."

His cheeks flushed. Now I felt bad. "There appears to be a disturbance in the vineyard."

"A disturbance? Like what?" I asked before Pierre could say anything.

"At first we thought it was local kids, but, well, I think you need to see this for yourself, sir."

If local kids were stealing grapes because they were hungry, I wanted to be a part of finding a resolution. But Jules made it seem like the answer was nothing so easily resolved. The grapes were almost ready for picking. We were planning a harvest festival for the end of the week. As far as I knew, only a few members of the palace staff would be in the vineyards until then.

There would only be—oh, no. What was Caleb trying to convince Queen Claudette to import after the harvest? Chickens or something. To live on the land over the winter? I said a silent prayer that my brother's shipment hadn't arrived earlier. A herd of chickens stampeding the vineyard was not a good look.

Pierre said, "Lila, why don't you come with us?"

He definitely only made the suggestion to pacify me. What I knew about inspecting crops fit on the head of a pin. But since I'd been looking for ways to get more involved, I appreciated the opportunity to feel included. It would be nice to do something other than attend princess lessons, smile pretty, and exchange pleasantries.

"I'd be happy to, my love," I said. "Jules, this doesn't involve chickens, does it?"

Pierre's head shot up. "Chickens?"

"Please, follow me."

I hesitated, looking at the picnic blanket and food on the

ground. Not because I wanted to stay and finish eating—because I suspected someone would clean it up while we were gone. The last thing I wanted was to create extra work for the staff.

But Jules said time was of the essence. We didn't have time to pick up dishes if something threatened the palace.

We left the picnic and followed Jules down a path to the nearest vineyard. The vines were picked clean. Grape leaves lay ravaged on the ground. It looked like a hurricane passed through. Local kids wouldn't have caused this type of destruction, not when it was their parents and families who counted on the land to yield crops to support them. As far as I knew, deer weren't indigenous to Corchenne.

But chickens... Oh, man. I wanted to strangle my brother. How did such small animals cause such a mess?

A series of grunts filled the air. Definitely not kids. Hold on. Chickens didn't grunt, as far as I knew.

Was it adults playing a prank? Protesters? Why would anyone protest growing the country's chief export? Without grapes and wine exports, taxes would increase to pay for necessary services, like paving the roads and providing unemployment benefits to people who needed them. Maybe the workers were trying to unionize for higher pay? That made no sense.

I started toward the noise, but Jules stopped me with a hand on my arm. "No, Madame. Just watch. You're here to observe."

"He's right, Lila," Pierre said. "Neither of us should get too close. We don't know what we're dealing with yet."

"How can I help from back here?" I asked.

"I'm afraid it's not safe to get any closer," Jules said.

"Then what are we doing here?"

"Observing, mostly. We need to give a full report." Pierre's hand on my shoulder was calming and firm, a reminder not to enter the fray. "Security will take care of the problem."

"They won't shoot the chickens, will they?" On the one hand, I didn't want anyone to harm a flock of innocent birds. On the other, I'd never realized they were such destructive little beasts.

Instead of answering, Pierre glanced at Jules over my head.

"We will try to contain them in other ways," Jules said. "We'll herd them out of the vineyard. If that doesn't work, we can put out feed and water, laced with drugs to help them sleep."

I heaved a sigh of relief. "Oh, good. Thank you."

A high-pitched shriek cut through the air. That was not a chicken. It sounded like someone in pain. I made it one step toward the vineyard when a creature came bursting out. Not a man. An animal. Big as a man, standing upright. My heart pounded in my throat. Although the beast stood at least fifty feet away, I froze.

What was I even looking at? My brain ridiculously refused to put together the pieces in front of me.

"Was that what I think it was?" Pierre asked.

"I hope you know, because all I'm thinking is 'whoa, giant bird-like thing,'" I replied.

Ignoring me, Jules said, "Yes, sir. I believe it was an Australian emu."

An emu? All of a sudden, I longed for chickens.

A feeling of dread settled into the depths of my stomach. "Are we closer to Australia than I think we are?"

"If you think we are approximately fifteen thousand kilometers away and that emus cannot fly, you would be correct. They can swim, but to my knowledge, no one has recently spotted a herd of emus traversing the Atlantic Ocean."

His words confirmed my sinking sensation, but I tried again. "Has there been an incident at the local zoo? Some kind of mass emu outbreak?"

"I'm afraid not. To my knowledge, the zoo would not have large birds in this quantity."

Pretty sure I already knew the answer, I forced myself to ask. "Are Australian emus by any chance native to Corchenne? An import from the seventeen hundreds as a gift from Queen Victoria, bred here for centuries?"

"Oh, *chérie*, how I wish that was the case," Pierre said.

"Then how...?" But the now gaping pit in my belly told me the truth. This must be the "amazing opportunity" Caleb kept talking about. As irrational as it sounded, it was the most logical explanation I could think of. Somehow my brother had brought a herd of emus to the palace, rather than the chickens I had been expecting.

And now they were destroying the country's primary cash crop.

Chapter Twelve

A string of expletives escaped me. My brother couldn't be that thoughtless, could he?

Of course he could. Caleb cared only about himself. He would only think how cool he might look importing "exotic" animals. He wouldn't care that they might get loose and wreak havoc. Nor would he stop to verify that the animals he expected to live in the vineyards following the harvest were actually being delivered once the grapes have been removed from the fields.

He must know this wasn't okay, or he wouldn't have been so cagey about what his actual business plan was. To think he'd let me believe he was bringing in chickens! That was bad enough, but this was beyond the pale.

"What do we do?" I whispered to Pierre. I couldn't afford to attract the emus' attention. Were they violent or playful? Would they attack a human? There are things I didn't want to know.

"I'll wait for Animal Control to show up," he replied.

"Shouldn't you get inside? Those things look fast."

He looked from the vineyard to me, to the castle, then back to the vineyard. "I think I'm safe enough for the moment. If they take a single step this way, I'll go inside."

That made me feel one iota better. I watched the birds for another few seconds, but they seemed oblivious to our presence. At the moment, Pierre should be safe . If I stayed here, he'd only worry about me. Here, I was in the way of the people who could resolve the situation. But there was something I could do.

Spinning around, I started for the castle.

"Lila, wait!" At the sound of Pierre's voice, I glanced over my shoulder. "Where are you going?"

"To find Caleb and give him one chance to explain why I shouldn't feed him to the emus."

He snorted. "If it helps, I'm pretty sure most emus are meat-eaters."

"Yes, sir," Jules supplied helpfully.

"I'll tell him that."

The thought made me smile as I snuck back toward the castle, praying the emus didn't follow me.

Finding someone in a building the size of the Chateau should be difficult, except for one thing: with three hundred staff members around, at least one of them nearly always had someone in eyesight. Even if he wanted to hide, it wouldn't occur to Caleb to look for a room empty of staff. He simply ignored them. Someone would know where he was.

Another reason most of the palace workers would happily help me: I talked to the people who worked in the castle, learned their names, and treated them with respect. Pierre had grown up doing the same. Caleb didn't pay any attention to anyone unless he needed something from them.

As suspected, it took less than ten minutes to locate my brother. He sat in one of the palace libraries, with a highball glass in one hand and a stack of books open in front of him. He was holding his phone out, taking pictures of something.

When I turned the corner, he jumped out of his seat. Trying to hide his reaction, he drank from his glass while shutting each of the books on the table. I tried to peek at what he was doing, but the title of the top one was written in French. Okay, I knew the word "Corchenne". *L'histoire* looked a lot like history. Weird that he cared enough to do any research. Maybe he was growing as a person.

Just kidding.

He was probably looking for the country's weaknesses so he could exploit whatever his stupid emus didn't destroy. Wait. One thing at a time. Giant birds, vineyards. Priorities.

"Caleb!" I hissed at him. Although this wasn't the sort of public library I'd been trained not to raise my voice in, it still felt weird to shout around these books. "Do you, by any chance, know why there are wild birds racing through the vineyard?"

He cleared his throat. "Um, apparently, there was a minor mistake in my purchase order."

"A little mistake? You said you were buying chickens!"

"I never said that. You asked, and I never confirmed either way. You and Pierre both assumed that I was talking about a small bird. Queen Claudette knew the truth."

"Then what was the mistake?"

"They were supposed to be delivered after the harvest," he said. "And sedated. Apparently, the sedation was an extra fee I wasn't aware of."

"Does Queen Claudette know what's happening now? She's been very tolerant of you, but I don't think she's going to be okay with losing acres of farmland that don't even belong to her."

"She was aware of the risks of this investment. I have a friend who can take care of everything. In a few hours, it'll be like nothing ever happened."

Of course he did. His "friend" would charge a hefty fee to round up the birds, then give half to my brother. Typical Caleb. I wanted to kick myself for even thinking about giving him another chance. I should have convinced Pierre to chain him up and carry him away on the private jet as soon as I spotted him cozying up to the queen.

"Your friend can regrow destroyed grapes? That's quite the superpower."

Caleb waved one hand. "Grapes are over. The money is in emu farming. Their eggs and meat are *huge* in Brazil."

"In case you haven't noticed, we're not in Brazil. We're in a country with one export, and you have intentionally imported a species that is destroying it! Who knows if the grapes will recover if we don't get out there!" Desperately, I said, "Come on. You've got to help me fix this."

"I'm sorry, sister dear, but I'm afraid I'm busy," he said. "I have research to do. These books aren't going to read themselves. A baron has to know about his land."

"That wasn't a request, Caleb." I drew myself up to my full height, doing my best to put on the veil of haughtiness worn by certain other members of the royal family. "As a Princess of Corchenne, I insist you accompany me to the vineyard."

"Nice try," he said. "I'm not a citizen of Corchenne. You're not my princess."

"That's not how laws work, I'm afraid. You can't go to a foreign country and decide none of the rules don't apply to you because you don't live there."

"Laws, no. But you don't have any authority here, either. You weren't born into the royal family. Queen Claudette hasn't bestowed a title upon you, and you have no official duties. You don't even have a flag. I'm pretty sure I outrank you. As Baron, I order you to go away and leave me alone."

I cursed under my breath. He shouldn't know any of those things. I balled my hands into fists and rested them on my hips. "Fine. Come help me, or I'm going to tell Mom and Dad that you tried to single-handedly destroy my husband's country's economy."

Finally, Caleb realized I meant business. He stood and returned his phone to a pocket. Then he bowed mockingly. "After you, *Princess Lila*."

Without another word, I turned and stomped toward the room designated as my office, hoping my brother did what he said for once and followed me.

As the least extravagant room in the castle, I felt more at home in this office than anywhere else. Plopping myself into the chair behind the small desk, I motioned to Caleb to have a seat across from me. He glanced around the room. "This is it? You're not going to offer me a drink?"

"There's a coffee shop down in the village. Go there when we're done. Stay as long as you want. No need to return."

"I don't understand this hostility. What did I ever do to you?"

The list of my brother's flaws could roll off my tongue as easily as my ABCs, but now wasn't the time. Caleb was already defensive, and I needed him to fix the immediate issue at hand, not dredge up old grudges. "You brought a herd of wild emus onto this island. That herd is right now trampling the vineyards that grow Corchenne's number one export. An export that has not yet been harvested for the year."

"Come on, Lila, where's your vision? Wine is in the past. Emu burgers, that's the future. That's the business opportunity I've been talking to Queen Claudette about. Short term, yeah, they might mess up the land a bit. But I'm telling you, once we get started harvesting eggs and breeding for meat, this country will make a killing. I'd have included you and Pierre, but his advisor—Blaise, was it?—never returned my call. I figured if you were interested, you would have told me."

"No, we're not interested." I leaned forward and crossed my arms over the desk. "I can't believe Queen Claudette approved this. We're talking about tens of thousands of dollars of damage to the land, and potentially millions if they're not stopped."

"What am I supposed to do about it?"

"They're your emus! Cage them, sedate them, take them out

to dinner. I don't care. But you've got to control them before Queen Claudette throws us into the dungeons."

"There are no dungeons under the castle anymore," he said. "Don't you know Queen Claudette turned them into a wine cellar about fifteen years ago?"

"How could you possibly know that?"

"Because, unlike you, I did my homework before I arrived."

"You mean you researched the best way to exploit my mother-in-law before showing up uninvited? I'm so proud. No wonder Mom and Dad are always asking me to be more like you."

"That's it, isn't it? This isn't about the emus. You're jealous because our parents love me more."

"Enough!" We turned to find Queen Claudette standing in the doorway. My cheeks flamed. "I could hear you shouting all the way in my private sitting area. While you carry on like children, a giant bird has stormed the throne room. I believe I have the two of you to thank for that."

Me? I wanted to ask what I did, but arguing with the queen only made me look childish. Besides, Caleb came to Corchenne because of me. This really was all my fault.

"Excuse me, Your Majesty," I said tentatively. "Did you say there's an emu *in the throne room?*"

"Why, yes, I did. One of the servants didn't expect to see a giant bird in the hall when she exited. Poor Yvette screamed and fainted in the doorway. The emu went in, along with its friends."

Beside me, Caleb looked like he wanted to laugh. My fingers itched to throttle him. Instead, I dropped into as deep a curtsey as I could manage. "I'm so sorry, Your Royal Highness. We would be happy to take care of this immediately."

"See that you do. Because if there are still emus in the castle when the Prince of Luxembourg returns from his day trip to France, I will personally declare your marriage to my son null and void."

Chapter Thirteen

OFFICIAL GUIDE TO BEING A PRINCESS: A princess shall maintain proper decorum at all times. There is never cause for behaving like a commoner.

Queen Claudette's ultimatum rocked me to my core. I didn't know if she could undo a marriage without either spouse's consent, but didn't want to find out. She could refuse to acknowledge it in her own country. She was, after all, in charge.

After she made the pronouncement, she swept away, back toward the residential area of the palace. I moved away from her, toward the throne room. Then I stopped and looked back. My brother hadn't moved an inch. "Caleb?"

"Yes. Er, I think I better go alert security." Before I could stop him, he scurried down the hall in the wrong direction like the rat he was. I wanted to go after him, but there wasn't time. Queen Claudette was pretty clear that I shouldn't make any detours before neutralizing the emus inside the castle.

Pierre met me in the hallway outside the throne room. How different from the last time we stood here together.

"Not to sound rude, but aren't you too important to be here?" I asked.

"We both shouldn't be here," he said. "If we get stampeded by giant birds, it's be a national tragedy. I'm here to ask you to wait for security to come take care of this. There is no reason in the world for you to enter the throne room. The birds are contained. The best thing we can do is make sure no one else stumbles in before the problem gets resolved."

"That doesn't feel like we're helping," I said.

"This is not our mess to clean up, *chérie*," Pierre said. "Keeping others safe is plenty of help."

"At least we're more useful than my brother," I grumbled, glaring at where Caleb had disappeared. He probably didn't even know where the security office was. I was definitely going to call our parents once this was resolved. "You're aware that your mother threatened me with dissolving our marriage if I can't fix this, right?"

Leaning over, he kissed me gently. "She's all talk. *Mére* knows that if she tries to get between you and me, it will send me out of the country again. And she's worried that I won't come back."

Those words made it sound suspiciously like the Queen had feelings. Maybe we were all human after all. With a deep breath, I threw my head back and gestured toward the doors.

"How long is it to get security here?"

"They're already on their way. Should be two or three minutes, tops."

Okay, that wasn't so bad. We could wait here. Security would definitely be better equip—

Frantic barking filled the air. I froze.

"Where's Preacher?"

"I haven't seen him. What time's his daily walk with Bernadette?" The Queen's chauffeur adored the little guy, and we were happy to let her walk him every afternoon. Even if Chef Eric spoiled him with treats on their way back to our suite.

Dread seized me by the throat. "Probably about twenty minutes ago. They might not be back yet."

More barking. It sounded very familiar—too familiar. Then a loud boom. It was unlike any sound I'd ever heard.

"Do you know where she takes him when they're out?"

Pierre started to answer, but then I heard a high-pitched whine and a yelp. That wasn't an emu noise. That was my little dog, and he sounded terrified.

Throwing the door open, I darted into the room. Pierre yelled for me to wait, but I ignored him.

About three steps into the room, I spotted the giant bird. Up close, it appeared even taller than it had from the hill. It squatted on the throne as if it belonged there. As I skidded to a halt, its beady eyes fixated on me. He—she? It?—cocked his head, as if debating whether I would make a tasty snack. For the first time, I realized I was defenseless. But these creatures could devour my dog in an instant. Especially if, as Jules said, they were really meat-eaters. I couldn't let poor Preacher become an emu snack. I had to save him.

My eyes darted around the room, seeking my little boy. He had to be in here somewhere.

There.

In the far corner beyond the throne, Bernadette cowered against the outside wall. Her face was white. She trembled. A second emu paced in the doorway to the courtyard, blocking her escape. He stopped walking to peck the bulletproof glass on the window, then resumed pacing. Wonderful.

Preacher wriggled in Bernadette's arms. Her gaze was firmly planted on the emu sitting on the throne. She didn't seem to have noticed me.

When he spotted me, he let out a high-pitched yelp. The bird in the door flinched but didn't move. The taller one, the one on the throne, spread his wings and stretched his neck out before settling back.

Perhaps running into a room full of wild emus was not the best idea. But now, how to save Bernadette and Preacher? I thought back to my summer days of watching Animal Planet when home from school with Hannah and Caleb. It was one of three channels my parents allowed.

With bears, you were supposed to seem as large as possible and not try to outrun them. Scare them away. Were emus like bears? No clue. But if the birds rushed me, Bernadette and Preacher could get away.

Distantly, I heard the door close behind me. Pierre had probably assessed the situation calmly and followed me into the room. Unlike me, he had the presence of mind to stop the emus from exiting into the main hallway. Great. He could help the others.

My mind raced frantically. Two exits—one to the outside and one back to the hall. Was that it? Shouldn't there be some secret door under the throne to whisk the Queen away if someone attacked?

I racked my brains, but I couldn't remember. I hadn't had enough time to study the castle's layout. Also, secret Queen-escape tunnels probably weren't on any of the plans found in the library.

Then I spotted it. Behind the throne—a small, unobtrusive door, barely visible. The only reason I noticed it was the giant bird plopped in front of it, attempting to preen a large crown.

Queen Claudette had mentioned three birds, hadn't she? More than one, at least. I prayed there weren't more.

Pierre stepped up beside me. "Security will be here in one minute."

"We have to get Bernadette out," I whispered, not daring to turn my head. The emu still stared at me.

All of a sudden, it squawked loudly. Preacher flinched before yapping furiously. Ignoring him, the emu spread its wings. Then it rose to its feet, still on the seat of the throne.

Between the emu's legs sat an enormous egg.

I gasped.

If the emu nested on the throne, we'd never get her out. Where was the security team?

At the sound of my voice, Preacher leaped toward me. The entire world went into slow motion. Bernadette cried out in pain. Then my little dog raced toward the bird. The giant mama bird protecting her egg. The bird behind the throne stopped preening, crown still in his mouth, and walked forward onto the dais. Headed straight for my dog.

Without another thought, I screamed and flapped my arms, racing toward them.

"LEAVE MY DOG ALONE!" I roared as I expected a bear would, stomping and making myself as large as possible.

Behind me, Pierre yelled. "Lila, no!"

Bernadette screamed. The mama emu pecked at Preacher, who hopped out of the way. Then she stretched again and sauntered to the door. I breathed a sigh of relief, cut off abruptly when the emu sentry plopped down on top of the egg.

Maybe if I could get Mama to leave, the others would follow?

Not with that egg on the throne. Sentry Emu seemed pretty intent on guarding it. And I didn't dare touch the egg, even if I could get him to stand up. I just needed to distract them enough to get Preacher and Bernadette out. Then the palace security guards could handle the rest.

As I stopped to catch my breath, I removed one shoe and chucked it at the chair beside the throne, hoping to scare the birds rather than actually hurt them. It glanced off the arm of the throne. Sentry Emu hissed at it.

Hissed.

With its gaze fixed on Preacher, I threw my second shoe.

A shot tore through the air. Wind whizzed by my ear. Mama Emu dropped. The emu that had been blocking the servant's entrance followed a second later. Finally, Sentry Emu went down. A loud silence filled the room.

Preacher paused and cocked his head, clearly confused. He hopped forward, sniffed Mama Emu, danced back. Then, when he realized they were out, he turned and raced into my waiting arms. A bunch of men in navy blue uniforms stampeded by me as Pierre enveloped me in his arms. My knees went weak. I collapsed against him.

Finally, security had arrived.

~

Out in the hall, Bernadette flung herself into my arms. "Oh, lady! Thank you so much! I can never repay your kindness!"

"It was nothing," I assured her. "Are you okay?"

"Certainly! It takes more than a giant bird to beat me." She pushed away from me and stood stiffly, putting on a brave face. "It's not every day you find human-sized fowl in the throne room. Especially not one trying to wear a crown."

When she held it up, I realized Bernadette clutched a ring of gold and jewels. Well, it used to be a ring. Now it was more of an oval. I didn't want to think about what that cost. Or that my brother's antics almost destroyed it.

Last year, I was making minimum wage at a big box store where I had to fight for enough hours to also qualify for health insurance. In five hundred years, I never would've made the cost of a royal crown.

"Is there a royal jeweler?" I asked weakly. Maybe he'd let me work for him to pay the debt.

"Of course there is," Pierre said. "But you should make Caleb take care of it. This is his mistake, not yours."

If my brother got his hand on a real Corche Crown, it would be on eBay before you could say "priceless stolen artifact."

Bridgette said, "Honestly, I wouldn't worry about it. That one isn't one of Claudette's favorites. She's got at least a dozen."

Weakly, I shook my head. "No, it's fine. If someone in security doesn't mind taking it over, the jeweler can send me the bill. I don't want to risk doing more harm by taking it myself."

"Certainly, Madame," Bernadette said. "With your permission, I'll take it to the jeweler now."

She turned and disappeared down the hall. I made a mental note to check on her later as Pierre's head of security came over to read me the riot act. I tried to apologize, but it wasn't until Pierre told him I went in to save my dog that Alexander calmed down.

He put his hands on his hips. Preacher trembled in my arms. "I understand your need to protect your pet. But if anything like this happens again, I will guard your suite door for the rest of your stay."

"Noted," I said. "And thank you, really, for saving us."

Alexandre bowed. "It is my duty and my great pleasure. Now, I must find the birds."

Despite Alexandre's dire warning, Pierre, Preacher, and I spent the rest of the hour before dinner scouring the castle for any signs of emu... including more freshly laid eggs. The last thing we needed was baby birds hatching in the portrait gallery.

Pierre forced me to stop by the royal infirmary, which I hadn't even realized existed. The busty, gray-haired nurse, Bertha, cooed over my husband the moment we walked through the door. When she wasn't checking me for injuries, she was telling me stories about Pierre as a little boy. I was almost sorry when she told me I was okay and we could leave. But Bertha promised I could come back at a less urgent time to visit. We had more important things to do.

Everything seemed okay. I didn't spot any emu tracks, bird poop, or eggs. Only a loose feather or two. I pocketed those, idly dreaming of leaving them on Caleb's pillow as a warning.

When I wasn't searching for signs of bird, I was ranting at my poor husband. How was any of this my fault? Why wasn't she blaming Caleb? Instead of forcibly divorcing me from the love of my life, maybe her Royal Majesty should remove the actual problem. Banish Caleb, strip him of the lands and title he never deserved.

But that would mean admitting her mistake. While Queen Claudette would have no qualms telling the people of Corchenne that her "errant son" had made a mistake by marrying an American commoner, she would never admit having been conned by the commoner's equally common-yet-more-smooth-talking brother.

One thing at a time. First, we needed to clean up Caleb's mess —something I was unfortunately very accustomed to doing. Then it was time to make myself presentable for dinner, which I managed fairly quickly. Luckily, Bridget's hairdresser taught me a few tricks to get my hair to look nice when I was short on time. I even remembered one of them. I wouldn't be making the lists of any "Best Hair" websites, but I looked perfectly acceptable.

Zoe had arranged the clothes Bridget loaned me by function, so it was easy enough to pick out a floor-length light green dress with a lace overlay for a state dinner. The long sleeves would keep the chill of the air conditioning off me. The vee neck was flattering, yet appropriate for dining with royalty. A diamond pendant from Bridget's collection twinkled at my neck. Since this dress touched the floor, I indulged myself in a pair of low-heeled sandals. My feet had been through a lot since arriving in Corchenne. These were nice enough shoes, if anyone caught a glimpse, without leaving me feeling like I walked on stilts. #ShortPeopleProblems.

Sure, the entire ensemble seemed a bit much for dinner, but I had to admit, I looked fantastic. Hopefully, I would one day grow used to being dressed to the nines every time I consumed a meal. More importantly, I hoped to one day eat without being terrified of a spill ruining clothes costing more than my parents' car.

Pierre was as wrung out from our afternoon as I, so we dressed in near silence. But when he took my arm to escort me to dinner, I once again drew strength from knowing he was at my side.

"Hey! Have you by any chance seen any giant flightless birds around?" I kept my tone light, but the nervousness shone through.

Pierre chuckled, although without much humor. "None of this is your fault. You know that, right?"

"That's not what your mother thinks," I pointed out. "She wants to dissolve our marriage and send me packing back to Boston."

He stopped in his tracks, bringing me to a halt. In the middle of the hallway, oblivious to everyone else around us, Pierre turned to me.

With one hand, Pierre cupped my face. He held my gaze for a very long time, letting me see his love for me replace the anger. Then he leaned in. His lips captured mine. Warm, firm, and conveying a promise I'd love to skip dinner to cash in.

It wasn't until someone nearby cleared their throat that we parted. Pierre's cheeks were flushed, and I was having trouble breathing.

He pulled back and spoke loudly, projecting his voice through the hall. "I know my mother has eyes and ears everywhere. Hear this. I love Lila. She is my wife. Nothing her brother does could change that. And if my mother won't accept that, if she tries to scare Lila into going back to Boston—I'm going with her. I'll never return to Corchenne. And I'll happily tell Mére the same as soon as she is prepared to listen."

My eyes widened with each word. We were married, sure, but that public declaration made me feel better than the kiss.

When he finished, I leaned closer and whispered. "Do you want to skip dinner and go to bed?"

He laughed, a rich sound that filled the room. "Later, *chérie*. Now, I want the Prince of Luxembourg to meet the brightest jewel in our kingdom. And I don't just mean how stunning you look in that dress. Lila Sinclair is the complete package, and I want everyone to know it."

His words made me feel much better. No matter how upset

the Queen got, she didn't get to control my relationship with her son. Our marriage was between me and Pierre. As long as I remembered that, we'd be fine.

"Thank you," I whispered, hoping he felt the emotion behind those words. "I think I'm ready for dinner now."

Together, we once again headed down the hall to the formal dining room reserved for royalty.

I'd never been one for big dinner parties. They always seemed like a loud affair where the most interesting conversations were taking place on the other end of the table, and I'd wind up sandwiched between someone I barely knew and Madison—meaning I spent the entire meal talking to my bestie, anyway. Years ago, we'd realized that it made sense to skip the headache of splitting a check fifteen ways and go out with two to four people so everyone could talk.

This state dinner reminded me why we did that. Oh, the table looked grand, all decked out for dozens of people to eat. Queen Claudette held court at the far end. As the guest of honor, the Prince of Luxembourg and his wife sat to her left, with Henri to her right. Pierre got seated beside Henri, with me to Pierre's right. Princess Serena sat across from me, as the next-highest ranking person in attendance. To my utter chagrin, Caleb sat beside her while I found myself next to Serena's Aunt Isabella.

The arrangement made little sense to me until I saw Caleb kiss Serena's hand in greeting and realized he must have switched the place cards. Queen Claudette opened the conversation in French, engaging everyone seated to my left. Serena and Caleb sat with their heads close together. That left me primarily with Serena's aunt as a dinner companion. Luc stood a few feet behind my chair, but I really preferred to communicate on my own when possible. Thankfully, Pierre had told me she spoke English.

Serena's laugh drew my attention to her side of the table. Caleb was sitting a hair closer than appropriate. Both of them beamed, and my brother eyed the princess of Spain as if she were a mouse and he were a hungry cat.

I should warn Isabella. She was Serena's aunt, after all. She wouldn't want to see her niece make a terrible mistake.

Adopting what I hoped was a friendly expression, I introduced myself.

She looked at me over the top of her glasses. "Do you think I'm senile? I know who you are, Dear Girl. I saw the seating chart. Next, you'll be telling me that the woman across from you is my niece, Princess Serena."

As her name was bellowed across the table, both Serena and Caleb jumped, then looked at us. Not knowing what else to say, I offered, "Corchenne is lovely this time of year, isn't it? I love the bright foliage in the vineyards."

"Yes, stunning," Caleb said. "It reminds me of our home in New England. Serena, you simply have to visit Boston one of those days."

I couldn't hear her reply over the din, and just like that, I was out of their conversation. I hadn't wanted to talk to them, but when I turned back to Isabella, she spoke toward the man to her right. I didn't know his name, couldn't hear what they were saying, and wasn't rude enough to interrupt. Not knowing what else to do, I tried to focus on my food.

The Chef had pulled out all the stops, opening with vol-au-vent and gromperekichelcher, which Pierre said were common to Luxembourg. The latter dish was a yummy fried potato pancake served with applesauce. I would've happily eaten them all night, but we had several courses left. It was important to pace myself if I didn't want to get sick.

Everything tasted delicious. Pierre and I never ate like this in Boston, even with all the fine restaurants downtown. Well, unless we went to Blaise's place. But that was expensive enough that we only dropped by on special occasions. He would usually come out from the kitchen to join us, making those restaurant meals feel more like dinner with family than this incredibly dull affair.

When I was a kid and Caleb had gotten me in trouble with our parents, I'd sit at dinner and stare at his head, trying to will it to explode. It had been years since I'd engaged in such juvenile behavior. And yet, I didn't have anything better to do.

After the servers cleared our appetizers, the guy on the other side of Isabella moved to talk to someone across the table. I seized on my opportunity before anyone filled his empty seat. "Excuse me, Señora, but I am concerned about my brother's interest in your niece. Do you have a moment?"

She heaved a heavy sigh. "Serena is a passionate girl. Always throwing herself into one affair after another."

That didn't help.

"It's not only that," I said. "I'm worried he's going to trick her into making an investment into one of his business schemes. They never work out."

Isabella lifted her napkin to her mouth to hide a snort. "As if my sister and her husband would let that girl touch any real sum of money."

What Isabella considered real money and what I thought were probably vastly different amounts. "She shouldn't give him anything she can't afford to lose--and that includes her heart."

"You don't seem to have much family loyalty, girl," Isabella said. "That speaks as poorly of you as of him."

With great effort, I sipped my wine to keep from biting her head off. "Ours is a strained relationship, tested by my brother's selfish actions repeatedly. I assure you, I am quite loyal to those who deserve it. Like our older sister, Hannah. Or Pierre."

"Oh? What about Pierre's brother?" When I didn't reply, she chuckled. "I've heard all about you, girl. Listen, if you want to do something useful, help me get to the washroom."

She had barely placed her napkin on the table when a server appeared to pull her chair back and hand Isabella a gorgeous cane. It was made of gleaming wood, with an ornately carved handle. Now that I looked closer, the symbols on the handle appeared to match her earrings. A nice touch. After she stood, she cleared her throat and gestured to me. I moved my chair back, but the server was faster.

As Isabella took my arm and we left the room, I glanced back at Caleb over my shoulder. He was clearly up to something—he wasn't even trying to hide it. Was he romantically interested in Serena, or was he trying to con her in plain view of everyone? Playing the Princess of Spain for a fool was a huge mistake. The last thing we needed was for my brother's action to turn a Corche ally against the entire country.

"Why so serious, girl?" Isabella asked as we headed down the hall.

"Just what I was saying," I said. "I'm worried that my brother is going to take advantage of your niece."

"If it would make you feel better, I'll have a word with my sister," she said. "You've got that fine man sitting beside you. You should be making new heirs to the León line, not worrying about a foreign princess."

You'd think by now I'd be used to all the comments about procreation, but never did I expect to get one from a member of the Spanish nobility, older than my mother, who I'd known for roughly seventeen minutes.

Before I could reply, we arrived at the bathroom. Isabella swept inside, closing the door firmly in my face. She didn't have to tell me to wait.

To be honest, waiting outside the bathroom was more interesting than being surrounded by conversations I couldn't hear or didn't understand. The food might be delicious, but I would be glad when this meal ended. I would be even happier when Princess Serena returned to Spain, safe from Caleb's clutches. Whatever he wanted with her, it couldn't be good.

By the time Isabella returned, I'd decided to let sleeping dogs lie. She didn't seem concerned about Caleb's influence on Serena, and she knew her niece better than a total stranger. We chatted about the menu, the wine, and Preacher on our way back to dinner. Turned out, Isabella was quite the dog person. Once the subject came up, she was happy to tell me all about her personal kennels, housed on her twenty-acre estate in the eastern part of

Spain. I promised to come visit the next time I was on the Continent.

We made it to the dining room as the soup course was being served. The mouth-watering fragrance of garlic, cheese, and onion greeted us at the double doors. It was all I could do not to dive face-first onto the table. Instead, doing my best to observe royal protocol, I waited for my companion. Yes, I might hypothetically outrank her at some point, but I didn't have a title yet, and she was my elder.

As Isabella took her seat, I gazed at the mound of cheese sitting atop the soup. Suddenly I understood the phrase "eating with your eyes." I devoured that bowl while a server pushed Isabella's chair in. At least I knew better than to seat myself. Once the server finished with Isabella, he pulled out my chair. As I went to sit, my gaze fell on two empty spots across from me. Serena and Caleb were gone.

In my surprise, I wobbled, missing the chair entirely and landing in a heap on the floor. Every head turned my way. My cheeks burned.

Isabella poked me with her cane. "Don't sit there gawking, girl. Act like you did it on purpose."

I didn't know what to say. Part of me wanted to crawl under the table and hide. But I couldn't. Not with my brother sneaking around trying to seduce a member of the Spanish royalty and steal her money.

Luckily, Pierre swooped in to save me. Standing up, he asked if I was okay while offering me a hand. He pulled me to my feet in one fluid motion. When I assured him I hadn't been injured, he announced to the room that everything was fine, then promptly dismissed them. A smooth move. I needed to ask how to do that. Everyone went back to their meal as if it was perfectly normal for someone to consume soup while lying on the floor.

"Thank you," I whispered when I sat. "Did you see where Caleb and Serena went?"

He shook his head. "Sorry, no. They weren't talking to us. Only to each other."

"When did they leave?"

"I can't be sure. Maybe a couple of minutes after you?"

"Did you hear what they were talking about?"

"No. It is my duty to give all my attention to the guest of honor. I'm so sorry." He kissed my hand, then turned back to the Prince of Luxembourg.

Great. They'd been gone together for at least five minutes. They hadn't been going to the restroom; I would've passed them. There were other bathrooms, sure, but there was no reason to go far.

Only one thing was certain: I needed to find them.

Chapter Fourteen

OFFICIAL GUIDE TO BEING A PRINCESS: A princess does not lurk in the shadows. She is a presence, a force of nature.

Oh, no. Here we went again. Every time I turned around, my no-good brother was doing something he shouldn't.

It would be weird to jump out of my seat less than thirty seconds after returning, but since I'd just fallen on my butt in front of everyone, no one would say anything. Most likely, they'd think I'd slunk off to die of embarrassment. Which was not entirely off the table.

But one thing at a time. After verifying that Isabella had her food and was already enjoying it, I squeezed Pierre's hand under the table and pushed my chair back. My stomach protested the idea of walking away from that amazing-smelling soup, but I ignored it. Whatever Caleb was up to now, I needed to stop him.

The problem was, I didn't have a clue where to find them. My intent had been to say a polite goodbye, then head away from the bathrooms, since we hadn't seen them when I was there with Isabella. There was no way to get down that hallway without passing us.

Alas, best-laid plans and all that nonsense. In reality, whoever designed the palace must have started their career as a maze builder. It took me roughly forty-five seconds to realize I had no clue where they were, and also that I'd gotten hopelessly turned around. They were gone, and I was still hungry.

Not wanting to pull Pierre away from a state dinner—especially when Queen Claudette would not be happy all the Sinclairs had left—I reached out to the next best person for help. As soon as Bridget heard I was in a "high-ceilinged room" with "lots of ugly old pictures," she told me to sit tight. As if there was anywhere to go.

A moment later, I heard footsteps heading briskly toward me. For a second, I expected that a security detail had come after me. But Pierre said I only needed them during the castle's public hours. We closed at dusk. Never had I been so relieved to spot a duchess.

"How did you get lost at a state dinner?" Bridget asked when she got close enough to pitch her voice low. "Or was the food so terrible you had to leave?"

"Nothing like that," I replied. "The food smelled divine. But I'm pretty sure Caleb is either trying to swindle or seduce the Princess of Spain."

All the blood drained from Bridget's face. "Please tell me I'm just not understanding your American humor."

Instead of answering, I pointed at the exits. "Help me find them? Where do all these doors go?"

"This one will take you to a hallway that connects to several offices. Including mine, Pierre's, and yours. If you turn left at the end, you'll find a door that opens behind the throne."

I couldn't think of any legitimate reason for Princess Serena and my brother to wander into private offices or the throne room.

"What's the other door?" I asked.

"The royal library."

I'd already found Caleb in the library earlier today. For many people, that wouldn't seem unusual, but my brother wasn't a big reader. He'd definitely been trying to find information. It was possible he'd roped Serena into helping him, especially if he couldn't translate the text.

What was he researching? Was he showing her pictures of the emus now? Wouldn't it make more sense to show her the real thing? He must know where the security team housed the ones that had been caught. But it was worth checking before dismissing the idea.

With effort, I said, "I'll go this way. Please text me immediately if you find anything."

"Are you sure?"

I nodded. "Just hurry, please."

Even the hallways here were ridiculously fancy. My footsteps clattered on the marble floors, making it impossible to move quietly. After about three steps, I stopped to remove the heels. Although I'd prefer not to be spotted slinking around the halls barefoot, holding my shoes in one hand like some Princess Walk of Shame, there was no way to sneak up on someone when your shoes announced your arrival from two hundred feet away. If Caleb had taken Serena somewhere private, I needed to get close enough to hear the conversation before they realized I was there.

The library was unfortunately empty. The head librarian's office was locked, which made sense considering the time. I was pretty sure there was an exit to a courtyard beyond the bookshelves. It was doubtless romantic this time of day, with the setting sun and vineyard views.

As I moved toward the French doors, something crashed behind me. I jumped and spun around. Nothing but a book on the floor. I must've shaken the floor or something to make it fall. With a sigh, I headed to pick it up and replace it before going outside.

Something rustled behind the bookshelf. I wasn't alone.

Were Serena and Caleb over there? Had I somehow walked right past them without noticing? Or maybe they doubled back. They could be making out in the stacks. My brother loved to do that in high school.

Taking a deep breath, I forced myself to exude confidence and determination. I was going to stop this, even if I had to tell Serena that Caleb was a married con artist. She should thank me.

Then the floor creaked again, and someone stepped out of the rows, directly into my path.

Check that. Not someone. Some*thing.*

It wasn't my brother. Well, not in the flesh, anyway. It was the product of my brother's ridiculous scheming. An emu pushed the books one at a time, onto the floor. Apparently, he wasn't a fan of ancient Russian literature. How it got here, I couldn't imagine. We had seen no sign of this bird when searching the palace earlier. It must've somehow escaped from its pen while we were at dinner. Or Caleb inexplicably brought in more. I put nothing past him at this point.

Ugh. As badly as I needed to find and stop Caleb, I couldn't just leave an emu wreaking havoc in the library. What if it got into the dining room? Queen Claudette would have a heart attack while she was banishing me from the premises. Or worse, what if other guests found it? The last thing we needed was for the internet to see the Corche palace overrun with emus.

How to get it out of here? I didn't have food to entice it. The smart thing would be to leave, lock the doors, and find the palace guards. But it was between me and the exit. Earlier, I'd been able to scare the emus by running at them... but chasing might send him out to the main hall where he could trample someone else. No, somehow, I needed to get it to follow me to the garden.

"Good emu," I said, hoping to sound calm. It ruffled its feathers but kept pushing books onto the floor. If this racket kept up, someone else would stumble across him soon.

A glance told me we weren't far from the courtyard exit. If the emu ran outside, I could lock the doors and keep the thing contained on the patio until the handlers arrived.

Without food to entice it, how to get the emu outside? All I could think was to open the doors, startle it, and hope for the best. As plans went, it wasn't terrific. But it was mine. My eyes never leaving the emu, I tiptoed to the door, grateful that I'd already removed my shoes. He ignored me. When I pushed the door open, a breeze came in. The emu lifted his head and turned toward me. Excellent.

Now what? I didn't want it to run toward me. Instead, I circled back around, so slowly I felt like I was moving backward. The emu alternately watched me and checked the door. Inch by inch, one step at a time, I got it between me and the outside. Now, I just needed to scare it away from me. Before, I had Preacher's help. Now I was on my own. What to do?

Well, I was a millennial, a bleeding heart liberal, an influencer, a soon-to-be princess. What could be scarier than that? Pulling out my phone, I started playing the alarm ring tone at full volume. Then I raced toward the bird, screaming and waving my arms over my head. The emu ruffled its feathers. Excellent!

It ran. Although it now held a book in its beak, it was moving away from me. Progress! It looked from me to the courtyard and back, then a second time. I feigned a lurch toward him. The emu ran away from me.

Dropping my shoes and my phone, I hiked up my dress and raced after it. As soon as it crossed the threshold, I slammed the door shut and locked it. Leaning against the wall, my body sagged with relief.

Outside, I heard a loud hiss. Hooves thundered on the concrete, then another hiss, farther away.

Followed by a blood-curdling, very human scream.

Princess Serena.

For a second, terror froze me in place. I had accidentally sent an angry bird to attack the princess of Spain. This was an absolute disaster.

Please, please, let her be okay.

A second shriek was enough to get me moving. Throwing the doors open, I burst out onto the patio. At first, I didn't see anyone. The garden stretched further than expected. Then voices rose beyond a trellis obscured by plants.

"Your highness?" I hoped that was the right way to address a princess I barely knew. Not waiting for a reply, I started toward the voices. "Are you okay?"

The reply sounded wary, but not terrified. She spoke in Spanish. Luckily, "who's there?" was one of the few phrases I remembered from my high school foreign language courses.

Note to self: even in an emergency, do not go anywhere without an interpreter. And guards. And maybe Pierre.

Barely had I finished the thought before spotting the poor woman I'd put in danger. She stood in a corner created by two hedges. Was she laughing? Although enormous for a bird, the emu stood a few inches shorter than Serena. It appeared to be sniffing her neck. Rather than being terrified, she looked delighted.

What was going on?

I racked my brain for how to say, "Do you need help?" in Spanish. Finally, "¿Auyudas?" came out. I was fairly certain that was wrong. Something about formal versus familiar verb tenses. Before she could correct me, however, another voice answered.

Until he spoke, I hadn't seen my brother standing beside her. The emu had stolen all of my attention.

"We're fine. I was just introducing the Princess to my friend here." He repeated his words to Serena, translating so seamlessly I wanted to throw up my hands. Just like that, all my fear for Serena's safety was replaced by aggravation.

Somehow, I'd wandered into a Bizarro World where my brother was a bird whisperer. Or a princess whisperer. Maybe both.

At least I wasn't alone. As I stood there trying to process the situation before me, a dozen guards appeared in the doorway leading to the throne room. Beyond them I spotted Bridget, Luc, and, thankfully, Pierre.

Our eyes met, and my shoulders relaxed. People more qualified than me would handle this. A guard addressed Princess Serena in Spanish. I moved toward the doors. They didn't need me for this. When I reached Pierre's side, he put one arm around my shoulders and pulled me close.

"Thank goodness you're here," I said. "How did you know?"

"Bridget came to get me." He shot his aunt a stern glance. "*Mére* is not happy so many of her guests have wandered off. I had to tell her you got lost. Bridget, I'm disappointed in you. The last thing I expected was for you to turn into a bad influence."

My spine stiffened. "I'm not a child, nor an unmarried virgin in Regency England. I don't need a chaperone."

"I apologize, I misspoke. But she was supposed to watch out for you when I couldn't. She should never have left you alone to fend off enormous birds."

Bridget's face turned bright red. "I am so, so sorry. I thought this problem had been contained. My goal was to help Lila find her brother as quickly as possible."

Beyond the doorway, three guards ushered the emu out a large gate, presumably back to whatever cage they were being stored in. Caleb and Serena were still talking to another guard.

"It's not your fault," I assured her. "You're not the one who brought the birds upon us. Excuse me, I need to go have a talk with my brother."

Pierre put a hand on my arm to stop me. "You realize he's speaking with the Princess of Spain?"

Internally, I sighed. It wouldn't be good manners to berate my brother in front of royalty. Maybe that was his plan. He would surround himself with extremely rich and powerful people so I couldn't tell him off. To Pierre, I said, "Would you care to introduce us?"

"Certainly, *ma chérie*." He took my hand and led me to the

corner of the garden, my interpreter trailing a few steps behind. As Pierre and Serena spoke, he told me what they were saying.

Pierre said, "Serena! Are you okay? My deepest apologies."

"I'm fine, just surprised," she replied. "It's not every day you find human-sized birds outside a palace library. Especially not one intent on bringing me a first-edition translation of *Anna Karenina*."

"I hear that's an excellent book," I said weakly.

"It was terrific when I read it as a child. Now, if you don't mind, it has been a long day. I am exhausted." Serena smiled tightly, avoiding my eyes. "Caleb, would you be so kind as to escort me back to my chambers?"

"No!" The word flew out of my mouth before I could stop it. Unfortunately, some things required no translation. "I mean, I'd be happy to go with you so we can get to know each other."

"That will not be necessary. Your brother was telling me all about these fascinating creatures, and I cannot wait to hear more."

Summoning my inner poise, I straightened up and addressed Serena as I thought one princess would speak to another. "I would never dream of depriving you of my brother's company. May we speak tomorrow?"

"Of course," she said. "Caleb?"

Caleb bowed beside Serena and offered her his arm. "I would be honored, Your Highness."

As they walked past, I muttered, "If you seduce her, I'm telling Mom."

My brother just chuckled. Helpless, I watched the two of them wander away. Once they were out of sight, I allowed Pierre to lead me back to the royal dining room. On top of everything else, the meal had ended. I wasn't even going to get to try that amazing soup.

~

After another long day watching my brother ruin my Corche life, in the morning, I wanted to hide in bed until he'd left the country. Okay, well, I wanted to get up, warn Serena away from him, then hide in bed until he left the country.

Darn it.

Every second I spent in my room was a second he was out there, putting his nefarious plans into action. Drawing Serena further into his web and probably ruining more Corche crops.

This internal debate raged until banging on the outer door of our suite forced me out of bed. Too bad. The only people I wanted to see or talk to were Serena and Pierre. Neither was likely to be in the hall. My husband had a breakfast meeting with the Prince of Luxembourg, and I couldn't think of any reason Serena would seek me out.

What had my brother done now? Bombed France? Swapped a load of exported wine for grape juice? Convinced Henri to marry him to show me up? The possibilities were endless, each worse than the last.

My traitorous stomach growled.

Darn it. I could ignore the noise, but now that I was awake and hungry, I needed to get up and face the day.

Might as well find out who it was and what they wanted. I threw back the covers, pulled a robe on over my nightgown, and went to greet my visitor. Preacher trailed behind me, like I might open the door to greet my visitor, then keep going until I got outside to take him for a walk. I loved this little guy's optimism.

When the door swung open, I was greeted with the sight of a dark wrist, raised to knock yet again. I threw my hands up to protect my face. "Wait! I'm here."

Candace burst past me and into the room without preamble. "Lila, we've got a problem."

"Don't I know it," I said. "Please tell me you didn't find more emus inside the palace."

"Not since last night. But we've got to work on damage control. I've got something to tell you, and it's bad."

A groan escaped me. "What now? Did Queen Claudette decide to reprint all the money with Caleb's face? Do we live in the country of Caleb now?"

"I want to reassure you, but the truth is worse," Candace said. "This isn't about him."

"Nothing would be worse than living in Caleblandia and having to spend the Caleb coin to buy things." I headed for my closet. Might as well find something to wear now that I was up. We could take Preacher out while we talked.

She followed me. "Lila. I need you to focus. I know that you're upset about your brother, but we have a bigger problem."

Her tone chilled me to the bone, enough that I stopped caring about how I was dressed. Turning around, I met her gaze. Although I was half-whining and half-joking, her face was dead serious. "What's wrong?"

"There's something you need to see." She tapped her phone and to show me the screen. A video was loaded, waiting for her to start it. "Ready?"

Now I was worried. "I think so. Should I be nervous?"

Instead of answering, Candace pressed play. The empty throne room filled the screen.

"What is this?" I asked.

"Just watch."

She hadn't even finished admonishing me when a figure entered the room, wearing a purple and white floral sundress with blond hair artfully piled on her head. Bridget had done such a good job turning me into a princess, it took me a minute to recognize myself.

I started to ask another question, but then the screen jumped, and I vanished. The throne came into view. The decidedly not-empty throne, occupied by that bloody emu.

"What is this?" I asked.

"Palace security footage," she said.

All of a sudden, the emu jumped up, revealing the egg beneath her.

"You spliced this together? Why?" My stomach somersaulted.

"Oh, no. No, I didn't make this. The cameras in the throne room are on motion detectors. There are other cameras, but this feed made itself when you entered. Someone cut the emu's entrance, but otherwise it's exactly what the cameras captured yesterday."

As she spoke, Preacher started barking frantically on the screen. Preacher in the closet with us hopped on his back feet, trying to see the video. To calm him, I picked him up. We might as well all watch together. The cameras shifted again, and there I was, running frantically and screaming at the giant beast. The emu darted toward me, and I gasped. Even knowing I escaped didn't make things better. Squeezing my eyes shut, I shook my head.

"Oh, man. That's so embarrassing. Has anyone else seen it?"

"That's why I'm here, Lila. Everyone has seen it."

The words barely penetrated the fog in my brain. "I'm sorry. What? Everyone?"

"Yes, everyone." She spoke slowly, as if worried she was using the wrong English words. "I need to do damage control. A lot of people saw this video."

"But it's just security footage," I said weakly. "No one outside these walls should ever see it."

"I'm afraid not, Lila." Candace's face was grim. "I got this off YouTube. It's gone viral."

Chapter Fifteen

OFFICIAL GUIDE TO BEING A PRINCESS: A princess shall never be caught with her pants down, so to speak.

At Candace's statement, the world swam before me. My entire life flashed before my eyes. Not again. The last time Pierre got caught in a media storm, we almost broke up. I couldn't bring more negative attention to the royal family, especially not now that I was one of them.

"What do you mean, viral? Just around the castle, you mean?"

She shook her head. "This has more than twenty million views. The original post has been shared thousands of times."

"But how? Why? Who would do that?" So many questions.

"I wish I knew who," she said. "The why is easy. Someone wanted to embarrass you. Do you have any enemies in Corchenne?"

A hollow laugh escaped me. "You mean, other than the Queen and the Crown Prince? Oh, and the Princess of Spain. Just a few unimportant people. And my useless, arrogant brother.

Unfortunately, he is also in Corchenne, doing his best to make me miserable. The rest of the castle seems to adore me, though."

She flushed and looked away. "Sorry. This can't be easy for you. For what it's worth, Her Royal Majesty is furious. Even if she dislikes you, I can't imagine she would bring this negative attention to the royal family. She would find another way to get rid of you."

Like by making my brother a baron and giving him my property? It wasn't worth asking. At the moment, I had other problems.

"Who else? How does anyone get security footage?" While my immediate gut reaction was that Caleb did this, it made no sense. He was with me before I went into the throne room. He wasn't a hacker like Hannah, and his title wouldn't give him access to top secret castle cameras. Very few people should have that.

"That's the thing," she said. "No one can. It's top secret. You need high, high security clearance to get it. My father has it. The head of security. His Royal Highnesses."

"Both of them?" While I couldn't imagine Pierre doing anything like this to me, I wouldn't put much past his brother. Unlike Caleb, Henri could absolutely get what he needed. No one would dare refuse him if they wanted to keep working here.

The enemy of my enemy is my friend, my foot. Maybe Henri hadn't been able to resist an opportunity to make me look like a fool.

Of course he hadn't. If Pierre cast me aside, Caleb would have no reason to remain here. Two birds, one stone.

"I know what you're thinking." Candace put one hand on my arm. "But after dinner, Prince Henri went with his mother to watch a show she'd brought in for the visiting royals. He was surrounded by people all night. Someone would have seen him. And to be honest, I think he loves his country more than he dislikes you."

"Does he have his phone with him? It would've been easy to

ask for the footage before dinner and post it while no one was looking."

Candace pressed her lips together. "I'll talk to him, but for both our sakes, you better hope someone else is responsible."

"Why?"

"Because, even if he intentionally leaked sensitive security footage, calling him out would be akin to accusing the Crown Prince of treason."

I snorted. "I've accused him of worse. Let me talk to Henri."

Of my three suspects, he was the one I wanted to avoid least. Might as well start there.

Unfortunately, I soon discovered that getting a private meeting with the Crown Prince of Corchenne was easier said than done, even for his sister-in-law. Henri was a busy man, and he didn't like me. His chief of staff offered to pass him a message for me, but that wouldn't help. I couldn't pass him a note that said, "Did you sabotage me by posting a humiliating video of me online? YES NO (Circle One)."

Pierre could, though. Not the note, the conversation.

As much as I didn't want to cause problems between the brothers again, I couldn't think of a better option. No one else hated me and could demand access to the security footage.

Adrienne? As Pierre's ex-fiancé, she could be expected to top the list of people who hated his new wife. But after learning that she'd been secretly sleeping with Henri behind Pierre's back, it was difficult to see her getting involved. She and Henri broke up years ago, so it's not likely she'd feel the need to get revenge. Also, I hadn't seen her anywhere near the castle. Last I heard, she was living in Boston. She might have friends on the security staff, but why would she care? How would she know about the emus?

Queen Claudette? As Candace pointed out, making me look bad in a way that reflected poorly on the monarchy didn't seem like her style. Now that a flock of emus breached palace security, everyone and their brother would try to break into the crown room. They'd be posing for selfies if they got a chance. She would never risk that level of chaos at the *Chateau de Serpentine*. Also, accusing her without proof would be worse than calling Henri out. I would have to eliminate all other possibilities before even considering either of them. Caleb would never admit if he had any involvement, so it wasn't even worth approaching him without proof. First, I needed to talk to the security guards.

The head of security was a dead end. He wouldn't even talk to me. I managed to get a few minutes with Alexandre. All he could tell me was that he didn't leak it.

No big surprise there. Given his loyalty to Pierre, it wouldn't have made sense for him to be responsible. Alexandre hadn't even crossed my mind as a potential suspect.

After what felt like hours of darting around the castle trying to talk to people (Candace had temporarily taken possession of my phone to make sure I didn't post an angry rant on social media), I returned to our suite to find Pierre waiting for me in the sitting area.

When the door opened, he stood. "How are you, *ma chérie?*"

One look at his face told me he'd seen the video. Tears filled my eyes. "I feel so stupid! I should've known there are cameras in the throne room? Of course there are!"

He opened his arms, and I fell into them. For a long moment, I sobbed against Pierre's shoulder while he stroked my hair. "This isn't your fault. There are cameras everywhere in the palace. All employees sign a confidentiality agreement. No one should have seen that footage except the guard working when it recorded."

"Then how did it get out there?"

He kissed my tears away. "I wish I knew. But trust me. I'll find out."

It was on the tip of my tongue to ask if he thought Henri did this. Or if he could think of anyone else who had the access and the resentment toward me. But the thought of starting an argument filled me with exhaustion. I couldn't do it.

Then Pierre's words penetrated my brain fog. "Hold on. You said no one would see it—except the person in the room when the footage was playing live. You mean someone is watching the security cameras at all times?"

"Yes, of course. I'll ask Alexandre who was on duty when the emus escaped, but you should know that all of our staff is thoroughly vetted. Anyone who betrayed the family would be fired, and never get a new job on the island. Most people wouldn't risk it."

"I know, and that makes sense." Still, something bothered me. "But what if someone paid them a lot of money to do it?"

"Who would know to buy the tape? The only people in the room were you, me, and Bernadette."

"We weren't the only ones who knew about the emu invasion," I said. Everything fell into place. "When you found me outside the throne room, Caleb had just gone to alert security. If he reported the incident when I entered the throne room, he saw everything."

"He would have no qualms in stealing, buying, or blackmailing a member of our staff to get the footage," Pierre said. "Forgive me, *chérie*, but I'm starting to seriously dislike your brother."

"Join the club."

"There is one problem. Stealing the footage would be difficult. The palace is extremely secure. No one could stroll into the security office unattended. Your brother would have to be a skilled hacker. There would be traces. When I spoke with him this morning, Alexandre saw no signs that our system had been breached."

I pondered that for a moment. "Let me talk to Hannah. She'd know if it's even possible."

"Would Caleb?"

"I don't think so. He was never great with computers. He'd be more likely to pay off a member of your staff. But he doesn't have any money. Does that new title include an income?"

"I'm sure it does, but from working the land. There's no immediate payment. *Mére* doesn't pay the nobility an allowance.

It would take several weeks at a minimum before he saw money from that property."

Nobility.

Allowance.

Money.

I sat up like a bolt of lightning hit me.

"What is it?" Pierre asked.

"Last night, when I was talking to Isabella, she made a comment about Serena's access to her parents' fortune. *Serena* gets an allowance. Serena is friends with Caleb. They've been plotting every time I've seen them. And Serena has hated me ever since she saw me dancing with her ex-boyfriend at the ball."

He heaved a heavy sigh. "That's a serious allegation, *chérie*. They barely know each other."

"They don't need to." I quoted Henri's words to me. "'The enemy of my enemy is my friend.' But I can't possibly prove it."

"Maybe not yet, but we can ask." He pulled out his phone and tapped on the screen a few times. A moment later, he started speaking in rapid French. My vocabulary had been growing daily, but it wasn't enough. I waited patiently until he said "merci" and disconnected.

"Any news?" I asked.

"The man working is a long-time employee, very loyal. He and his wife have four kids. I played with the youngest as a child."

"Any sudden medical bills?"

"We have government-funded health care," Pierre reminded me. "Alexandre is going to do some research. I can't believe it would be him. We'll keep looking."

I put my arms around his neck. "Thank you so much. I'm sorry to be such a burden on your family."

He gazed into my eyes. When he spoke, his tone was fierce. "Listen. You are not a burden. You're having a string of bad luck. And I will find the culprit."

Leaning down, he kissed me. I tilted my head upward to meet his lips with mine. Although only a few days, it felt like weeks since we arrived at the palace. We barely got any time alone. After a moment, he pulled back. "Are you sure you don't want to talk more?"

Wordlessly, I kissed him again. I didn't need conversation. I needed comfort. Pierre would figure out who betrayed us, and I trusted him. I only hoped my enemy wasn't a member of the royal family. Lila Sinclair wasn't about to be responsible for the destruction of the monarchy.

∼

After lunch, as soon as Pierre left for his first in another long afternoon of official activities, I sat up in bed and grabbed my tablet. He'd begged me to come with him, insisted that today's event would be a lot of fun. I just wasn't up for it.

The only person I wanted to talk right now wasn't in Corchenne. It was still early in Boston, but my sister slept little. She should be awake.

As soon as Hannah's blue eyes and green-dyed hair entered the screen, the screen blurred with my tears. Corchenne was lovely, and this honeymoon let me get to know my new family, but I missed my big sister. Talking on the tablet every few days wasn't the same as seeing her in person.

Her smile changed instantly into a look of concern. "Lila! What's wrong? Is Pierre mistreating you? Do I need to murder him?"

My lips twitched at that. "No, Pierre's great. And we don't joke about killing people here. The palace has eyes and ears everywhere." Oh, how well I knew that.

"Oh, hey, speaking of committing crimes—"

"Now there's a segue if I ever heard one."

She snorted. "I can't help what reminds me of things related to you. Listen, I was going to call later, anyway. I found this article. I'm going to share my screen for a sec. Isn't this your store?"

Hannah's face vanished, replaced by a news article in the

Globe dated a few days ago. SIDMART MANAGER CRACKS SHOP-LIFTING RING. My eyes widened, but as I scanned the text, everything felt heavier.

"Oh, no. Hannah, I know that family." The image of a young boy sneaking handfuls of *Fruit Loops* swam before me. They shopped at the store often, buying whatever was on sale. According to the article, both parents were unemployed. They'd been arrested, and their kids were in the custody of Child Services. "This is terrible. Jail won't help them."

"I know." She held up her hands and wiggled her fingers. "Want me to make it all go away? Someone could 'accidentally' erase the files."

I smiled weakly. "I wish. But let's try to help them the legal way."

Shortly before my wedding, my sister had set up a non-profit organization for me to help the poor. In all the events that happened since, I hadn't quite settled on a charity. Posting bail for a family in need seemed like a decent start.

"What are you going to do?" Hannah asked.

"Not sure yet. Call their lawyer? At least I can put up the money to get them released. Although I might have to borrow from Pierre."

"It's not borrowing when it's your husband."

"Isn't that exactly what Caleb thought about taking your money? Family helps family?" Shortly before moving to Brazil with his wife, my brother "borrowed" several thousand dollars from my sister. She'd yet to see a penny of it back, despite his claims of success in multiple business ventures.

Hannah grimaced at the reminder. "Touché. How is the Baron of Moose enjoying his new title?"

"That's actually why I called."

My sister was an accomplished hacker. Quickly, I filled her in on the previous day's events—and what happened this morning.

"You're wondering if I broke into the castle's security office and stole footage of you doing something ridiculous so I could make it go viral and force you to come back home? Because I'm flattered but—"

"Hold on. You saw it?" My words were flat and dull. It would have been beyond belief if she hadn't, and hope springs eternal.

"Of course I have. Sorry to tell you this, but I think everyone's seen it. I didn't want to bring it up and make you feel worse. What happened?"

"I don't know. That's what I wanted to talk to you about. Do you think someone could have hacked the security system here?"

"How would I know that?"

"Because you're you, and I'm me, and you were desperate with curiosity the moment you found out who Pierre was."

Her cheeks flamed. "Maybe a little. But no. I never tried, and if you tell anyone I did I will absolutely, categorically deny it. But between you and me—I couldn't get in. It's way beyond my capabilities, and I'm pretty good."

"Do you know anyone at that level?"

Hannah thought for a minute. "Maybe? But the ones I know, the people who could do something like that, are in it for bragging rights. They have no reason to want to embarrass you. Most regular people have mad respect for the ordinary girl who married a prince. And also, my hacker friends aren't out to weaken a country. Corchenne's currency is way down in the foreign markets today."

That caught my attention. From the moment Candace showed me the video, I'd assumed someone was out to get me personally. It never occurred to me that there might be a bigger purpose. "Hold on. Do you think this was political?"

"I'm just saying it could be. But that's assuming an outside job. It really could be as easy as Henri walking into the security office, asking for the footage, and posting it." She tapped her keyboard a few times. My sister rarely stopped typing, even when we were in the middle of a conversation. "The account it came from was brand new, no prior posts. I could pull an IP address, but if they know what they're doing, it's fake. It would never be the one attached to the palace."

"Yeah, I know. And as much as I don't like Henri, I'm hoping it's someone else. If he did it, that causes way too many problems. Could you ask around for me?"

"I'll look into it." Her fingers flew across the keyboard a second time. "Anything else?"

"Can you get into Caleb's financials?"

"Is the Pope Catholic?" Hannah replied instantly. "But why?"

"He was near the security office when the emus broke into the throne room. The camera footage is visible to anyone in there. I don't see how he would have gotten it, though. He doesn't know anyone here well enough to blackmail them. Which leaves me wondering if he bought the video somehow. I'm just not sure where he'd get the money."

"Consider it done," she said.

"Great! Also, if you're not too busy, could you check out—" I lowered my voice to just above a whisper, "—Serena, Princess of Spain?"

"Lila!"

"You know I wouldn't ask if it wasn't important. But Caleb's hanging around her. He definitely wants something, and she doesn't seem inclined to tell him to go away."

"Fine." She let out a long-suffering, very fake sigh. "The things I do for you."

"Come on, you know you're excited."

"Oh, yeah." She laughed. "Now we're talking. Let me see what I can find—phone calls, texts, emails. This is my jam."

"Only my sister would get excited at the thought of felony hacking."

A voice from the doorway made me jump. "Did the Princess of Corchenne just ask someone to commit a crime?"

Chapter Sixteen

At the sound of the voice coming from behind me, I groaned. Another day, another scandal. All I wanted was to know who set me up. Even with Pierre looking into it, it helped to have Hannah as a backup. Of course, someone would find out what I was up to.

With great trepidation, I lifted my head to see who had overheard my conversation.

A massive sigh of relief escaped me. "Bridget! You nearly gave me a heart attack."

Her eyes danced mischievously. "That's what you get for not locking your doors. You're royalty now. You don't just want anyone walking in. Also, you shouldn't be hiring petty thieves yourself. You've got people for that."

Bridget's expression told me she was joking. But I absolutely couldn't tell her everything I'd asked Hannah to look into, so I coated the truth a bit. "Nothing illegal. My sister is going to check some public records."

By logging into highly classified databases. What Bridget didn't know wouldn't get me arrested.

"I hope you find what you're looking for," she said. "When I saw that video, I felt terrible for you. Which is why I'm here. I'm sure your plan for today was to hide in bed, cower under the covers, and never show your face again."

"Actually, yes. I'm glad you under—"

"Nonsense! Get up, get dressed. You're coming with me."

Since I was still holding my tablet, I pulled up the day's calendar before replying. "Did we have something scheduled? I'm not seeing anything."

Bridget snatched the device out of my hand. "Candace called me. This is called 'damage control.' It overrides everything else. The only thing you're going to do today is put on a brave face, show yourself to the people of Corchenne and let them see just how fabulous and sane and devoted to our country you are. Also that you love emus and are not a bird terrorist."

Wonderful. No problem there.

Before I could ask more questions, Bridget pulled me out of bed. Then she pointed me at the shower and shoved me lightly. Since my rainfall showerhead would do wonders to lift my mood, I didn't argue. When I came out, she refused to tell me where we were going.

"How do I know what to wear, then?" I asked, reasonably.

"Wear something comfortable that you don't mind getting dirty."

What on earth was she up to? If I found myself shoveling fertilizer onto the vineyards to encourage growth... Well, it wouldn't be the most disgusting job I'd ever had. And it might endear me to the people. With a resigned sigh, I pulled out one of Bridget's knee-length casual summer dresses in a deep purple pattern. It shouldn't show dirt, and it was washable. Did I look like a Princess? I couldn't tell, but I didn't look like an embarrassment.

For twenty minutes, Bridget ignored all my questions while she braided my hair out of my face (something I'd been meaning to learn for about twenty years), took me to a limousine, and asked Bernadette to drive somewhere so quietly it was impossible to make it out.

Since Bridget wouldn't tell me what was going on, I used the car ride to call her assistant. Zoe listened to me explain that the Wilson family in Boston needed help. She promised to speak to their lawyer and send money over to bail out all of them as soon as possible.

I hesitated. "One more thing. Can you see if there's a way to keep my name out of it?"

"What's that point of doing charity work if no one knows about it?"

I rolled my eyes. Right there, that was what was wrong with the world. But instead of giving her a lecture, I simply said, "I want to help them. If they know it was me, they'll try to pay me back. I don't need or want that. Listen, while you're at it, see if you can get a thousand-dollar gift card to their local supermarket. No one should have to steal to have enough to eat. Then look into how we can get the parents decent jobs. I'm not sure how to do that, but I want to try."

"Madame, forgive me for overstepping, but this is not how charities are usually run."

"Maybe it should be. But it doesn't matter. Use my personal accounts." Before she could argue anymore, I hung up.

"What was that all about?" Bridget asked.

I gave her a sly smile. "You tell me what you're up to, I'll tell you what that was about."

She shook her head. "Nice try."

Most likely, since Zoe was Bridget's Chief of Staff, she'd know everything within the hour, anyway. We spent the rest of the drive lost in our own thoughts.

What was I doing over here? While I'd wanted to use my power and influence as a spouse of the Corchenne royal family to do good, so far, all I'd done was smile and wave and chase rogue emus. Not exactly achieving world peace. There had to be something more, something longer-lasting and more beneficial than throwing money at one family's very specific problem.

Finally, we arrived at the bottom of the hill, outside the entrance to a winery I was pretty sure the León family owned. A giant banner overhead announced the day's activities.

My jaw dropped. "You brought me to a grape-stomping competition? You want me to jump on grapes, barefoot?"

A mischievous grin split her face. "It's more a festival than a competition. Corche citizens come together, many from miles away, to celebrate the ancient wine-making technique. It's common for members of the royal family to take part, and at the end, everyone drinks to a profitable year and fertile crops. It's a great time. Pierre originally intended to bring you himself. But after the video went viral, he worried you wouldn't want to face everyone."

"He knows me well," I said dryly. "So why am I here?"

"Because Pierre knows what you want, but Zoe and I know what you need. And what you need right now, Lila, is to participate in one of our nation's greatest traditions."

"You want me to put my feet in grapes and then drink the wine? How is that sanitary?"

"Participants wash their feet before stepping in, of course. The acid in the grapes kills any toxicity found on human feet. It's perfectly sanitary."

"Oh, no. I'm not drinking feet juice."

At that, Bridget chortled with laughter. "You should see your face."

"You mean, you made that up?"

"No. That's actually all true, but most wine requires removing the skin from the grapes—the stomped grapes are in the skins. We use a wine press to do that. Skinless grapes make up the vast majority of our crop, and that's what we'll be tasting throughout the festivities. It *is* perfectly healthy to drink wine from stomped grapes, but my dear sister decided a few years ago that it was unseemly for the Queen to drink, as you so charmingly put it, 'feet wine.'" The car drew to a halt as I gazed around at the stunning leaves on the grapevines.

"Smart lady," I muttered.

"Yes. The two of you have a lot in common."

Before I could think of a response, Bernadette opened the back door to help Bridget exit. I was half a step behind her.

That woman was fast. She took off for a large stage set up in a clearing. By the time I caught up to her, she stood directly in front of three tubs of grapes, set on an elevated platform. Festive music filled the air. On the stage, three men danced vigorously with their backs to me. Under the platform, three clear plastic tubs slowly filled with grape juice.

Then the first man turned around, revealing his face. And the second. And the third. With a start, I realized I knew all three of them.

Standing in front of the crowd, dancing as if he didn't have a care in the world, stood my husband with my two least favorite people—his brother and mine.

The music paused between songs, and I realized they were calling out to each other. Laughing, joking, tossing the good-natured barb. In all the time I'd known Pierre, never had I viewed anything that resembled a loving brotherly interaction between him and Henri. Until now. Although my heart ached to see what they had lost when Pierre moved away, I reminded myself that the tension in their relationship wasn't because of me. Adrienne had been the catalyst, and Henri himself had widened the rift by trying to break us up.

Right now they looked so happy. I vowed to strengthen their relationship if I could.

At the same time, I could barely look at Caleb. I knew it was hypocritical to want Pierre and Henri to give each other another chance while refusing to do the same for Caleb. But one thing at a time. Despite the fun he was having up there, charming the entire crowd—including Queen Claudette, who would see the coverage—I couldn't forgive him for coming here and causing such upheaval to my life.

Which brought my thoughts full circle to the festival. I needed the people of Corchenne to accept me. Henri would never give me a chance if I remained a national embarrassment. If Bridget wanted me to dance in grape juice, I would, and I would play the crowd while I did it. Smile, wave, all that jazz.

When the music stopped, Pierre, Henri, and Caleb clasped hands and bowed as one. I clapped furiously. Beside me, Bridget put two fingers in her mouth and let out an ear-piercing whistle.

I laughed. "I wouldn't have thought you could be so unladylike."

"There are benefits to being the black sheep of the royal family, you know," she said. "For me. That role is taken."

"I wouldn't dream of trying to displace you," I assured her. "I'm here to win the crowd's respect."

"Wonderful!" She gave me a light push. "Now go up and see your man."

Although I had my doubts about the wisdom of this plan, most of the regular citizens hadn't seen Pierre and I make a casual public appearance yet. As I slowly climbed the steps, Pierre looked up from where he was brushing grapes off his feet and met my eyes. The smile lighting up his face showed that joining him was the right move.

In three steps, Pierre closed the gap between us. Before I could react, he picked me up and twirled me around. Back on the ground, he dipped me over backward and gave me an exaggerated kiss. I felt it down to my toes.

The crowd exploded, filling the air with cheers, whistles, and cat-calling.

"Wow," I said once standing upright. "What was that for?"

His eyes danced. "The crowd picks the winner based on applause. You just sealed it for us."

"Better make it a good show then." Popping onto my toes, I kissed him a second time. Then we held hands and waved at the crowd.

The event's emcee came to stand beside us. I hadn't noticed her before, but she wore a fabulous dress that appeared to be made of vines and grape leaves (although it couldn't have been). Atop her head perched a hat made of several clusters of grapes. She towered over me and Pierre, partly because of her six-inch platform heels. How did she even climb to the stage in those things?

"Well, well, well," she said, looking right at me. "What do we have here?"

Pierre took the mike and smiled at her, his amazing grin that made hearts flutter worldwide. "Wayne, this is my wife, Princess Lila."

The crowd roared again. Behind Pierre's back, Caleb grimaced and muttered something I thankfully couldn't hear.

To me, Pierre said, "Lila, this is Corchenne's most popular entertainer, Sparkling Wayne."

I grinned up at her. "The perfect name for a grape festival."

"Well, I wanted to call myself Sham Payne, but I wasn't born in the appropriate region of France. I'm a Corche girl, through and through." With an exaggerated laugh, she moved over to Henri and Caleb, introducing everyone to the crowd again, as if they could forget.

Then it was time for the vote. Wayne started with Caleb, who got a polite smattering of applause for "the Royal Brother-in-Law." It took every ounce of willpower not to roll my eyes. Then she announced Henri, and the crowd went wild. Especially, it didn't escape my notice, the women about my age. No surprise there. He was a good-looking guy. A handful of the men glowered, which amused me. It couldn't be easy to compete with the Crown Prince, even jokingly.

Then Wayne got back to us. She held up a clear container full of grape juice. To my eye, it looked exactly the same as the ones Caleb and Henri produced. But that didn't matter. She turned to the crowd, brandishing it overhead. "And who thinks our winner is Prince Pierre, back from his journey overseas with his beautiful new wife?"

The applause thundered so loudly, I barely heard the tail end of Wayne's sentence. It wasn't even close. She declared Pierre the winner, planted an exaggerated lipstick kiss that left a bright red mark on his cheek, and presented him with a crown made of grape leaves.

I lowered my voice and put my voice close to Pierre's ear. "Is this whole thing rigged in favor of the Royal family?"

He shook his head. "Not at all. This is all in good fun. The actual competition starts when we're done. That carries a cash prize and a year's supply of wine. Henri and I just get bragging rights. It used to be us and Dad, then me and Henri last time I was here."

His voice trembled a little, prompting me to give him a squeeze. Even though Pierre had always been closer to his mother, he missed his father dearly.

"Okay, lovebirds, that's enough!" Wayne's voice sent us jumping apart. "Our royal winner needs to go finish his photo opp with the adoring crowd. And you, my dear—are up."

"What? Me?" Until Wayne said the words, I'd almost forgotten that Bridget suggested I should smash grapes with my own feet.

"That's right, Sugar. It's your turn." Behind Wayne, workers had already whisked the original three tubs away. Three new tubs filled to the brim with luscious, vibrant purple grapes stood in their place. Good thing my dress wouldn't stain.

"Who am I up against?" I asked as we walked across the stage.

"Other nobles, of course," she said. "Queen Claudette couldn't take part, but Princess Serena of Spain is here. Also Lady Adrienne of Corchenne."

I almost tripped at her words. Not only was I about to dance in a vat of grapes to prove myself, but I had to do it between Pierre's ex-girlfriend and the woman being scammed by my brother? The woman who might have helped him buy security footage to humiliate me? Thankfully, I caught myself by pretending to be stopping to remove my shoes. Last thing I needed was to fall on my face in front of everyone.

As I stepped into the tub, my eyes met Pierre's. He gazed back, steady as always. I would be okay. We would be okay. Stomping on grapes couldn't take any exceptional talent. We'd dance around and someone would win, and who cared if it was me? If the prize was bragging rights, I didn't need them. I just needed to paste a smile on my face and be a good sport.

One of the men gave me a small pitcher of water and a hand towel. So we wouldn't get the grapes dirtier, I guessed. The idea made my lips twitch, but I dutifully washed and dried my feet. Gathering all my courage, I stepped into the tub. Grapes squished between my toes. It felt weird, but not unpleasant.

Sparkling Wayne announced Adrienne and Serena, to the crowd's great delight. Before I knew it, they stood in tubs on either side of me, and Wayne started explaining the rules.

"Okay, ladies. You've got two songs, which will last approximately five minutes. When the music starts, STOMP! You're here to smash as many grapes as possible. The juice goes out of the drainage holes in the bottom of the tubs, into the clear plastic bins below the stage. Once you're all done, we'll bring the containers up here, and the crowd will determine a winner." She winked at me. "Once upon a time, the woman who made the most grape juice won a date with the winning Prince. Guess that's off the table, right, Lila?"

She shoved the microphone in my face, startling me. "Not at all, Wayne. I certainly intend to go on a date with my husband after I win."

The crowd laughed their approval, and the music began. I lifted one foot tentatively, then dropped it. Wow. Grapes were more slippery than I expected. I wobbled, but remained upright. I shuffled my feet, not lifting them more than absolutely necessary.

"Is that how you fight for your man?" Serena asked beside me.

On my other side, Adrienne joined her. "That's not how you stomp grapes, Lila. *This* is how you stomp a grape!" She flapped her arms, lifted one leg so high I feared she might hit her nose with her knee, and brought it down with a resounding thud.

Grapes splattered everywhere, including onto the hem of my dress.

"Oops." She didn't sound the slightest bit sorry.

Just an accident, I assured myself. Let it go.

Ignoring her, I threw myself into the task, trying to imitate what Adrienne and Serena were doing. Both clearly had practice. Squish, squish. Squish. Okay, this was working! It had to be. The grapes slid in the tub, and the volume was... maybe a millimeter lower? It was a start.

Out of the corner of my eye, Adrienne kept coming closer. Her grapes flew at me in a way that must be intentional. Oh, well. She would not get me to snap at her. I would maintain my composure if it killed me.

I spun around, focusing my gaze on Serena instead. If I couldn't see Adrienne, she couldn't get me. Serena was gliding around the tub, looking as full of joy as if it had held a mountain of bubbles and a flute of Corchenne's finest sparkling wine.

Something cold hit the back of my neck. Something slimy. Ew. I didn't even know how Adrienne would have done it without intentionally chucking grapes at me. I refused to look at her.

Then I saw where Serena's gaze was focused. As she danced in the tub, swaying her hips seductively, she stared into the crowd. Eyes locked on Caleb's.

Oh, no.

I couldn't watch this.

Once again, I spun around. Too fast this time. The grapes slipped under my feet. With a gasp, I wheeled my arms.

Another well-aimed target flew out of Adrienne's tub,

smacking me in the open mouth. I jerked backward. The sudden movement was too much. The grapes slid under my feet, throwing me back as I tried to right myself. I overcorrected. I flailed.

Then, to my immense horror, I toppled out of the tub and landed in a tangle of limbs at Adrienne's feet.

Chapter Seventeen

Another day, another viral disaster. The grape-stomping video was even more popular than the emus. Or maybe it just seemed that way because so many people caught the live event. At least ten different people posted the footage on their social media, and, apparently, everyone in the world needed to view them all. For the next two days, n the coaxing and assurances in the world couldn't bring me out of our suite. On Day 1, Pierre remained with me, swearing up and down that the negative press wasn't that bad. After all, I'd want to prove I was human. Making mistakes was not only human, it was relatable.

"Which was really the goal all along, wasn't it?" he asked.

That earned him my steely glare.

On Day 2, he showered and dressed before perching on the edge of the bed. "I hate to leave you alone again, but these meetings can't be missed."

"Go," I said. "If you're there, people can't talk about what a loser your wife is."

"Hey." He pulled the pillow off my face. "None of that. My wife is delightful, and possibly not great with the balance."

I groaned and flopped over.

"Listen, *chérie*. It will blow over, I promise. One embarrassing video is not the end of the world."

"What about two?"

"Not even two. Soon, they will have other things to talk about." He paused. "*Mére* thinks we should announce a royal pregnancy to get minds moving in other directions."

I snorted. "Thanks for the laugh."

"I thought that would help." Someone knocked at the outside door. Pierre stood and returned a moment later with a tray of chocolate croissants. "These are yours, but you have to get up to eat them."

"You don't play fair," I grumbled.

Deep down, I knew he was right. But I wasn't ready to stop hiding. The wound was so raw, I couldn't even call Hannah or Madison to share the misery. Instead, I grabbed the tray of croissants, moved to our couch, and hunkered down with Preacher for a morning of bad reality TV.

Unfortunately, on the third day, Preacher got out of our rooms. He probably did it on purpose, running out into the gardens and refusing to come to anyone else. Either way, it worked.

Chasing animals on viral video once was enough for me for a lifetime. Instead, I stopped by the kitchens and picked up some of his favorite treats, plus a coffee for me. The chef created a full tray with Eggs Benedict, bacon, and croissants.

"That's way too much trouble!" I protested when I saw what she was doing. "All I need are the treats. Forget everything else."

"Nonsense. You could sit all day, waiting for Preacher to appear. Besides, I'm under strict orders to get you to eat anything that would make you happy." She held the tray out. "Here, take it."

I'd long since learned not to argue with palace staff when they wanted to take care of me. Instead I thanked her, took the tray to a patio table overlooking the garden where Preacher had last been spotted, and created a trail of treats to the nearest rose bush. As soon as he smelled them, that little Yorkie would eat out of my hand. Literally.

Settling into a chair, I took the lid off the platter. My mouth watered when the scent of fresh Hollandaise and bacon hit my nose. Oh, wow. Two days of hiding in bed had left me *starving*.

A rustling in the rose bushes behind me suggested Preacher would appear shortly. I glanced over, but saw nothing. Maybe.

Pulling out my phone, I discovered messages from Zoe and Hannah. Zoe assured me that every member of the Wilson family had been released from custody and returned home. The public defender told her that SidMart would drop all charges if they paid for the items, plus a fine. A pang of guilt hit me. Had I not been wallowing, this could have been resolved yesterday. I texted back immediately, asking her to pay whatever amount was needed. I didn't know yet how non-profit accounting worked, but I would not leave that family hanging while I figured it out.

When that was finished, I texted Pierre and asked him to join me on the terrace. He appeared so quickly, I suspected he'd been waiting. Glancing from the rosebushes to my husband, a thought formed.

"Did you let Preacher out, so I'd have to find him?"

He took an empty plate and filled it with eggs and bacon before raising his right hand. "On my life, I swear to you it is not in my best interests to answer that question. Especially not before I've had anything to eat."

At the sound of Pierre's voice, Preacher bounded across the patio and catapulted into his lap. In a flash, he'd put his paws on Pierre's chest and started licking his chin. "Good morning! Who's a good boy?"

"Traitors, both of you." I tried to sound stern, but it was impossible not to smile at the sight of my dog and husband snuggling. "Well, thank you."

"Some rather interesting news came across my desk this morning," Pierre said through a mouthful of eggs.

"Oh?" 'Interesting news' could be anything from him buying a seat on a trip to the international space shuttle to a getting a robotic pooper scooper. I'd honestly prefer the scooper. Less pollution, less ostentatious.

"Yes." He picked up his mug and drank, savoring the moment. "Alexandre had a long talk with Finn."

"The guard I met at the ball?"

"Yes. He is also the one who was on duty when Caleb entered their room to report the emus."

"Well, now you've got my full attention." To show how serious I was, I set my fork down on the tray. "What did he say?"

"First, he confirmed that Caleb was standing beside him when you entered the throne room on the cameras. He said he moved in front of the screen and turned it off, but he's sure your brother saw enough."

I knew it. Every time I wanted to believe in my brother's basic decency, he showed me why I shouldn't. "Did Caleb say anything?"

"Not at that time. Finn said he radioed to send help to the throne room and ushered Caleb out. Thanked him for the report but said no one could be in the room during an ongoing incident. Mostly because he didn't like Caleb sneaking glances at the screen."

"Do you believe him?"

Pierre took a moment before answering, really contemplating the question. "I do. As I said the other day, I've known him most of my life. Growing up, I played with his kids. I can't imagine that he would betray me, or you, or the castle by giving away classified security footage. Also, he's near enough to retirement to not want to risk his pension. Loyal members of the staff receive a very attractive retirement package at the end of their tenure.”

While I was glad to hear it for their sake, the thought of losing one of our few non-royal suspects deflated me. “No dark secrets? Nothing Caleb could exploit through blackmail?”

“I don’t think so,” Pierre said. “But Finn wasn’t the only guard in the room. One of the newer hires, Carlos, had stopped in. They were discussing his schedule.”

“You found a disgruntled employee. One who knows my brother.”

“He doesn’t just know your brother,” Pierre said. “Carlos accompanied Caleb down the hall back to the public areas of the palace after Finn asked him to leave.”

Which gave Caleb the opportunity to win him over.

“Is this guy working now? I need to talk to him.”

“I’m afraid that’s impossible, *chérie*.”

At that, my hopes crashed down. “Why? We’re so close to finding out who did this. I know you trust all the palace staff, but someone betrayed you.”

“It’s not that,” he assured me. “I want to find the person who did this as badly as you. But we can’t talk to Carlos. Last night after supper, he boarded the ferry to France.”

“Did he know you were looking for him?”

Pierre shook his head. “I can’t be sure of that. But what I know is that he wasn’t alone on the ferry. Princess Serena was also a passenger.”

My mouth dropped open. “You’re kidding me.”

“Not just that, Lila. She flew home from France this morning. The news footage of Princess Serena’s return to court shows her traveling with a recent addition to her entourage. My sources inside the palace have confirmed that Carlos went with her.”

Chapter Eighteen

Pierre's revelation shocked me. Was Serena that outraged that I danced one song with her ex after they broke up? That seemed so petty, considering I hadn't met either of them previously. It didn't make sense. More likely, my brother had put her up to it. If only I knew how he convinced her. Was Caleb so powerful?

At the moment, Serena didn't matter. The princess and her companions had returned to Spain for the foreseeable future. According to Pierre, there were no upcoming events before Christmas that she might be invited to, and no reason for us to visit Spain. Since Pierre and I weren't staying much longer, Serena didn't present any sort of immediate threat. Exposing her deeds to the world would only make me look petty.

It was time to redirect my attention to where it belonged: stopping Caleb.

Whether I liked it or not, Caleb was becoming firmly entrenched in Corchenne. Part of me thought it might be time to walk away and let the chips fall. It would serve Queen Claudette right when he ruined everything. Let giant birds overrun the crops. What did it matter to me?

At the same time, I cared enough about Corchenne not to want to subject its citizens to Caleb's endgame. While my mother-in-law hadn't been exactly welcoming to me, I still wanted to help her. Someday, Pierre might regret not having a better relationship with his family. I didn't want to be part of the reason he never repaired things.

Out of desperation, I went to Henri's office after lunch one day. I'd simply run out of ideas for fixing the problem of Caleb. It was every bit as opulent as I'd expected, but better lit. Enormous windows kept the rich blue draperies and dark furniture from feeling oppressive.

For a full minute after I knocked, he remained focused on his work as if he hadn't heard me. But he had. "Lila! If it isn't my favorite member of the Sinclair family."

I snorted. "Considering my competition, that's not saying much. Listen, did you mean what you said earlier?"

"I say a lot of things, and I mean most of them. To what are you referring?"

"The enemy of my enemy is my friend."

"Oh, yes." He motioned to a sitting area against the far wall. "Please, let's talk. I'll have my steward bring tea."

A month ago, if someone had told me I'd be sitting on a dark blue velvet couch overlooking a garden while sipping tea and munching on scones with my brother-in-law, I would have politely asked what drugs they'd been taking. But now, I settled in and relayed all of my concerns over Caleb's apparent decision to stay in Corchenne indefinitely.

When I finished, Henri nodded sagely. "Out of curiosity, why are you asking me? Why not Pierre?"

The question made perfect sense. Henri would sense a lie, so I needed to be as honest as possible. I wanted to say that my husband didn't have Henri's seething hatred of my brother, but that wasn't entirely accurate. In reality, I wanted to prove to Pierre that I could resolve problems on my own. I didn't need him every time something got difficult. We needed to be equals in this marriage, not the nobody and her savior. But I also didn't want to disclose any of my insecurities to someone so likely to exploit them.

Instead, I went for a half-truth. "Pierre's been in America so long, hiding from his roots. I assumed you would have more resources at your disposal."

"Certainly." He waved one hand. "I'll need something from you."

I eyed him warily. The list of things Henri might want from me was short, and it rhymed with "bivorce tie nother."

"I'm not going to leave Pierre," I said firmly. My eyes never left his. My marriage was off the table, period. It wasn't a negotiation chip.

"It's not that." He took another bite of his scone. This guy even ate with arrogance, and I wouldn't have thought that possible. "I have to admit—my brother seems happier when you're around."

"That's because we love each other." I refrained from adding, "Something you would know nothing about."

"As you know, my mother's birthday is approaching. There will be an enormous celebration."

"I will do everything in my power not to embarrass you or the family, or to allow giant birds to ruin the occasion," I said, trying not to roll my eyes. "If nothing else, I promise that I will not invite the emus."

"It's not that, Lila. I know you know how to behave appropriately," Henri said. The unexpected compliment filled me with warm fuzzies. "I'm worried about your brother. How do we keep him from causing another disturbance?"

"Personally, I recommend tossing him in the dungeons and losing the key," I grumbled. Why did I always become my brother's keeper?

"That might be extreme at the moment. I need to know what he's doing. Other than embarrassing you, what is his end goal?"

"Money," I replied immediately. "With Caleb, it's always about money."

"How? The emus were a complete disaster. *Mére* figured it out soon enough to avoid investing most of what they'd talked about. He has to pay her for the damage they caused to the vineyards. He got none of the required import permits, and it's illegal to bring wild animals onto palace grounds. If he doesn't fix everything, he's looking at criminal charges. He didn't make money from that venture. He would be deported if we didn't need his help containing the emus."

"Thank goodness for small favors." I thought for a minute. "What about the land your mother gave him? Maybe he wants to sell it."

Henri shook his head. "No, the property is entailed. It belongs to the person holding the title. It can't be sold or transferred."

"Could it be converted to an Air BnB and rented out?"

"I suppose there's no law prohibiting it," Henri said after a long moment of contemplation. "We don't have a large tourist trade here. Corchenne is rather self-contained, as you know. You barely knew we existed before you met Pierre. The rest of the world is similar."

I conceded the point. "Do you think he's planning to bring Corchenne onto the world stage?"

"That is my question," he said. "If necessary, I can speak to Parliament about banning short-term rentals in private homes. But I'm not sure that's necessary at this stage. Speak with Caleb, find out what his plans are."

"How am I supposed to do that?"

He shrugged. "Have you considered being nice to him?"

I faked retching at the suggestion. Henri was not amused. "Okay, fine. I'll try. Then what? You want me to find out what he's doing and then convince him to give up? Abandon his plans and go back to the States?"

"Where he goes is not my concern. But yes, I would like him to leave the country, and in a way that *Mére* doesn't suspect me of being behind it."

I thought for a moment. My parents had never been interested in controlling Caleb. I supposed I could tell him one of them was sick and he might leave—he was the golden child. But what if he insisted I go with him? Or called to verify my story before he left? No, that wouldn't work.

"You have a lot of faith in me," I said.

"I have always thought you were very capable, Lila. Not wanting you to marry Pierre had nothing to do with your abilities."

"Careful, now. Compliments will make me blush."

He shrugged. "It is a simple statement of fact. I know you can accomplish this task if you put your mind to it. Are you in?"

Pulling myself to my feet, I held out my right hand. Henri clasped it. We shook. "I'm in."

Chapter Nineteen

Official Guide to Being a Princess: A princess is never dishonest or deceitful.

Ingratiating myself to my brother seemed like a daunting task, after all we'd been through. The one thing that made it easier was Caleb himself. He was so self-absorbed, he had no idea that I hated him (for good reason). More importantly, when I started being nice to him, he would take it as his due as my older brother. He was a smart guy, but his ego would be his downfall.

He lived in the palace while his castle was being cleaned and repaired. After decades of it being empty, he'd wanted to make sure the property was structurally sound before moving in. Although he had the skills to do it himself, he decided instead to source a report from local engineers. The results were as expected: water damage, wind damage, lots of need for cleaning. The land itself was overgrown, and most of the smaller buildings also needed work. It would be at least a couple of months before the property could be made habitable—assuming he had the money to do the work. He might live in the palace forever.

That made finding him easy. After ten minutes of making faces and gagging noises, I picked up my phone and texted politely to ask if he was free for lunch. His reply came almost immediately.

Caleb: So sorry, sister dear. I'm about to leave to explore my new estate. Her Royal Majesty wants me to see how much work is needed before taking the next step.

That didn't make sense. Queen Claudette was furious with Caleb for the entire emu incident. If she actually sent him to the estate, it was to get him away from her, unless she hoped the building would collapse. More likely, he was lying.

Me: Great! I'll come with. Can't wait to see it.
Caleb: I'm headed out now. Not a good time.

His not wanting me to come only made me more determined to go. Normally, my brother would be happy to brag about his perfect for a few hours. He must be up to something.

Me: Luckily, I'm already at the garage. Which car are we taking?

Although I had any of the palace drivers at my disposal as Pierre's wife, I didn't expect that same courtesy to extend to my brother. He didn't need an entourage of security guards, after all.

Now that I thought about it, I wasn't supposed to leave the palace by myself. Instead of getting into a car with Caleb, I should call Bernadette and arrange for an escort. But if I did that, I risked my brother leaving without me. I would have to wait to find out what he was up to, and his schemes would get that much closer to fruition.

Everything would be fine. We'd only be gone a couple of hours. Surely I didn't need a security escort to view my brother's home. What was going to happen? Caleb wasn't going to kidnap me and ransom me back to the palace.

Probably.

Caleb: I don't think a construction site is appropriate for a princess. It might not be safe.

The more he didn't want me to go, the more determined I became.

Me: Nonsense! Thanks to you, I know all about construction now. Did I tell you about the time I fell through the floor upstairs?

Three periods appeared and vanished, then appeared again. I had him now. There was nothing Caleb loved more than a good, embarrassing Lila story. The viral videos were proof of that.

Sure enough, we had been on the road approximately eight seconds before he asked for the story. I drew it out, trying to be as entertaining as possible, solely to gain his trust. Only about forty percent of what I said was actually true, but it didn't matter. I was halfway through when the part where I asked Preacher to go get help when his phone rang.

He answered in French, using a Bluetooth in his ear rather than the car's interface. I turned my head to watch the scenery. At first, I didn't pay attention. It could be virtually anyone in Corchenne, including the chef or even a contractor working to fix up the property. Then, unmistakably, I heard the French word for sister. My ears perked up.

I would've given anything to pull out my translation app to find out what he was saying about me, but I didn't think it would work with the road noise. Besides, Caleb certainly would notice and stop talking. He was self-involved, but not oblivious. Instead, I would have to rely on my own French knowledge to figure out what he was saying about me.

"Doesn't know?...Hide... sight?" That made little sense. Who would Caleb be trying to hide from me? And why? Who would be at the estate other than construction workers? Had Serena left Spain and doubled back for a secret rendezvous? That would certainly explain why he didn't want me to come along. But nothing else.

After he hung up, Caleb resisted my efforts to find out what he'd been talking about, so I turned my attention to the gorgeous countryside. Boston had great foliage, and fall was one of my favorite times to live there, but my neighborhood at home didn't have the stunning backdrop of the Mediterranean Sea. When the property finally came into view, its beauty took my breath away.

No wonder Pierre wanted to live here. The estate wasn't as large as the *Château de Serpentine*, of course, but it was stunning. Massive turrets at each corner reminded the world that this wasn't a house; it was a *castle*. The main house was easily four times the size of the place Caleb and I had owned in Boston, and there were several smaller buildings in the surrounding countryside. I hated to admit it, but this place was gorgeous. I would have loved living here. Once it was repaired, at least. I was definitely over living in a construction zone.

The façade crumbled in places, as expected. Hairline cracks zigzagged across several windows. I couldn't see a lot of the roof from the ground, but at least a couple of spots on the tower nearest me needed some stones replaced. Outside, the vineyards were overgrown. At first glance, it appeared to be a giant lawn rather than a place where anyone expected to grow crops. Then again, soon enough, it would be overrun by emus, so whatever. This field might be barren forever.

The crowning glory of the estate, however, was the shoreline beyond the castle. Located on a stunning white beach, the house overlooked a gorgeous, glittering blue expanse of the Mediterranean Sea. Caleb also had his own dock, which I wouldn't have expected. Then again, what good was a private beach if you couldn't launch boats?

I forced myself to tamp down my jealousy at how amazing this place was. Pierre and I had a lovely home. In Boston. Where we belonged. I didn't marry him for castles and private beaches.

But I also didn't marry him for my brother to exploit his

wealth. Darn it. This wasn't jealousy. This was legitimate fury. I hated my brother for taking my attention off helping people, for playing with my life and my marriage. And I became even more determined to take him down.

∾

After Caleb parked, he took me through the property on what couldn't accurately be called a tour. He pointed out different rooms, but mostly was nervous as a cat. He peeked into a room, looked around, jumped, retreated. Then he'd mutter a few words and move on. Repeat.

"What's going on, Caleb?" I asked. "Who are you planning to meet here?"

He stopped dead, wringing his hands. "I don't know what you're talking about."

"No? Then what are you looking for? Worried there's a stray emu in your dining room? After the trouble you've caused, I have to admit, that would be perfect." I smirked at his stricken impression.

"Why are you here?" he asked. "If you wanted to insult me, couldn't you have done it at the palace?"

"I told you, we've barely spent any time together since you arrived. It's a shame that we're finally in the same place, and I'm too busy learning my new role as Pierre's wife to even have lunch with my brother." I stopped and looked around as if a thought had just hit me. "Were you planning to cook something after the tour? Does this place have a working kitchen?"

"Actually, it doesn't. Everything needs to be cleaned and the floor is rotting. It's not safe." Caleb clapped his hands together. "That's an excellent idea! Let's go have lunch."

The trip here had been mostly long, winding roads. We hadn't passed through any town or village for at least half an hour before we'd arrived. "Are there restaurants nearby? Ooh, can we sail over to France for some fondue?"

He looked at me like I'd grown a second head. "Does the car we borrowed convert to a ship? It's a long swim to France."

"You've got a dock back there." I moved toward a rear window and pointed out. If I were trying to hide someone, on the ocean seemed a pretty decent place.

Something fluttered in the distance, causing me to take a second look. Trying to look casual, I focused my gaze in that direction. This castle sat atop an inlet, with a small mountain range on the eastern edge. The beach would have afforded some protection in the old days, and there were places a person might hide.

There!

A yacht lurked in the distance. Not a boat, a yacht. It was easily twice the size of the suite Pierre and I shared back in the castle. It looked brand new. The surrounding water was calm, so I didn't think the boat was moving. I would've bet anything it didn't belong to Caleb, and it wasn't just a casual fisher from another port. Someone was here. Someone my brother didn't want me to know about.

"Oh, wait. Looks like you have one." I tapped on the window.

Caleb came to stand beside me. "A ship? I don't own a ship. Are you sure? I don't see anything."

As if I might be hallucinating a yacht. Too bad I couldn't read the name from here. I'd have loved to have seen Caleb's face when I said it to him. But his too-casual tone told me what I needed to know. My brother wasn't in the least surprised that someone floated off the coast. He didn't want me to know about his guest. Who could it be?

"How far is it to Spain?" I asked, trying to sound casual. "Do you think Serena will come visit?"

Caleb snorted. "The Princess of Spain has no interest in me."

"Really? You looked awfully cozy at the Royal Dinner a few nights ago."

"She was using me," he said. "She was furious when she saw her ex-boyfriend dancing with you at the ball. Pierre is a newly-wed; trying to flirt with him wasn't working. She didn't think he even noticed. But she saw how it bugged you when you spotted us together in the library, and she latched on."

"Was it her idea for you to steal the footage of me chasing the emus?"

At that, his cheeks grew red. Caleb looked out the window. "I had nothing to do with that. She's the one who paid off the guard to give her the video."

Although I didn't believe my brother was blameless for what happened, I appreciated him confirming what I suspected about Serena. It was small potatoes at this point. "Does that mean I'm safe from here on out? No more security footage unexpectedly turning up online? No more embarrassing stories about me spreading like wildfire around the world?"

"Of course. You know I wouldn't do that to my little sister. I'm the one who persuaded her to leave the country once the damage was done."

I didn't believe him for a second. Forcing a smile, I said, "Thanks, Caleb. I really appreciate that."

"This must have been hard for you. I'm sorry." He spread his arms wide. "Can't we hug and make up, like old times?"

"Of course," I said with as much sincerity as I could muster. As I wrapped my arms around my brother, I lifted my phone behind his back and snapped a silent picture of the yacht through the window. Maybe if I zoomed in, I'd get enough information to find the owner.

Who was on that ship?

Before we left for lunch, I asked Caleb to point me at a functioning restroom. Not because I needed to go, but to ensure Henri got my texted image as soon as possible. Thank goodness the phone Candace had assigned me came with satellite internet. No need for Wi-Fi. It only took a second to send the message. Henri was thrilled with the photo. He promised to forward it to his security staff and find out whether it was as simple as a lost fishing vessel or someone with a more sinister purpose.

Maybe I'd missed my calling as a spy.

When I returned to the hallway where I'd left my brother, he was gone.

"Caleb?" I called. "Are you ready to go?"

No answer.

Well, this place probably had a lot of bathrooms. Maybe he'd gone to find another one. I walked around, calling again, to no avail. Were we supposed to meet outside? I didn't remember him saying anything, but I'd been pretty distracted by my mission. Surely my brother wouldn't just leave me—

—to go meet with whoever was hiding on that yacht? Yes, he probably would.

I raced for the stairs as quietly as I could. Hugging the wall, I tiptoed down, listening all the while for any sign of my brother. When I got to the bottom, I moved toward the rear of the building. That was the direction of the beach, for one thing. For another, the car was parked out front. Caleb wouldn't expect me to go looking for him out back.

The sound of a man's voice made me jump. Not Caleb. This voice was deeper, and the French accent much better. Was someone else in the house?

Then I realized that the sound was filtering through a crack in the window. Flattening myself against the wall, I tilted my head.

Nope. I still didn't speak French well enough to understand. And since I couldn't see Caleb or the man he spoke with, it was impossible to get another clandestine photo. The only way to attack my dilemma was head-on. I needed to get close enough to Caleb's companion to describe him. I could do this.

I took a moment to pull myself together, borrowing heavily from Dame Judi Dench's role in *Shakespeare in Love*. She really was a treasure. Then I smoothed my hair, straightened my shoulders, and moved briskly toward the back door.

I flung the door open and strode onto the porch with the confidence of a Kardashian. Then I turned and feigned surprise. "Caleb! There you are!"

"Lila! I thought we were meeting at the car."

"Silly me. I must have gotten turned around. Aren't you going to introduce me to your friend?" I turned my attention to my brother's companion, a fifty-something man with thick, graying hair, a strong nose, and an air of superiority. Everything about this guy screamed money. It wasn't just in his clothes, although they were well made. It wasn't the enormous watch on his wrist or the way he looked down his nose at me.

Okay, maybe it was that one. But I wasn't about to let this stranger derail my mission. I lifted my nose even higher. "Never mind. I'll introduce myself. I'm Lila Sinclair, also known as Lila de León, his royal highness Pierre's wife."

"I know who you are." A wide smile crossed the man's face as he bowed deeply. "It's a pleasure to finally meet you, Madame."

"Lila, I'm sorry for this tiny delay. This, uh, neighbor, was just leaving."

It didn't escape my notice that Caleb had stopped this guy from giving his name. My brother's attempt to keep me from knowing his associate only made me more determined to learn more.

My eyes not leaving the stranger's face, I said, "You must forgive my brother for interrupting. I'm sorry, I didn't catch your name."

"Antoine Lambert," he said smoothly.

"It's a pleasure," I said. "And you live nearby?"

"No, Madame. My family hales from the South of France. We have quite an interest in wine. I'm here to advise your brother on some uses for his new vineyard. But I'm afraid I got my days turned around. I wasn't supposed to be here until next week."

"That's okay, Antoine. We'll talk when I come back," Caleb said quickly. "It was nice to meet you in person."

"How wonderful for him to have such a capable advisor. The vineyards are quite overgrown." I'd assumed this role, and I would be gracious if it killed me. But I also would not give them more time to scheme behind my back. "I'm sorry to disrupt you, Caleb, but we really must leave for lunch soon. I have a meeting at three, so I must get back to the castle."

"I didn't see anything on your calendar," he said.

That was because the meeting was one hundred percent fictitious. "It was scheduled recently." Approximately eight seconds ago, in fact.

Antoine furrowed his brow. "Is something wrong? Did you change your mind about our project?"

"No, no, not at all." Caleb forced a nervous laugh. "Just a minor setback, that's all. Let's go, Lila."

"Antoine, it was nice to meet you," I said.

Although it probably wasn't appropriate for someone of my station (what was my station, anyway?) to shake hands, I extended mine to Antoine. He grasped it firmly. Good grip. Strong, extended eye contact. Not a single callous on that smooth, soft palm. This man hadn't spent a day working in a vineyard. Antoine Lambert. I'd remember that name.

"The pleasure was all mine, m'lady."

Caleb escorted me to the car. The moment he got in, I pulled out my phone and Googled the name under the pretext of looking for a good restaurant.

It didn't take long for results to come up.

Antoine Lambert was a French billionaire. He didn't make his money in wine, though. Or any type of agriculture. A few years ago, he'd tried to expand the French oil industry. Corchenne didn't have any oil, did they? What was he doing here? Why was Caleb determined to meet him in secret?

The car slowed at the end of the driveway. "Find anything good?"

I most certainly had. But I shut off my phone to avoid the temptation to keep digging until I got away from Caleb.

We found a hole-in-the-wall pub and got a table in the back. I kept my sunglasses on and faced the wall. The server's eyes widened when she saw me, but I slipped her a fifty and she never said a word. It was worth the money to have some privacy for a bit.

How I made it through the entire meal with my mind racing was beyond me. Luckily, Caleb needed no help in carrying on a conversation. After dodging all of my questions about Antoine, he returned to his favorite subject: breeding emus. He barely noticed that I didn't contribute another word until we arrived back at the Chateau.

When we pulled into the garage, men dressed all in black swarmed the vehicle. My heart pounded. From my conversation with Alexandre, I knew that most palace security guards were heavily armed, even if I couldn't see the weapons. I couldn't move. Couldn't breathe. What happened while we were gone?

"Caleb? What did you do now?" Part of me didn't want to know the answer, but I had to ask.

"Me? Oh, no sister dear. This is all about you."

"Me?"

Caleb tapped the rear-view mirror. "That's your husband coming toward us. Man, he looks angry. What did you do?"

Pierre? Confused, I twisted around in my seat. Sure enough, my husband strode toward the car. Thunder clouded his face.

Chapter Twenty

OFFICIAL GUIDE TO BEING A PRINCESS: A princess does her research. She is never taken by surprise.

The full contingent of palace guards awaiting my return took me completely by surprise. Seeing my husband with them confused me more. What could have gone wrong? Did something happen to Queen Claudette? To Bridget? Pierre was supposed to be in meetings all morning. He wouldn't have left unless it was for something really important.

Pierre reached the passenger door of the borrowed car in three long strides. He wrenched the door open. "Are you okay?"

"Yes, fine. Why? What's going on?"

I took off my seatbelt and turned toward him. Pierre pulled me out of the car and set me on my feet, doing a rather thorough pat-down. I might have enjoyed it if not for our audience. This was rather unexpected. On the driver's side, Caleb got similar treatment from a guard I didn't know. What was going on?

Did they think the Americans took a few hours to load up on assault rifles?

Okay, that wasn't an entirely unfair assumption these days, but still. I was a pacifist.

Finally, Pierre stopped checking me over and met my eyes. "You're okay."

"Yes, of course. Why is that in question?"

He exploded. "Why? You disappeared! There's nothing on your calendar. Preacher is in our suite alone, and you weren't answering your phone. I thought you'd been kidnapped!"

"Pierre, I told you, that's ridiculous. No one is going to kidnap me. We went to see Caleb's new place." With my brother in earshot, I couldn't explain why. "We were never in any danger. I'm sorry I didn't mention it, but it's unnecessary for me to travel with an escort for a quick trip."

"And I told you, never to leave the palace without an escort! Alexandre told you. Everyone told you! You need a driver and a bodyguard, both trained to keep you safe. Caleb doesn't have the first clue how to protect you in an attack. He'd be more likely to use you as a human shield."

He had a point.

As he raged at me, I realized I'd scared him. Pierre had been worried something bad happened. A wave of guilt washed over me. I should have talked to him before we left, but I figured we'd be back before anyone noticed. Mousseux wasn't far.

It truly didn't seem worth bothering the palace staff. Caleb had been so eager to leave without me, any delay might have cost me the chance to go along. Considering I'd met one of his associates that he didn't want me to know about, I absolutely wasn't sorry for leaving.

"It was a couple of hours. I figured it wouldn't be a big deal," I said.

"A couple of hours could kill you! When will it sink in? You're not a nobody anymore!"

Nobody. The word made my spine straighten. I glared at my husband. "Don't you mean *you* aren't a nobody?"

He ran a hand through his hair in exasperation. "Lila, hold on. That's not—"

"No, I am a nobody. What you mean is, people care about me now that I've married someone who matters, right? I'm not important, but my husband is."

"You know that's not what I meant."

"Do I? It certainly sounds like you meant it."

I refused to listen to this. Pierre had no right to tell me where to go, who to go with. He was my husband, not my father. And how dare he call me a nobody? I might not have been a rich fancy Royal, but I was still a person. There was value in who I was, apart from my family's money and influence.

For the first time, I saw myself the way he must. Why would he want to marry me if that's what he thought? And all of a sudden, I didn't want to be in the same room as him anymore. I couldn't look at him, this man I loved who thought I was no one.

"Get out of my way." I stepped toward him, forcing him to step back. I just needed to create a space large enough to walk through. "I'm sure you have more important things to do than talk to a *nobody* like me."

A stunned look crossed Pierre's face as I moved past him. He opened his mouth to speak, but it was too late. Head high, I marched past them all and back into the castle. So much for asking for advice. I'd figure out what Caleb was up to all by myself. I didn't need help from him or Henri or any member of the royal family. I'd show those hoity-toity snobs what a nobody could do.

Halfway back to our suite, I realized that I'd arrived back at square one. The original plan had been to ask Pierre to give me more information on Antoine Lambert. Now, I didn't want to talk to him until I figured it out myself. Unfortunately, I wasn't entirely sure how to do that.

My last message from Henri said he'd flown to France to meet with their President. Even knowing someone where that was an ordinary day boggled my mind. It also meant he wouldn't check his messages for several hours. No help there.

If only I could get my hands on Caleb's phone. His text messages or email should tell me explicitly what was going on. Unfortunately, he always had the thing on him unless he was showering. Bursting in on my brother au natural wasn't an option, so I'd find another way.

Shortly after naming Caleb the Baron of Mousseux, Queen Claudette gave him an official laptop on the castle's server. Complete with castle-level security. Hannah couldn't break into that, even if I were prepared to ask her to. No, I'd have to get this information the old-fashioned way. Besides, I'd brought this mess to Corchenne. I shouldn't have to rely on my big sister to save me. I was a grown woman, and I could do this myself. All I needed was to break into Caleb's suite and find his laptop.

I tried to picture the castle's layout, but there were so many rooms, I needed a map. The western turret only held our rooms at the moment. At the bottom sat a guest suite that remained empty. Pierre had said something about their grandparents using that wing when he and Henri were younger. It sounded like it was reserved for family.

On the floor below us, I believed I'd seen the French ambassador entering the staircase the day of the ball. Someone had mentioned that the visiting politicians were housed near each other. It didn't seem likely that the housekeeping staff would put my brother up on the same floor.

He'd gotten here long before them. He also would have had a room assignment before he finished ingratiating himself to Queen Claudette. Not that I thought Her Royal Majesty paid any attention to placing guests in her home. But he would have a room for someone of minimal importance.

Since I didn't have a map, I called Zoe. She answered immediately, which was one of about two thousand reasons I appreciated her.

"Hey. You don't know where my brother's rooms are, do you? Or does he have an office?"

"Yes. He's in a guest suite in the eastern wing. He wasn't given an office when he arrived because he was here as a personal guest, not representing a foreign government."

Thank heavens for that. The last thing we needed was for the Queen to base Brazilian foreign policy on her interactions with Caleb.

After thanking Zoe, I hung up and sat back to figure out my plan.

According to the official schedule, Queen Claudette took tea at three-thirty in the afternoon. Every day, Caleb had joined Her Majesty for tea if she were here. Today should be the same. While he was out, I could sneak into his suite. Caleb wouldn't expect me to be nosing around his rooms, nor would he be looking for me at tea.

Unfortunately, it was barely past one. Briefly, I scanned through the public schedules for the past week, but Caleb didn't have his own. He'd only pop up if he were meeting with a member of the royal family, and apparently he wasn't. Nothing with Antoine Lambert. That didn't surprise me. You didn't drive an hour to meet with someone, hide their boat, and lie about who they were if your prior interactions were all part of the public record.

The library!

On the day the emus overran the vineyard, when I found Caleb, he'd been reading a stack of books about Corchenne. He'd also been in there with Princess Serena after they left the state dinner. I'd assumed he spent all that time looking up information on housing and raising emus, but what if he wasn't? His books would have long since been put away by the staff, but I could find the one I saw. Something about Corche history.

Since the castle was open to the public during the day, I resisted the urge to sprint to the library. But I walked as quickly as I could without drawing attention to myself. Two tour groups stopped me, forcing me to grit my teeth and smile graciously until I could make my escape.

Finally, though, I swept through the double doors. Inside the library, I halted, trying to figure out where to get the information I needed. Although I didn't know whether Corchenne used the Dewey Decimal System, Caleb wouldn't have carried the books far. They must have been near where he was sitting. I started at that table, running one hand along the polished surface as if it could speak to me.

Not a spot, not a scratch, not magical answers to my questions. Fine. I'd go find the history books. They should be nearby.

The shelf nearest the table appeared to be about wine and vineyards, based on the few words I recognized. Pulling one out, I flipped through idly, looking at the illustrations. Vineyards, grapes, even a picture of a grape-stomping competition. I wondered if it included the helpful advice not to fall on your butt.

The shelves above and below looked the same. How many books did you need about making wine? No history books. But then something caught my eye.

Ressources Naturelles. That had to mean what I thought, didn't it? The book wasn't quite in line with the others on the shelf. It sat back a fraction of an inch more than the rest, as if put back hurriedly. Like maybe Caleb shoved it back to hide it when we were rushing out?

No. He never picked up after himself. Maybe whoever put the books away was annoyed with my brother. I was grasping at straws, but straws were all I had until Henri returned.

Pulling the book out, I held the spine and let it fall open. The book had been written in the nineteen-eighties, so quite a while ago. My French still wasn't great, but I gleaned that it was a study of the things found in soil. Iron, natural gas... And oil.

Antoine was an oil baron, and Corchenne had untapped oil under the vineyards.

I needed to find Pierre immediately. Before Caleb finished the plan he'd set in progress.

No. Maybe I was jumping to conclusions. I didn't want to look so desperate to catch Caleb doing something wrong that I falsely accused him. That there were books on oil in the library meant nothing. This library had thousands of books, easily. I couldn't swear Caleb had been reading this one. Before embarrassing myself in front of Pierre yet again, I needed to be one hundred percent sure. This nobody was going to prove herself.

Holding the natural resources book close to my chest, I continued looking for the history books.

"Can I help you?"

A man's voice made me jump like someone caught trying to steal the Crown Jewels. I turned to find a tall, thin man with unlined brown skin and closely cropped black hair. He wore a name tag identifying him as Jean, the Palace Librarian.

"Hi! I don't know if we've met. I'm Lila."

"I know who you are, Madame." His voice carried no trace of friendliness.

"Right, sorry." I wiped my damp palm on the side of my pants. His eyes followed the path, missing nothing. "I was looking for a book on Corche history."

"Of course." He offered me a thin smile. "The Sinclair family seems to have taken quite an interest in what Corchenne can offer them."

That gave me pause. "Jean, were you here when my brother was studying the books?"

He pulled himself up. "Of course. I am here every day."

"Did you happen to see what he was researching?"

For a long moment, Jean studied me. I'd just concluded that he wouldn't tell me anything when he spoke. "That book in your hand? He spent a lot of time reading and taking pictures. He also had this one here..."

A Corche history book! A-ha.

"Other than grapes and wine, what are Corchenne's primary exports?" I asked.

"Not emus, if that's what you're asking."

I snorted. "Listen, I realize you don't trust me. But I am not my brother. I want to stop him. Do you know who Antoine Lambert is?"

"Oil baron," Jean said promptly. "He's been trying to drill under the vineyards for years. Her Royal Majesty won't even consider it. Forbid him from entering the country. Since then, he's been trying to befriend Henri."

"Does Henri want to drill for oil?"

"Not. He humors Monsignor Lambert to see what he is up to." Keeping his friends close, of course. "Drilling Corchenne for oil is out of the question. There's no room for heavy equipment, and the cost of bringing it in would be exorbitant. A spill or leak would devastate the beaches, the vineyards, the economy. Our way of life. The de Leóns would never endanger their people like that."

The royal family wouldn't, but my brother certainly would. He felt no loyalty to anyone other than himself. "Jean, we can't let that happen. I want to tell the Queen. But first, do you know what other books Caleb read? I need to be prepared."

For the first time since approaching, Jean smiled. "Certainly. We have cameras in this area, and I walk the stacks several times a day. Please, come with me."

Chapter Twenty-One

Now that I had proof of my brother's treachery, I moved triumphantly down the hall, pages clutched in one hand. Here was irrefutable evidence that, from Day 1, Caleb had come to Corchenne to exploit my connection to the throne for his own benefit. He didn't care about the people. He wasn't here to get to know his extended family: it was all about money. Money and stripping the land of natural resources.

When those emus arrived, I knew it wasn't a mistake. They hadn't been too early or the wrong shipment. He didn't care if they wrecked the vineyards. It just hadn't been immediately clear that he wanted to destroy the vineyards, so there would be less outrage when he started drilling. After all, no one would want to trade their wine for oil, but if the land couldn't produce any more wine, why not dig?

It was kind of brilliant. Yet evil.

At the end of the hallway, I skidded to a halt when I realized that the t-shirt and Capri pants I'd worn to walk around a construction site with my brother were far from appropriate for tea with the queen. Even if I was only going to tell the truth about Caleb, I'd get a better reception if I changed first.

Nearly skipping down the hall, I didn't realize that our door stood ajar until reaching for the handle. Weird. Pierre should be here, but he would never leave it open. It wasn't yet time for Bernadette to walk Preacher. She wouldn't leave the suite open, either. What was going on?

Through the opening, I called for my dog, hoping he hadn't gotten out again. Pierre and I actually met for the first when the little guy insisted on tunneling under the fence between our properties. That was the start of our entire friendship.

While I loved Preacher with all my heart, I really didn't want to spend the entire afternoon searching for him. My mother-in-law needed to know about Caleb's plans as soon as possible. Preferably in time to catch Antoine before he sailed back to wherever he had come from. Now that I'd left Mousseux, he was probably waiting for Caleb to return alone and seal the deal. I expected he would do that right after dinner.

In response to my call for Preacher, I expected to hear excited yapping, maybe the scrabble of claws against the marble floor. Nothing. I tried again. "Pierre? Are you in there?"

Silence.

Now my spidey senses were tingling. If he were here, Alexandre would tell me not to go into that room. There was no way to know who might be in there or what they wanted.

But this was *the palace*, I argued to myself. The safest place in the country. We had like fifty security guards on duty.

Then again, I'd just broken into a room at the palace, so who was to say no one else could do it?

That was enough. First, I needed to talk to Pierre, then I'd find my dog. Since he didn't always notice his texts when he was working, I tapped his name to call.

No answer.

Okay, I definitely shouldn't go in there without talking to him. Not after our argument earlier. Entering after what appears to be a break-in would probably be considered disregarding my safety.

While Juan might tell me where to find my husband, I gave Pierre time to cool off. Instead, I tapped Alexandre's name.

Inside the suite, the phone rang. Weird.

Pushing open the door, I stuck my head inside.

"Hello? Pierre? Alexandre? Anyone there?"

The ringing abruptly stopped. Instead of Alexandre's voice in my ear, the man himself appeared at the end of the hall. His expression was completely blank.

"What's going on? Did someone break into our apartment? Is Preacher okay?"

"Come with me, please."

Alexandre came and took my elbow, then escorted me to our living area. When I saw the damage, I gasped.

Our suite had been completely torn apart. Clothes everywhere. Drawers turned upside down. The couch cushions and bedding had been tossed aside.

"Holy guacamole. Isn't this a bit of an overreaction to me going for a drive without a guard? Where's Pierre? He can't know about this."

Beyond the closed bathroom door, Preacher whined at the sound of my voice. He pawed against the wood. At least he was okay.

When Alexandre saw me, he approached and held one hand out. "Ms. Sinclair, I'm going to need your official phone."

"My phone? Why?"

"Don't make me ask again."

"Okaaay." Since I'd been too busy worrying about Caleb to post on social media much, I barely used the thing. I pulled it out of my pocket. "Do you need to do a security update or something?"

"Or something."

"Okay, seriously, you're freaking me out. Where's Pierre? What's going on? This can't be just because I left my security detail for a few hours."

"No, it isn't." Alexandre cleared his throat. "The throne is aware of your plan. Your visa is terminated, effective immediately. I have been ordered to deliver you to the Queen for further action."

Ten minutes later, two additional members of security staff met us, along with Zoe and Bridget, outside the front door to our suite. The women I'd considered friends and allies in this strange world avoided meeting my eyes. No matter how hard I tried, it was impossible to get additional information from anyone while we walked toward the throne room. I didn't even know what they suspected me of doing. Surely, just being Caleb's sister wasn't a crime?

No, that was ridiculous. Queen Claudette actually liked my brother. In her eyes, marrying Pierre was far worse than letting giant birds destroy the island. She couldn't be that mad because I'd fallen over while grape stomping, and the viral videos weren't bad enough to justify this type of treatment. It's not like I'd done that on purpose. There had to be something I was missing.

Where was Pierre? Was he waiting for me with his mother? Surely, if someone thought I'd done something wrong, he would come stand by my side. If not to offer a defense, at least to provide moral support.

When we arrived inside the throne room, I realized that the

emails I'd printed from Caleb's laptop were still clutched in my right hand. Okay, well, once I got this all sorted out, maybe she'd be willing to read them.

"Alexandre," I whispered. "I know you're upset with me, but please, look at this. You have to see what's been happening. Can you show these to the queen?"

"I know what's happening. Your brother told Her Royal Majesty everything. Maybe you didn't know he's been passing her information since arriving."

My mouth dropped open. Sounds of outrage escaped me. Beyond that, it was impossible to form a coherent sentence. The pages fluttered from my fingers to the ground. "What?"

On the dais, Queen Claudette sat on her throne. Henri was in his spot beside her, with Caleb in the chair where he'd first been spotted. But Pierre was nowhere in sight.

As I remembered the way she'd threatened to annul my marriage with or without my consent, an icy wave of fear swept over me. I needed to get out of here. I needed to find Pierre immediately.

But I wouldn't get the chance.

The doors behind me slammed shut with an ominous thud. Queen Claudette stood and stepped toward me. When she spoke, I recognized her "official" voice. "Delilah Sinclair! There you are. What have you to say for yourself, girl?"

She was trying to cow me into submission, but I hadn't helped Madison prep for every single mock trial during law school for nothing. Drawing on those old lessons, I drew myself up until my spine was as straight as hers. "I'm sorry, Your Majesty, but I am unaware of the allegations against me. What am I accused of doing?"

"Come now. Aren't we past that?"

"I would say, yes, but I honestly don't know what I did. I was coming to tell you that my brother, your Baron of Moose, has been conspiring against you. He contacted an oil baron, and they plan to strip Corchenne of its natural resources."

Queen Claudette laughed hollowly. "Oh, that's rich. First, you try to ruin my island. Then you plot behind my back. Now, you're not only lying to my face, but you're trying to blame your poor, defenseless brother for your misdeeds? After he came here, broken-hearted from his failed marriage, to repair his relationship with his beloved sister?"

That was so ridiculous, I would have burst out laughing if not for the seriousness of the situation. "With all due respect, Your Majesty, that sounds more like the plot of a Hallmark Original Movie than anything happening here. Caleb has been conning you this whole time, and I can prove it."

"Do you deny sneaking away from the castle to meet with Antoine Lambert? Slipping away from your security detail so no one would know?"

Okay, that definitely looked bad. "There was no time to alert Alexandre. I needed to get into the car with Caleb before he left. Henri! You asked me to find out what was going on! I didn't know Antoine would be there—or even who he was—until we arrived."

Henri shifted in his seat. "I did ask Lila to watch her brother. I didn't like the way he wielded influence over you."

She snorted. "Influence? Everything that boy did, I asked him to do."

"You asked him to destroy the vineyard and drill Corchenne for oil?" That completely boggled my mind. Was the Crown broke?

"That vineyard was full of rot. The intent was not to ruin it, but to get my younger son to realize how completely unsuitable you were for him. Your reaction, the way you treated your family, all of it, should have driven a wedge between you."

"All you did was help us grow closer," I announced.

"Strong words from a woman about to be sent home in disgrace," she said.

What? No way. Disgrace for what? And where was Pierre?

Desperately, I looked at Henri. He was the closest thing I had to an alley in this room. "Come on, Henri. I know you've never liked me, but you have to believe I wouldn't do this to you, to Pierre. I love him. Why isn't he here?"

Ignoring my last question, Henri said, "I wish I could, Lila, but I've seen the evidence with my own eyes."

"What evidence?" My tone came out sharper than it had a right to, but all this pomp was really chapping my circumstance. Did they actually think I'd helped Caleb mastermind this whole charade? For what reason? No one ever says, "Gee, I hope I can make my in-laws hate me!" even when said in-laws don't own a country.

Desperately, I flung my arms into the air, waving the papers. Queen Claudette flinched. "I have evidence, Your Majesty! Please, read these emails. They lay out everything."

She gestured to one of the guards, who took the pages to the throne. After a moment of flipping through the pages, she sighed heavily and passed them to Henri. "Yes, I've read these."

"So you believe me?"

"On the contrary, I'm not sure why you think these messages exonerate you."

This was bananas. How did she not see the truth in black and white in front of her?

"Did you read the emails? Henri?" Someone here must have some common sense left.

He scanned the first page. Then he narrowed his eyes, flipped to the next, and kept reading. Again. One by one, he read each email with a look that could only be described as bewilderment. When he finally looked up, he wore a dazed expression. "Lila, these are your emails."

His words punched me in the gut. My emails? I'd gotten them from Caleb's computer. Every single one was written in his words. "What are you talking about?"

Henri held one document out toward me. "The email address is right here. Every single one says 'DelilahLeon@monarchy.-corchenne.gov' at the top."

I blinked at him, sure that I'd misheard. These emails came from Caleb's official computer. From his web browser. The browser he had logged into and left open after sending these emails. They all said...well, I assumed they were from him. I hadn't thought to specifically check the "from" field.

Beside me, Alexandre spoke. "Your Royal Majesty, I have confirmed there are copies of each of these messages stored on the server. I accessed them using Ms. Sinclair's phone."

Suddenly, everything clicked into place. The email address I refused to use because they got my name wrong. When Caleb appeared in my suite out of nowhere to take an interest in the dog he abandoned more than a year ago. Maybe he hadn't specifically planned this, but he'd been looking for something to benefit him.

The list of names and passwords had been on the table in the front hall, right by Preacher's leash. He must have seen it and taken a picture when we were out. I knew I never should have left the suite door unlocked for him.

When we spoke with Antoine, I thought it weird that he looked at me when asking about a change in plans. But he had *actually been talking to me.* He thought I knew about the plans.

"Damn you, Caleb Sinclair," I muttered. Then something hit me. The name! My head snapped up. "Henri, please. Look at that email address again. It's *Delilah Leon.* That's not me."

Ignoring me, Queen Claudette addressed Alexandre. "Was that not the email address established for my son's wife? The one using her correct legal name?"

"Leon isn't my legal name," I yelled. No one even looked at me.

"Yes, Your Royal Majesty. I set it up myself," Alexandre said. "It's the account Candace installed on Ms. Sinclair's official phone before giving it to her."

Ms. Sinclair. The second time Alexandre used my name, it hit me. This was the only time anyone associated with the queen got my name right. As the implications of that sank in, all the air left my lungs. I fell to my knees. This couldn't be happening.

Alexandre held up the device. I wanted to scream. After they'd presented me with the wrong email address, I never even opened the app. I'd been waiting for them to send a new one—but never thought I was enough of a priority to follow up right away. Apparently, I should have. Maybe someone could have informed me that "my" account was being used. Caleb stole my username and password, then logged into my account and sent the messages as me. I'd even bet he intentionally left the window open on his laptop, hoping I would find the message and not make the connection. He knew I'd be so excited to get my hands on the smoking gun, I wouldn't stop to check the details. My brother set me up.

And when push came to shove, they'd made sure that the one person who would defend me wasn't here. I wondered how they'd orchestrated that.

"Did you send Pierre away? Is he okay? Why can't I see him?" Balling my hands in fists, I turned to Caleb. "How could you do this to me? What did I ever do to you? I always knew you were selfish but—"

"ENOUGH!" Queen Claudette's voice sent me reeling backward. Being on this end of royal wrath was no fun. "Lila, you will cease blaming your brother for your actions at once. The past few weeks haven't been easy for you. I understand you feel out-of-place, and that having your brother's welcome to the country outshine your own must have hurt."

"To be honest, Your Royal Majesty, I've been overshadowed by my brother for my entire life. I appreciate the opportunity to protect others in the way I wish I had been protected."

"Is that what this is all about then? Revenge?"

"No, Madame." I prayed she heard the truth of my words. "I want to help people. It's why I set up my charitable foundation. To give people a better life. If Corchenne is stripped of its natural resources, drilled and left bare, the people will ultimately suffer. That's the opposite of what I want."

She studied me for a long moment. "It is of no matter now.

Your actions are inexcusable, no matter what the motive. I'm only sorry that it has come to this. My son loved you once, Lila. Which is why it pains me to do what I must do."

A chill went down my spine. My mouth went dry.

Queen Claudette stood pulling herself upright as if embracing a royal mantle on her shoulders. She'd intimidated me from the start, but nothing like this. All of a sudden, I saw why rulers from other nations had cowered at her feet.

When she spoke, the words landed slowly, as if she wanted me to have time to appreciate the full meaning of each before moving on. "The Sinclair family has been nothing but trouble since you arrived, Delilah. Your brother and I were getting along marvelously, but your sibling squabbles have ruined even that rapport. My country's economy is in danger because your first 'investment opportunity' ran roughshod over our vineyards. We will be lucky to make any profit from the wine this year. Worse, if you'd gotten your way, our wine exports may have been ruined for a decade, or longer. None of that would have happened if you hadn't drawn your brother to our country."

This was so unfair. None of those things were caused by me. In fact, I'd actively tried to stop her from giving Caleb her time, attention, or, most importantly, money.

"Once again, Your Majesty, I apologize for my brother."

She waved one hand. "It is too late for your apologies. Continuing to blame Sir Caleb tells me you have learned nothing. I do not believe you can fix this. Actions must have consequences."

A chill went down my spine. My mouth went paper dry. It took several attempts to swallow before I could speak at all. "You aren't going to have me beheaded, are you?"

Queen Claudette said, "Of course not. We haven't had capital punishment in Corchenne for decades. I'm not Marie Antoinette. But you must leave the country immediately. My staff is in your suite now, packing your things and collecting your pet dog. When we are done here, Bernadette will drive you to the airport. You may return to the United States using the plane that brought you here."

Pierre's private jet. She was exiling me in my husband's plane. I pulled myself up to my full height. "I want to see Pierre."

"You're not in any position to make demands now, are you?"

Henri cleared his throat. "*Mere*, while I do not agree with Lila's actions, perhaps we should allow her to see Pierre before she leaves."

The look Queen Claudette gave him would have peeled the white off of rice. I shrank back, and she wasn't even looking at me. "Would you like to go, too?"

"I daresay you're not prepared to lose both of your sons today," Henri replied, not cowed in the least. This might be the first time I respected him. "My position here is secure."

Queen Claudette waved one hand. "It is of no matter. I spoke with Pierre not ten minutes ago, and he was in complete agreement with me. He was horrified to realize how easily Delilah pulled the wool over his eyes. Like her namesake, I might add. I warned him."

Her words punched me directly in the heart, each of them. Pierre knew what was happening, and he chose to abandon me. He'd left me here to face this humiliation—these baseless accusations—alone.

"Is he coming with me?" I asked. "Do I get to say goodbye?"

Although the circumstances were awful, returning home didn't bother me. I could check on the Wilson family, see how they were doing. Maybe I'd volunteer for Habitat for Humanity. I'd learned a little about construction over the years. If nothing else, I was terrific at rubbing away my frustrations with sandpaper. With Pierre at my side, we would get past this. But the queen's response did not instill confidence in me.

"I do not have the power to annul your marriage, unfortunately," Queen Claudette said. "But you are not married in Corchenne. Pierre will start divorce proceedings first thing in the morning."

My knees tried to buckle, but I forced myself to stand firm. "This can't be real."

"It's as real as you and I," she said. "But my son asked me to leave you a message. He said, 'I'm sorry, Lila, but I must protect my country. I thought highly of you and your brother, but you betrayed me.' My son understands loyalty and respect."

The room blurred beneath my tears. I couldn't even reply. None of this made any sense. That wasn't the man I knew. How could he let me go without a fight?

But of course he could. If he believed anything they told him, he wouldn't want to see me. When had we grown so far apart that he would lose faith this easily?

Queen Claudette spoke again, but the words meant nothing. Our marriage was over. After a moment, I allowed someone to turn me around and escort me to our chamber.

Excuse me. To Pierre's chamber. The rooms of His Royal Highness, who didn't care enough to say goodbye.

One thing gave me pause. Caleb's voice, too low to make out the words. And Henri's reply, "You are blameless in none of this, sir. I strongly recommend you leave the country at once. *Mére,* please begin stripping his title and recovering his lands."

"No need for that, dearest," she replied. "The transfer hasn't gone through yet. I never signed the deed."

Caleb's sound of outrage was a tiny consolation as I moved down the hall toward the suite that I once occupied with my loving husband. At least he wouldn't be allowed to stay, either. The land was safe from oil barons.

To my surprise, I found Bridget in our suite, folding and packing my clothes. That made sense—she would know what was mine versus hers. I stood in the doorway holding Preacher, not able to move or speak. Even if I'd wanted to, the security guards had accompanied me to watch. This was beyond humiliating. No one looked at me until the end.

Finally, when Bridget handed me the suitcase, she said, "I'm sorry, Lila. For what it's worth, I think my sister is wrong to blame you."

Bridget's opinion didn't matter. Queen Claudette's opinion didn't matter. The only thing that mattered was what Pierre thought, and he thought I betrayed him.

With great effort, I took the suitcase and walked outside to the waiting car.

Chapter Twenty-Two

Tears blurred my vision so much, when a tall shape appeared beside me in the driveway, I thought it was a mirage. Then I heard a voice and realized there was no scenario where I would dream up my brother as the person who had come after me. I'd hoped to be back in Boston before Queen Claudette finished reading him the riot act.

"I guess you're pretty mad at me," he said.

I snorted. It wasn't even worth replying.

"Would it help if I told you I'm sorry?"

"You're sorry you ruined my marriage and got me banished from a foreign country? Gee, that makes everything better!" I gritted my teeth. "Get away from me."

"I'm banished too, remember?"

"Yes, but you deserve it," I said. "You'll be lucky if I don't ask Bernadette to run you over on our way out."

"I suppose that means a ride to the airport is out of the question?"

I shot him a withering look. The limo turned t corner on the far side of the castle and headed our way. For a hot second, I debated shoving my brother in front of it.

It was only moving like 5 mph, though.

Caleb touched my arm gently enough that I didn't immediately throw him off. "Come on, Lila. Look at me. Please. We're family."

It was the "please" that got me, as always. Silently, I cursed myself. Everything would be easier if I could just stop caring about others. But when I turned to look at him, I didn't see the creep who ruined my life. I saw my big brother who taught me how to climb trees and showed me all the dirty parts of the Bible to annoy Mom. Stupid bleeding heart. I deserved everything I got.

I forced myself not to say anything. The car stopped, and Bernadette got out. "Are you ready, Madame?"

"No need to stand on ceremony, Bernadette. I'm no one now. Just Lila."

"You could never be no one, Lila. Remember that." She put my bag in the trunk. "Is he coming with you?"

Caleb gave me these beseeching eyes that made me want to punch him. "Please??? I want to make things right."

It was beyond the furthest stretch of imagination that he could make this up to me. On the other hand, he might tell our parents if I abandoned him, and I didn't want to deal with them now. "I will allow you to sit silently in the car, only because I don't trust you not to steal another one. But you're getting your own flight back to Brazil. You are NOT coming with me."

"I can't go back to Brazil, remember?" he said.

"Not my problem. I don't care where you go, as long as it's away from me. And don't mooch off Hannah, either. I'm calling her as soon as I can form a coherent sentence."

I slid into the car but didn't stop him from following me. Bernadette waited until I gave her a disgruntled hand wave before closing the door. A moment later, she slid into her seat and the front door slammed shut.

"Where are we taking him?" she asked through the lowered partition.

"I haven't decided yet," I said. "Do you have any places where he might spontaneously catch fire?"

"The airport, please," Caleb said.

I shrugged. What did any of this matter? The partition went up. A moment later, the car moved down the driveway.

Finally, I sighed. "What do you think will make anything better?"

"I don't know, but I wanted to apologize."

"Do you actually know what that word means?"

"After you and Pierre got married, it hit me how perfect your life was. Everything works out. You always land on top."

I laughed hollowly. "So you set out to destroy me?"

"No, not at all. This wasn't my idea. Her Royal Majesty reached out to me after your wedding."

I gaped at him. "Excuse me?"

"Come on, Lila. You didn't really think I could pull one over on royalty, did you? I'm flattered, but this was all her idea. Her sources told her you had a brother, that we were estranged, and that I'd had a couple of investments go bad. She offered to pay me to come stay in Corchenne long enough to drive a wedge between you and Corchenne." He paused and made a dramatic show of checking his watch. "To be honest, I thought it would take longer."

I resisted the urge to strangle him. "You intentionally sabotaged me! How could you do that?"

"Nothing could rock the boat if your relationship was strong enough. I figured I'd come here, do my job, get paid, and go home after a few weeks. What actually happened isn't my fault. Okay, I got excited by the oil, and I shouldn't have. But the rest was all her."

The worst part was that he believed he was blameless. After

we left Corchenne, I never wanted to see him again. For all I knew, he was still lying. Maybe the queen was as much a victim in all this as me. But given the way she'd spoken to me, even if that was true, I was out of empathy.

"You used to have a soul. What happened?"

"When I got to Brazil, we bought properties to flip. Her father helped put up some of the capital by mortgaging his house. Then the cost of materials skyrocketed, and the property values plummeted. All of a sudden, I was in debt up to my eyeballs. My other investors ditched me. I got stuck selling several homes for less than we paid to get them."

The same thing happened to me after he left Boston. Poor Fernanda. If she really threw him out, I understood.

It took everything in me not to sound sarcastic as I asked, "Did you consider getting a job?"

"I tried! The economy in Brazil dried up. There was no work in construction. The supply chain disruptions made it nearly impossible to get materials, even if we could find clients. Fernanda and I were fighting. She took a job sewing to make ends meet, and I was home with Alberto all day. I wanted more. I needed something bigger and better. She deserved more. I wanted to prove I was good enough."

"I thought she lied and cheated and Alberto wasn't yours," I said, remembering his reason for coming to Corchenne.

His cheeks turned pink. "No. Uh, I made that up. I was embarrassed to tell the truth."

It said so much that he would prefer I thought his wife was a liar and a cheater than that he lost some money. But I didn't have time to unpack that.

Wearily, I asked, "Why should I believe you now?"

"I don't have a great reason, but it looks to me like I'm all you've got."

Nope. Never would I be so low that Caleb was my only option. When I got home, I had Madison; I had Hannah. I still had the non-profit she'd set up for me. Pierre and I had a joint bank account in the US. It would probably take him a couple of days to close it. My brother wasn't part of what I had at all.

I wished I'd never let him in the car. He wasn't even sorry for all he'd cost me. He didn't care. Worse, he blamed me for his actions.

He was still searching for a way to take advantage. Not today, Satan. I was done.

I knocked on the roof of the car.

Bernadette lowered the partition. "Yes, Madame?"

"Let him out," I said. "I've heard enough."

Caleb gaped at me. "You're not serious. We're in the middle of nowhere!"

Corchenne wasn't that big. It wouldn't take long to walk to a town. "Bernadette, can you please remove my brother from the vehicle?"

"It would be my pleasure."

"Never speak to me again," I said to my brother. "We're done. Forever."

"You don't mean that."

"I really do. Bernadette?"

When she opened the rear door, Caleb sprang into action. He unbuckled his seat belt and scurried out the back of car like a roach running from the light. Apparently, the thought of being bodily removed from the vehicle was too much. Bernadette never had to touch him.

I smiled as she got back into the car and buckled her seat belt. "Are you sure about this?"

"I only wish I'd done it years ago. Thank you for your help." I paused and let out a sigh. "But if you want to get him after you drop me off, that would be okay. It's a long walk to the airport."

A tiny smile crossed Bernadette's face, and I could tell she approved of my decision. With a nod, she raised the partition. The engine roared to life, and the car pulled slid forward.

Leaving my brother stranded by the side of the road in a foreign country shouldn't have filled me with joy, but it did. I was done. One hundred percent finished. I didn't care what he said or did. Let him tell my parents. Hannah and I would set their ears on fire with Caleb tales.

It was time for me to distance myself from Caleb entirely. With that in mind, I pulled out my phone and turned to Instagram live. Luckily, my official accounts hadn't been disabled yet.

"Hello, Corchenne! First, thank you for the warm welcome you gave me. I have loved being here and getting to know you. I wish we could have more time together. But I inadvertently brought bad things to Corchenne with me. My brother Caleb saw my new husband and family as only dollar signs. He never looked at the person within. He just wanted to exploit you all for his own selfish gain."

My voice trembled, and I paused. "I wish I had been strong enough to stop him sooner. I wish he had never come to Corchenne, and for that, I apologize. I am working to repair the damage he caused to the vineyards. But it's time for the Sinclair family to leave Corchenne in peace. As I speak, I am heading to the airport, preparing to return to Boston.

"I hope to see you all again, on my terms. No brother, no drama. Just me, Lila Sinclair. Because I am somebody."

Chapter Twenty-Three

When we arrived at the airport, the limousine drove to the back instead of pulling into the public parking lot. Right. The private plane. Really, I should insist on paying my own way. I shouldn't get used to traveling like this. Nah. Maybe it was petty, but I wasn't gonna do that. Pierre could afford to fly me home, and if he was going to let me go without so much as a goodbye, he deserved to foot the bill. I couldn't believe he'd just give up on us so easily. But we'd talked a lot about making the world a better place. If he believed I'd been responsible for the things Caleb did, walking away was his only option. I wouldn't stay married to someone who acted that way, and neither should he.

After Bernadette parked the limo on the tarmac, the pilot who brought me and Pierre to Boston exited the plane. Douglass, that was his name. He had flaming red hair, freckles scattered across his face, and a friendly smile. The first time we'd flown together, I'd liked him, but something told me this trip wouldn't be so pleasant.

Bernadette insisted on carrying my bags one last time. I wanted to argue, but was too heartsick to bother. In that moment, I didn't care whether my luggage made it back to Boston.

All the way down the tarmac, I dragged my feet, praying Pierre would run out of the terminal and stop me. He had to know that Caleb set me up, that I had nothing to do with this. Drilling the country for oil went against everything I believed in. Supporting Caleb went against everything I believed in. How had he become so brainwashed?

But if he believed me, he would have shown up. He would have stood by me and not sent a message through his mother. His mother! I'd have preferred to hear it from Henri.

I stopped and gazed around one more time, letting Preacher sniff the ground. There was no sign of my husband.

"Go ahead," I told him. "Lift your leg on Corchenne once and for all."

Bernadette tugged at my elbow, and although I glared at her, I bit back a scathing remark. She was only doing her job. Her boss, Queen Claudette, wanted me on that plane, and on the plane I would go, whether using my own feet or dragged kicking and screaming. For the benefit of the media that most likely lurked inside the windows of the tiny airport, walking seemed preferable. At least I could keep some shreds of my dignity.

Not many, but some.

The three of us continued toward the plane. It had been nice pretending to be someone. Thinking that my actions mattered, that I could help save the world. A bitter laugh tore through my lips.

Douglass glanced back at me. "Are you okay? Most people seem happier to be boarding the queen's private jet."

"Most people aren't being sent into exile without the love of their lives. At least, I hope they're not."

"So it's the real thing with you two? Queen Claudette said the marriage was for show, that Prince Pierre only picked you after they argued."

"Of course she would think that." I rolled my eyes. "She doesn't remember what it's like to have feelings. Pierre wanted to stay in America to irk his mom, sure. Really, it was more about Henri. But that's not why we fell in love."

When we reached the bottom of the stairs, I picked up Preacher to carry him inside. Then I turned and gazed back at the lone building, at the parking lot beside it. No one but Bernadette, who was getting into the car. Nothing. Apparently, the media didn't even care about in my departure. Why should they? I was no one. Just the woman whose brother nearly destroyed a year's worth of crops and their entire ecosystem.

But that wasn't what stung. I didn't care if the press watched me go.

Pierre wasn't coming.

Although it was futile, I checked my phone again. Caleb had sent some texts, which I didn't read. Nothing from Pierre.

This was it. If I left Corchenne, I wasn't allowed to come back. Pierre wasn't coming after me. I'd never see him again, here or in America.

A tear slid down my cheek. I pressed my lips together, determined not to lose it until I got to my seat. Taking a deep breath, I buried my face in Preacher's silky fur, gathering strength from my little Yorkie. He licked my eyes.

"At least Caleb didn't take you, too." I loved this little guy. Good thing, since it was just the two of us from here on out.

"I'm sorry, Madame, but we have to go," Douglass said behind me. "We're scheduled for wheels up in three minutes."

"What happens if we're late?"

"I've been instructed to do whatever is necessary to ensure we're not."

Of course he had. Queen Claudette wasn't leaving anything to chance.

It was time to stop stalling. My fairy tale had ended. It was nice to be royalty while it lasted. I only wished I'd been able to achieve anything positive during my tenure.

Today, the inside of the plane didn't seem inviting and luxurious. The expensive fabric of the seats mocked me. The gourmet food stocked in the fridges did nothing to tempt me—if anyone had bothered to fill them. Queen Claudette may have figured I'd be fine with a pack of crackers and a cup of tap water from the airplane restroom.

The outer door thudded into place, sounding remarkably like a prison cell slamming. Douglass pointed toward the back corner. "There's a crate for your dog over there. It'll be safer for him during takeoff. You can let him out after we're in the air. Once you put him in, please take your seat and fasten your seat belt."

"Thanks."

He headed toward the cockpit, leaving me alone.

As soon as I unclipped Preacher's leash, he bounded toward the back of the plane. He must have smelled the food. Whatever the palace chefs had made for my little Yorkie, he loved it. It was an insignificant gesture, but it made me smile to see someone provide for my dog, even under these circumstances.

Once I ushered Preacher into his crate, I moved back toward the main cabin for takeoff. Not caring at all where I sat, I sank down onto the couch beside the windows. The view blurred.

My eyes remained glued to the tarmac. Despite everything, I couldn't stop hoping that Pierre was coming to stop me from leaving. I desperately wanted to believe that he still loved me.

He never appeared.

Douglass's voice came over the intercom, reminding me to put on my seatbelt and letting me know it should take three hours to get to Boston. Three hours or three days, it didn't matter to me.

The plane rolled forward. I told myself to stop looking out the window, but my eyes stubbornly refused to obey. In torturous slow motion, I watched my past move away from the plane, toward the horizon.

Finally, I burst into tears. Lying across the window seat, I sobbed until it felt like I would run out of tears, then I sobbed some more.

I didn't know how much time passed before a weight dropped onto the seat beside me. Great. Douglass was back, and he clearly didn't realize I needed some time to myself.

"Shouldn't you be flying the plane?" I asked, without lifting my head.

"No, I believe Douglass has that covered."

It couldn't be. I was hallucinating. And yet—

Sitting upright, I blinked repeatedly. Then I lifted my eyes to find Pierre grinning at me. My heart soared. "How? When? Why? How?"

"An excellent question, *ma chérie*. Let's start with the why. Because I love you." He pulled me into his arms and kissed me.

I leaned into him, savoring the moment. He'd come for me! He'd really come for me. I couldn't believe it. My hands roamed over his arms and back, as I desperately tried to reassure myself that he was real.

But finally, I had to know. I pulled back and eased myself away. "I didn't think you were coming."

"I came the second I heard what she had done. Henri told me everything."

I shook my head, confused. "Your mother said you didn't want to say goodbye. That you were filing for divorce."

He cupped my face in his hands. "She lied, Lila. I swear she lied. I had no idea they were confronting you. After we argued, I went for a walk. Then *Mere* asked me to check one of the southern estates—I was halfway across the island when Henri called me."

"You didn't know?"

"I didn't know."

"You didn't abandon me?"

"No, *chérie*."

My brain was having trouble accepting that things were really going right. "How did you get here so quickly?"

"Henri sent his helicopter."

"Forgive me for asking, but—why?"

Pierre laughed. "That's a fair question. He knows how much I love you. He heard *Mere* tell you what high regard I have for Caleb, and he knew I didn't really send that message."

I snorted. "I should have caught that."

"He wanted to be sure I knew the truth before you disappeared. He didn't want me to think you'd abandoned me," Pierre said. "I know you've had your differences, but we used to be very close. He may have made mistakes—a lot of them—but he loves me."

As far as I was concerned, Henri was forgiven for everything. I ran my hands up and down Pierre's arms, hardly daring to believe he was real. "You didn't call."

"Sorry about that. I needed to hide on the plane before anyone got here," he said.

"You mean the media?"

"Well, yes. But more importantly, *Mére* has spies everywhere."

Everywhere. Yes. Including in the cockpit. "Douglass—"

"—works for me. He has for years," Pierre said. "He let me hide in the co-pilot's seat until after takeoff."

"This is so amazing." Unable to resist, I leaned forward and kissed him again. Then I stopped, resting my cheek against his. "I thought I'd lost you forever. I was so scared."

"*Ma chérie*, you could never lose me. Especially not over something your brother did."

"He said your mother paid him to break us up."

Pierre heaved a sigh. "I am sorry to say, I believe him. It didn't make sense when she let him stay after the emu incident. She should have stripped his title immediately. But if you forgive me for my mother, I certainly forgive you for your brother."

"Deal." I sniffled, trying to understand what had happened. "Will the economy be okay? In the throne room, she said something about vineyard rot?"

"That's a fact of life when you make wine. But I got a report earlier today. We were not going to get wine from that vineyard."

She hadn't been lying. "I can't believe it. Your mother really was in on it the whole time."

"It looks that way. I'm so sorry. But if it's any consolation, Henri told me Caleb was going to get paid once I filed for divorce. He won't see a penny now."

"Thank goodness. If he made money off of all this…" I sighed and shook my head. "It doesn't matter. I told him I never want to see him again."

"I told *Mere* the same. As soon as we took off, I sent a message from the cockpit. We're not coming back. We're going away, to be together, away from anyone's interference."

That sounded like the best idea anyone had ever had. I sniffled. "I didn't want money or fanfare. All I need is you."

"I know, *chérie*. Me, too." He wiped the remaining tears from my face before putting his arms around me. "Are you okay?"

"I am now. As long as I've got you, we can figure the rest out." I snuggled into him, then a thought hit me. I chuckled.

"What's so funny?"

"Your mom should have let Henri in on her plan earlier," I said. "He enlisted my help in stopping Caleb."

He snorted. "Henri has been trying to convince me to stay since the moment our flight landed. If he'd known what she did, he would have helped me pack. Mere has too much control over us."

"Too bad. We would have fled the country days ago. Where to now?"

"The plane has set a course for Boston, but Douglass can change it. Where do you want to go?"

I contemplated his words. We'd been traveling since we got married, more than a month ago. Corchenne was beautiful, with its sweeping vineyards and glittering beaches. But it wasn't where I belonged. It wasn't where Pierre belonged either, not anymore. We didn't need five-star hotels or private planes and castles. All we needed was each other. And Preacher, of course.

"No. I've seen enough of the world," I said. "Let's go home. Madison's got a room waiting for us."

"Nothing would make me happier."

Author's Note

I hope you enjoyed A ROYAL PAIN. Getting to write and publish romantic comedies over the years, both on my own and traditionally, has been a true privilege. Writing and publishing books was my childhood dream, and I am so grateful that I managed to do that for so long. Thank you for being part of this journey by reading my books.

Special thanks to everyone who helped this book come to life, especially Carly Winter and Marty Mayberry I appreciate you more than you know.

The best thing for a writer is to know when readers liked their book. If you did, please consider leaving an honest review on BookBub or with your favorite retailer.

As Gwen gives in to temptation, everything's in play for a major heartache. With the rounds heating up and players eliminated, she knows she's gambling a lot more than a seat at the final table in Vegas. But Cody's kisses promise more than a fleeting romance. If she plays her cards right, Gwen just might walk off with the championship *and* the man of her dreams.

Read on for a sneak preview!

The conference center buzzed with anticipation. Palpable excitement filled the air. Some of the other participants fidgeted. I stood alone, an island of calm in the sea of activity. Nerves were for the less prepared. I'd done my homework, I'd played endless games, and I planned to make it to the final table in Las Vegas, where I'd win the $10,000 grand prize.

In about six months, anyway. One thing at a time.

My first game started in about twenty minutes, leaving me plenty of time to sip my Diet Coke and survey the competition. If someone said, "I'm going to the local American Explorers of Islay Competition," most people would picture a room full of pasty twenty-ish guys with glasses and high water pants, living in their parents' basements. We had those types, sure, and my collection of geeky t-shirts fit in perfectly with that crowd. But the room also contained people of all shapes, sizes, genders, and colors, ranging from eighteen to about eighty. We hailed from all over the region, possessed a variety of interests.

And one of us was a very good-looking guy with curly brown hair, surveying me over his coffee cup with gorgeous chocolate brown eyes. He wasn't pasty at all, with a deep tan and lean muscles making his jeans and black t-shirt look a lot more exciting than they sounded. When I met his gaze, he smiled, flashing beautiful teeth, the kind typically found on the wealthy and children of dentists.

Although I'd never seen him before, he chatted with a guy who showed up at these things every now and then. Tall, with thin black braids trailing down his back, the most beautiful light brown eyes I'd ever seen, and dimples. The two of them upped the hotness average in this room by about thirty percent, but both were unfortunately off-limits to me. I didn't date gamers. Don't poop where you eat and all that.

"Not bad." My former roommate, co-competitor, and close

friend Holly appeared beside me. "Looking for a little after-competition action?"

I rolled my eyes at her. "Whatever. I won't have the energy for hooking up after I kick butt."

Participants in the American Explorers of Islay Competition competed in a popular resource-sharing board game. The original game accommodated three or four players, and the expansion allowed for more, but the tournament assigned everyone to tables of four. This morning, everyone would play three games and receive a score based on their final rank in each. Table placement was determined in advance by a random draw.

Holly and I weren't playing each other in the first round, but it wasn't a big deal. At some point, we'd inevitably face off. And if we didn't, well, the trash talk would still kick into high gear. The way the tournament was set up, we could both move onto the next round. After three years of grad school and playing together, we'd still be friends after the final scores were announced. It didn't matter whether one of us got knocked out on Sunday or the two of us made it to the final table.

"*Almost* everyone here. I personally plan to wipe the floor with you." Holly corrected me with a wink and a smile. Trash talk and "game hate" ruled at these events. No one meant anything they said. Usually. "Oh, hey, I forgot to mention—last year's winner is here. I talked to him when he transferred his registration from Florida."

With her background and tech know-how, Holly helped set up the registration database for the competition. After years of acting as tech support and back-up registrar, she knew practically everyone's name. We weren't a large community, at least not locally.

Playfully, I swatted at her arm. "What? I can't believe you didn't tell me!"

Last year's winner was a legend. He'd won four years in a row, more than anyone except John, the current competition host. Rumor had it he was calm, collected, and dominated the table during games. Many a gamer imagined testing our skills against C. McKay. The thought of getting to play him here made my mouth water.

Unfortunately, he lived in Florida, so our paths had never crossed. I'd never been able to afford go to the finals. Usually, I volunteered at the local and regional competitions, then dreamed about the rest. But not this year.

"Sorry. Things have been busy with the wedding planning and everything. But there he is."

She pointed at the list of first round match-ups on the wall behind me. Directly below H. McDonald, also known as Holly, the sheet said, C. McKay. A name I'd never seen on the lists in this state, but sent a little thrill through me. Was he as good as everyone said? I couldn't wait to find out.

"Excellent! I can't wait to scope out the competition, find his weak spots, and destroy him."

"You were checking him out a second ago," a voice said behind me.

John, the only person who won more tournaments than C. McKay, stood behind us. He was medium-height, medium-build, probably around my dad's age, with close-cropped, curly dark hair and a salt-and-pepper goatee. Only his whistle and clipboard made him stand out from the rest of the crowd. And the twenty years he'd been around, playing with everyone, making friends. He and his wife Carla co-owned the local game store with his parents, so I'd known him since I was a baby. "That's him over there. Cody."

Following John's finger, my eyes once again landed on the hottie. So that was C. McKay. My number one competition. My ridiculously buff number one competition. My stomach dropped. Why did he have to be an excellent player *and* totally hot? He reminded me of my very first crush as a child, Jonathan Crombie from *Anne of Green Gables* (who reminded me of my second crush, Megan Follows). Those crushes may have played into my utter fascination with the entire series.

He winked at me. For some reason, winking always weirded me out. Maybe because it was mostly old men who did it, looking at twenty-something women. I'd never seen anyone my age do it. As I rolled my eyes, he flashed a grin. My stomach flip-flopped.

Mentally, I revised my assessment: a good player, hot, and a shameless flirt. He probably thought that made him a triple threat. Whatever. I'd been one of only about a dozen females at these events for years: There wasn't a single pick-up line my friends and I hadn't heard. This guy didn't have as much game as he thought.

"Did he wink at you?" Holly rolled her eyes. "Like he's gonna win because he's cute?"

"I think he did."

"If only he frosted the tips of his hair or wore a popped collar, he could be a total walking cliché."

"Or both," I agreed.

A high, clear tone filled the room: the bell, alerting us that we only had ten minutes to get to our tables and settle in before the first game started. The guy started toward us, eyes still fixated on me, and I groaned.

"Ugh. I'm not up for introducing myself."

"I'd love to say hello," Holly said, "but I need coffee before we start."

"Yeah, I've gotta go, too," John said. "Talk to you later."

"You don't want to say hello yourself?" My question went to both of them, but John had turned away, tilting his head the way he did when someone spoke into the earpiece he wore during these events.

True friends wouldn't abandon me with this guy. If he opened with "Hey, is your name Sonic? Because you've been running through my dreams," I'd never forgive them. And, knowing Holly, she'd be sorry to miss such a horrible line. She'd been attached to her fiancé for so long, most everyone around here knew not to bother trying their luck. Every once in a while, though, a newbie got sucked in by her perfectly polished sorority girl look and decided to make a move. Usually with amusing results.

Holly grinned as she stepped away. "Not with the way he's looking at you. See you later."

Before I could argue I wasn't here to flirt, she vanished back into the crowd, and C. McKay arrived in front of me. He looked even better up close, if possible. A wave of disappointment hit me. Part of me hoped he was like a Monet–beautiful from afar, but a total mess up close.

"Carrots?" he said.

As pick-up lines went, this one stumped me. It beat the Sonic line some creeper tried on me a few months ago, but largely because it made no sense. With no idea what he was talking about, I said the first thing that came into my head. "Squash? Rutabaga?"

He chuckled and pointed at my chest. Oh, right. My t-shirt: *Don't Keep Calm, He Just Called You Carrots.*

My face grew warm. "Sorry, I forgot. It's an *Anne of Green Gables* reference."

"I got the reference. I was trying to be funny. Sorry." He held out one hand. "Cody McKay."

In all the times I'd worn this shirt, no guy my age had ever caught what it meant. Of course, I'd never met a guy who looked like Gilbert Blythe. Under other circumstances, I'd have been impressed. But now I was mostly intrigued to meet the guy I'd heard so much about. Not that he could know. "Gwen Williams. I'll be kicking your ass here shortly."

"Gwen? That's a pretty name." He smiled. "Think I prefer Carrots, though."

My stomach fluttered traitorously at the way he looked at me. My hand tingled where our fingers still touched, but I quashed those emotions. If this guy thought he could charm me to throw me off-guard, he had another think coming. Just because he was better-looking than the average gamer didn't mean I'd fall at his feet once he flashed those gorgeous brown eyes. I came here to win games, not to hook up.

Hoping he couldn't see how flustered he made me, I said, "Then maybe you should hit up the snack room. They've got plenty of carrots for you."

"Sorry. I didn't mean to offend you. I'm usually much better at this."

"Well, if you're not great at playing games, you're in the wrong place." I flashed a broad smile at him to take the bite out of my words. "Excuse me, I've got a tournament to win."

"Actually, *I've* got a tournament to win," he said, smoothly maneuvering around me. Still walking, he turned to look back at me. "After all, I'm the four-time American Explorers of Islay Competition champion."

"That's because you've never played against me." The parting shot had the desired effect in that it made him pause for a second. He shook his head, grinning, which left me dying to wipe the smug look off his face.

So that was the guy I needed to beat. He apparently thought charming the other players gave him an advantage. Little did he know, I'd had plenty of experience with silver-tongued gamers who relied on their good looks to get girls. They didn't impress me. Our interaction only made me more determined to hand Cody his ass in a game.

With a small smile, I tugged at my t-shirt, bringing the v-neck a bit lower. My boobs couldn't compete with Holly's, but I could give him something to look at. Then I shook my long hair out of its braid and pressed my lips together to redden them. Two could play Cody's game. But only one of us would win, and it was going to be me.

Buy now!

More by Laura Heffernan

The Reality Star Series

America's Next Reality Star: Jen went on a reality show to compete for the $250,000 grand prize. But when she finds herself battling another woman for co-competitor Justin's heart, she finds herself wondering what the true prize is.

Sweet Reality: After a killer competitor threatens her new business, Jen sets sail on a new reality show adventure to save the day. But Ariana's back, and she's determined to end Jen and Justin's relationship once and for all.

Reality Wedding: After retiring from reality TV, Jen receives an offer she can't refuse. The Network wants Jen and Justin to film their wedding to fill an empty time slot—and if they refuse, the Network will get Justin fired.

~

The Gamer Girls Series

She's Got Game: Gwen's dedicated to becoming the American Board Games Champion, and she never ever mixes gaming with pleasure. But when she meets Cody, trying to resist his charm becomes a losing proposition.

Against the Rules: For years, Holly has harbored a secret crush on her best friend's dad. Nathan is young, he's hot. What's a little harmless flirtation while playing games? But when she discovers that Nathan returns her feelings, Holly may have to choose between two of the most important people in her life.

Make Your Move: Shannon's more interested in designing games and rising to the top at work than dating. She's surprised to find herself falling for her roommate, Tyler. Worse, he's dating her boss's daughter. If she makes her move, Tyler's girlfriend could get Shannon fired.

≈

Push and Pole Series

Poll Dancer: A delightfully modern twist on *My Fair Lady:* When a promotional video for her pole-dancing classes goes viral, Mel comes under fire from a local politician running for senate. Desperate to save her studio, Mel decides her only option is to launch her own campaign — and win!

The Accidental Senator: After accidentally finding herself elected state senator, Lana Chen is determined to prove her worth. But when a mistake aids the passage of a bill that's going to put her best friend out of business, Lana has to find a way to set things right before it's too late.

≈

Retail to Riches Series

A Royal Farce: After years of secretly crushing on her friend Pierre, Lila is thrilled when he proposes they start a fake relationship. For weeks, she finds herself hoping their farce could turn into the real thing—but Pierre's hiding a secret of royal magnitude.

A Royal Pain: When Lila and Pierre arrive in Corchenne to meet her in-laws, she's shocked to discover that her scheming brother has already arrived. Can their marriage survive Caleb's shenanigans and the weight of royal expectations?

≈

Standalone Books

Finding Tranquility: Christa Cooper finds the courage to transition after she nearly loses her life on September 11. Eighteen years later, she's confronted by the wife she left behind: Jess, who discovers that the person she knew as Brett is now Christa. Can they find a future together, despite the past?

Anna's Guide to Getting Even: Anna's perfect life has turned into a string of disasters: After a hurricane destroys her house, her ex publicizes private photos of her — which costs Anna her job and her current boyfriend. And after hitting rock bottom, she decides that revenge is the only way forward...

Friction: Britt's always avoided relationships. Then, weeks before she's set to move away, she meets Colin. To her surprise, she finds herself wanting more.

Time of My Life: She's a poor dance teacher. He's her rich student. If they can only overcome their differences, this could be love. A gender-flipped update of *Dirty Dancing*.

Books Written as Ada Bell

Welcome to Shady Grove...

Aly doesn't believe in psychics. Too bad she just had a vision.

Future scientists don't have visions. Aly's got enough on her plate, with finishing her degree and taking care of her nephew and starting her new job at the antique store while drooling over the owner's gorgeous son. No visions.

Alas, the universe doesn't care what Aly believes. When she turns 21, she starts to feel psychic impressions left on objects. A disorienting power for someone surrounded by antiques. Then cranky customer Earl is killed, and Aly's new boss Olive is the prime suspect. Who hated Earl enough to kill? Police would rather make a quick arrest than investigate, so it's up to Aly to clear Olive's name.

Shady Grove is reeling from the first murder in decades. If Aly can get her hands on the murder weapon, she should be able to solve the crime. Can she learn to control her visions before the killer sets their sights on her?

Mystic Pieces
The Scry's the Limit
Sight Seering
Mystic Treasure
Seer Today, Gone Tomorrow
The Pie in the Scry
Mystic Persons